P9-CDK-178

NANCY DREW
DREW
girl detective
®

PAPERCUTZ™

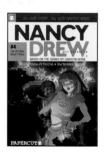

NANCY DREW

#1

DREW

girl detective ®

The Demon of River Heights

STEFAN PETRUCHA • Writer
SHO MURASE • Artist
with 3D CG elements by RACHEL ITO
Based on the series by
CAROLYN KEENE

PAPERCUTZ™

The Demon of River Heights
STEFAN PETRUCHA – Writer
SHO MURASE – Artist
with 3D CG elements by RACHEL ITO
BRYAN SENKA – Letterer
CARLOS JOSE GUZMAN
SHO MURASE
VAUGHN ROSS
Colorists
JIM SALICRUP
Editor-in-Chief

ISBN 10: 1-59707-000-9 paperback edition
ISBN 13: 978-1-59707-000-3 paperback edition
ISBN 10: 1-59707-004-1 hardcover edition
ISBN 13: 978-1-59707-004-1 hardcover edition

Printed in China.

10   9   8   7   6   5   4   3

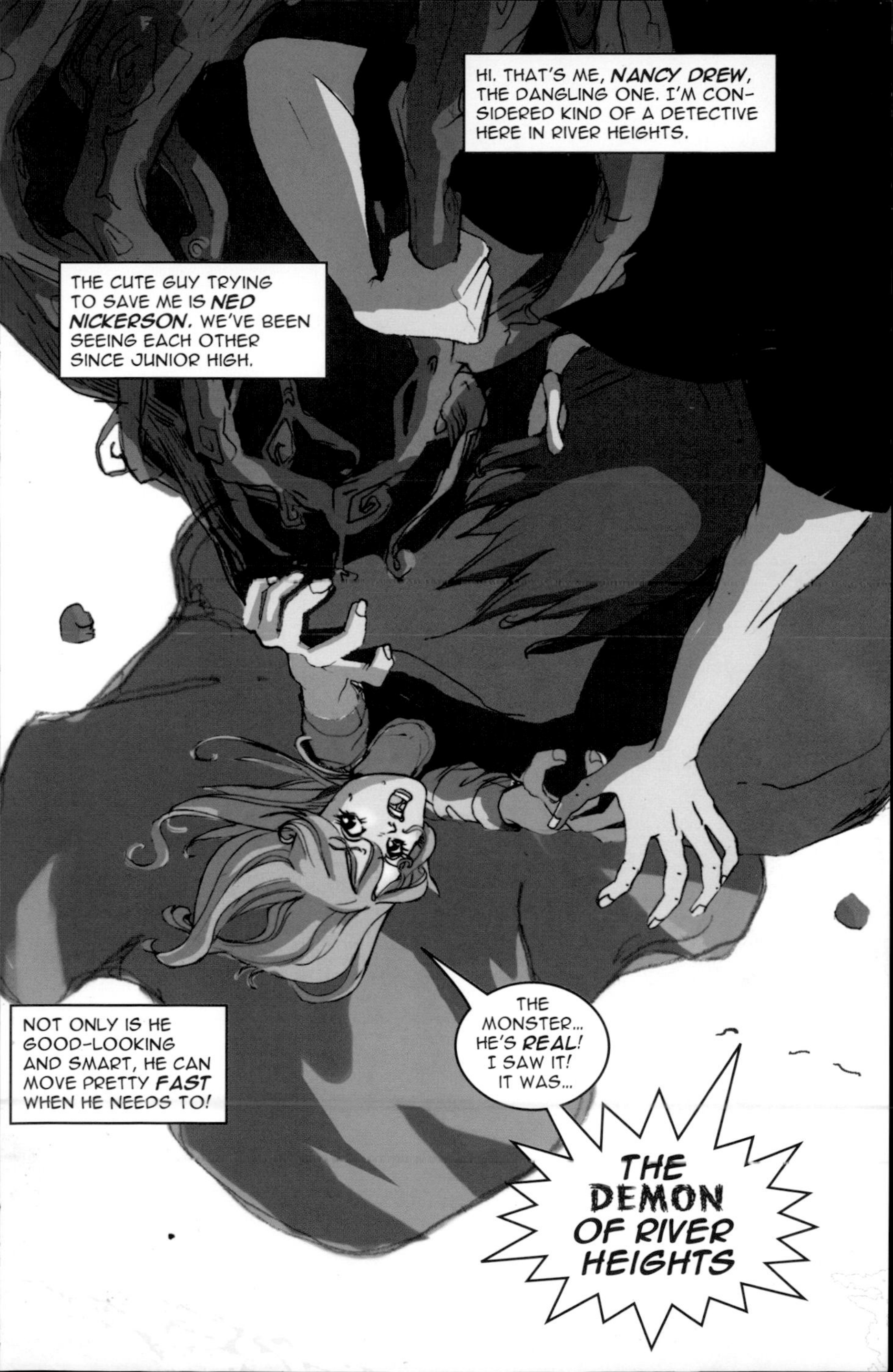
HI. THAT'S ME, NANCY DREW, THE DANGLING ONE. I'M CONSIDERED KIND OF A DETECTIVE HERE IN RIVER HEIGHTS.
THE CUTE GUY TRYING TO SAVE ME IS NED NICKERSON. WE'VE BEEN SEEING EACH OTHER SINCE JUNIOR HIGH.
NOT ONLY IS HE GOOD-LOOKING AND SMART, HE CAN MOVE PRETTY FAST WHEN HE NEEDS TO!
THE MONSTER... HE'S REAL! I SAW IT! IT WAS...
THE DEMON OF RIVER HEIGHTS

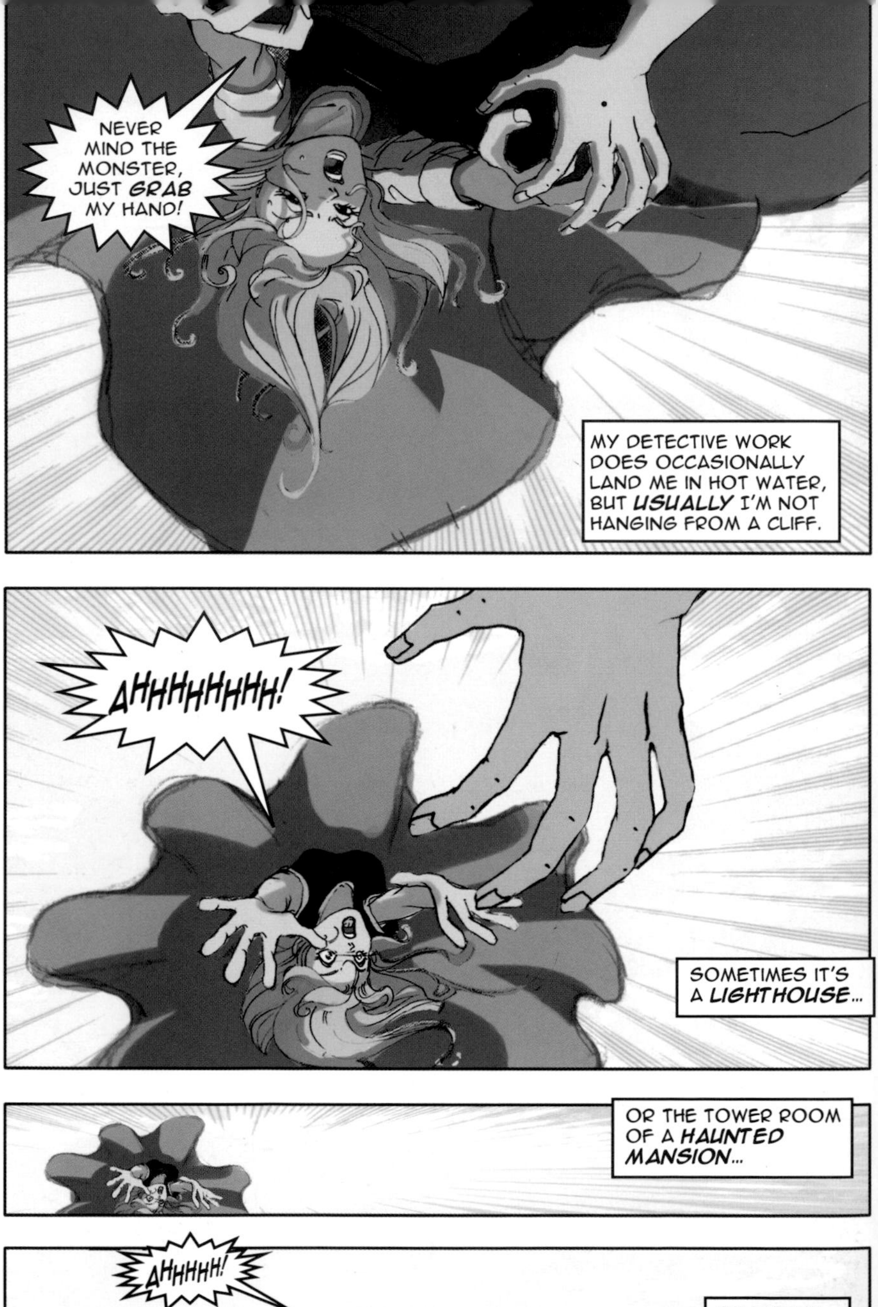
NEVER MIND THE MONSTER, JUST GRAB MY HAND!
MY DETECTIVE WORK DOES OCCASIONALLY LAND ME IN HOT WATER, BUT USUALLY I'M NOT HANGING FROM A CLIFF.
AHHHHHHHH!
SOMETIMES IT'S A LIGHTHOUSE...
OR THE TOWER ROOM OF A HAUNTED MANSION...
AHHHHH!
OR WORSE...

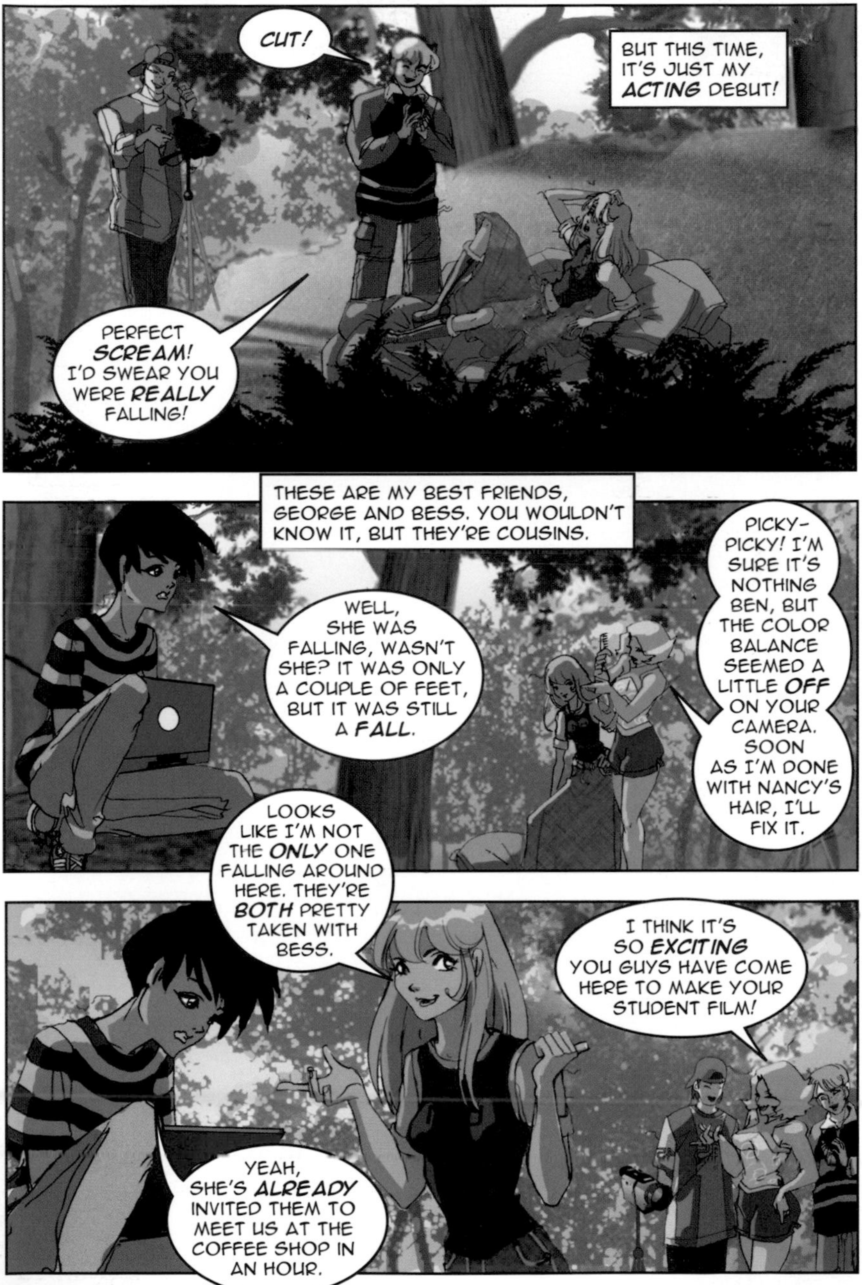
CUT!
BUT THIS TIME, IT'S JUST MY ACTING DEBUT!
PERFECT SCREAM! I'D SWEAR YOU WERE REALLY FALLING!
THESE ARE MY BEST FRIENDS, GEORGE AND BESS. YOU WOULDN'T KNOW IT, BUT THEY'RE COUSINS.
WELL, SHE WAS FALLING, WASN'T SHE? IT WAS ONLY A COUPLE OF FEET, BUT IT WAS STILL A FALL.
PICKY-PICKY! I'M SURE IT'S NOTHING BEN, BUT THE COLOR BALANCE SEEMED A LITTLE OFF ON YOUR CAMERA. SOON AS I'M DONE WITH NANCY'S HAIR, I'LL FIX IT.
LOOKS LIKE I'M NOT THE ONLY ONE FALLING AROUND HERE. THEY'RE BOTH PRETTY TAKEN WITH BESS.
I THINK IT'S SO EXCITING YOU GUYS HAVE COME HERE TO MAKE YOUR STUDENT FILM!
YEAH, SHE'S ALREADY INVITED THEM TO MEET US AT THE COFFEE SHOP IN AN HOUR.

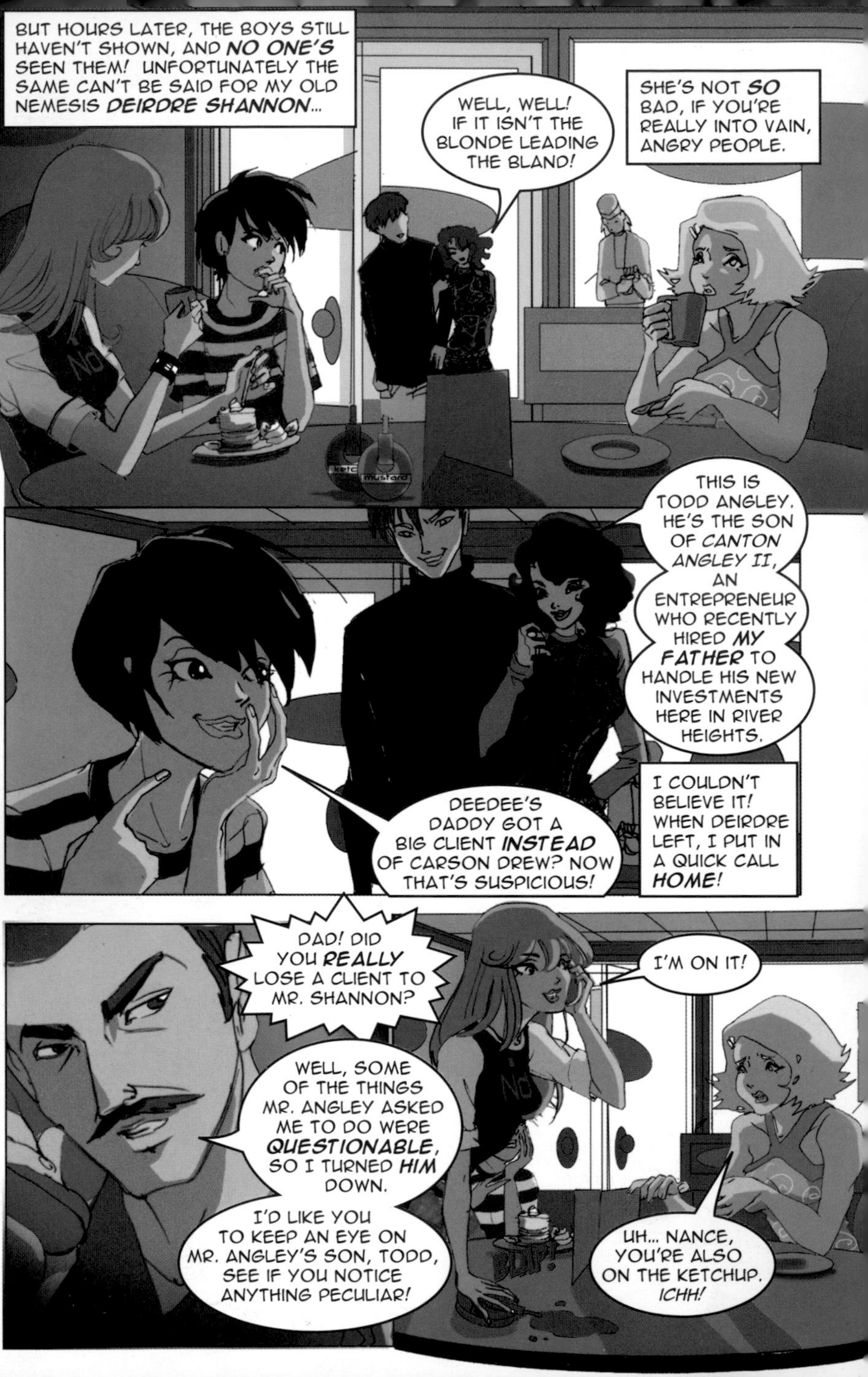
BUT HOURS LATER, THE BOYS STILL HAVEN'T SHOWN, AND NO ONE'S SEEN THEM! UNFORTUNATELY THE SAME CAN'T BE SAID FOR MY OLD NEMESIS DEIRDRE SHANNON...
WELL, WELL! IF IT ISN'T THE BLONDE LEADING THE BLAND!
SHE'S NOT SO BAD, IF YOU'RE REALLY INTO VAIN, ANGRY PEOPLE.
mustard
THIS IS TODD ANGLEY. HE'S THE SON OF CANTON ANGLEY II, AN ENTREPRENEUR WHO RECENTLY HIRED MY FATHER TO HANDLE HIS NEW INVESTMENTS HERE IN RIVER HEIGHTS.
DEEDEE'S DADDY GOT A BIG CLIENT INSTEAD OF CARSON DREW? NOW THAT'S SUSPICIOUS!
I COULDN'T BELIEVE IT! WHEN DEIRDRE LEFT, I PUT IN A QUICK CALL HOME!
DAD! DID YOU REALLY LOSE A CLIENT TO MR. SHANNON?
I'M ON IT!
WELL, SOME OF THE THINGS MR. ANGLEY ASKED ME TO DO WERE QUESTIONABLE, SO I TURNED HIM DOWN.
I'D LIKE YOU TO KEEP AN EYE ON MR. ANGLEY'S SON, TODD, SEE IF YOU NOTICE ANYTHING PECULIAR!
UH... NANCE, YOU'RE ALSO ON THE KETCHUP. ICHH!

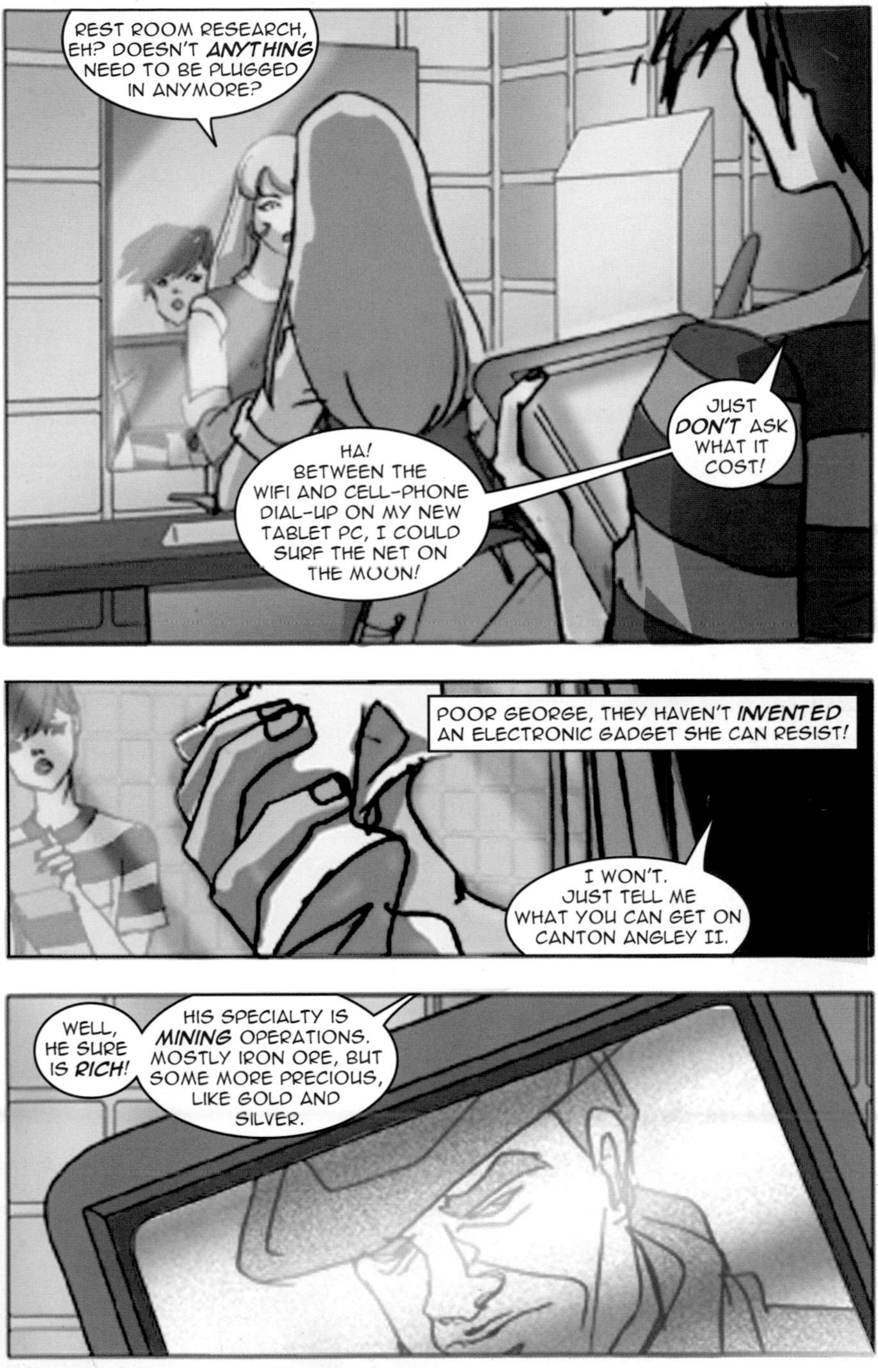
REST ROOM RESEARCH, EH? DOESN'T *ANYTHING* NEED TO BE PLUGGED IN ANYMORE?
HA! BETWEEN THE WIFI AND CELL-PHONE DIAL-UP ON MY NEW TABLET PC, I COULD SURF THE NET ON THE MOON!
JUST *DON'T* ASK WHAT IT COST!
POOR GEORGE, THEY HAVEN'T *INVENTED* AN ELECTRONIC GADGET SHE CAN RESIST!
I WON'T. JUST TELL ME WHAT YOU CAN GET ON CANTON ANGLEY II.
HIS SPECIALTY IS *MINING* OPERATIONS. MOSTLY IRON ORE, BUT SOME MORE PRECIOUS, LIKE GOLD AND SILVER.
WELL, HE SURE IS *RICH*!

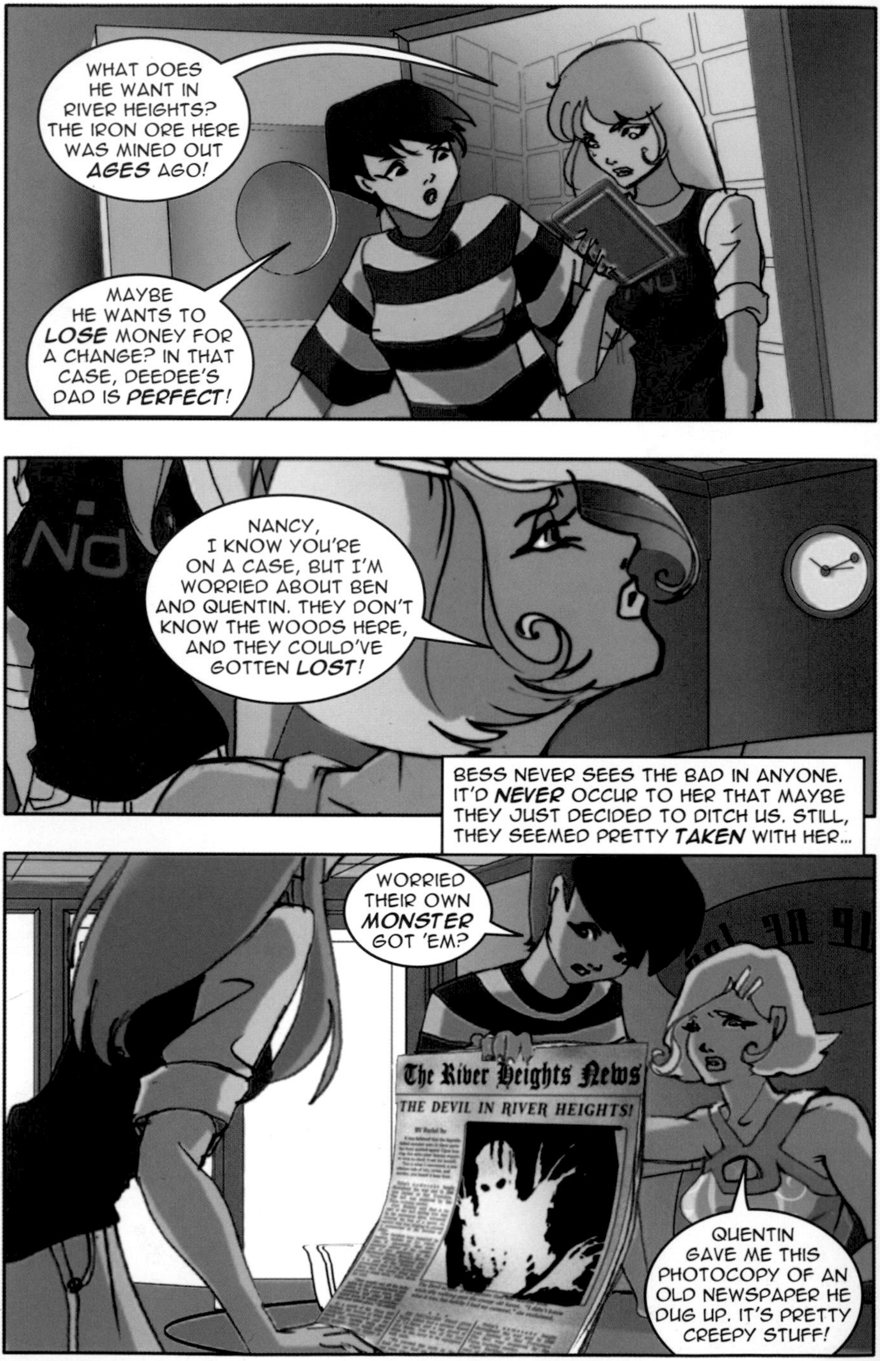

WHAT DOES HE WANT IN RIVER HEIGHTS? THE IRON ORE HERE WAS MINED OUT AGES AGO!
MAYBE HE WANTS TO LOSE MONEY FOR A CHANGE? IN THAT CASE, DEEDEE'S DAD IS PERFECT!
NANCY, I KNOW YOU'RE ON A CASE, BUT I'M WORRIED ABOUT BEN AND QUENTIN. THEY DON'T KNOW THE WOODS HERE, AND THEY COULD'VE GOTTEN LOST!
BESS NEVER SEES THE BAD IN ANYONE. IT'D NEVER OCCUR TO HER THAT MAYBE THEY JUST DECIDED TO DITCH US. STILL, THEY SEEMED PRETTY TAKEN WITH HER...
WORRIED THEIR OWN MONSTER GOT 'EM?
The River Heights News
THE DEVIL IN RIVER HEIGHTS!
QUENTIN GAVE ME THIS PHOTOCOPY OF AN OLD NEWSPAPER HE DUG UP. IT'S PRETTY CREEPY STUFF!

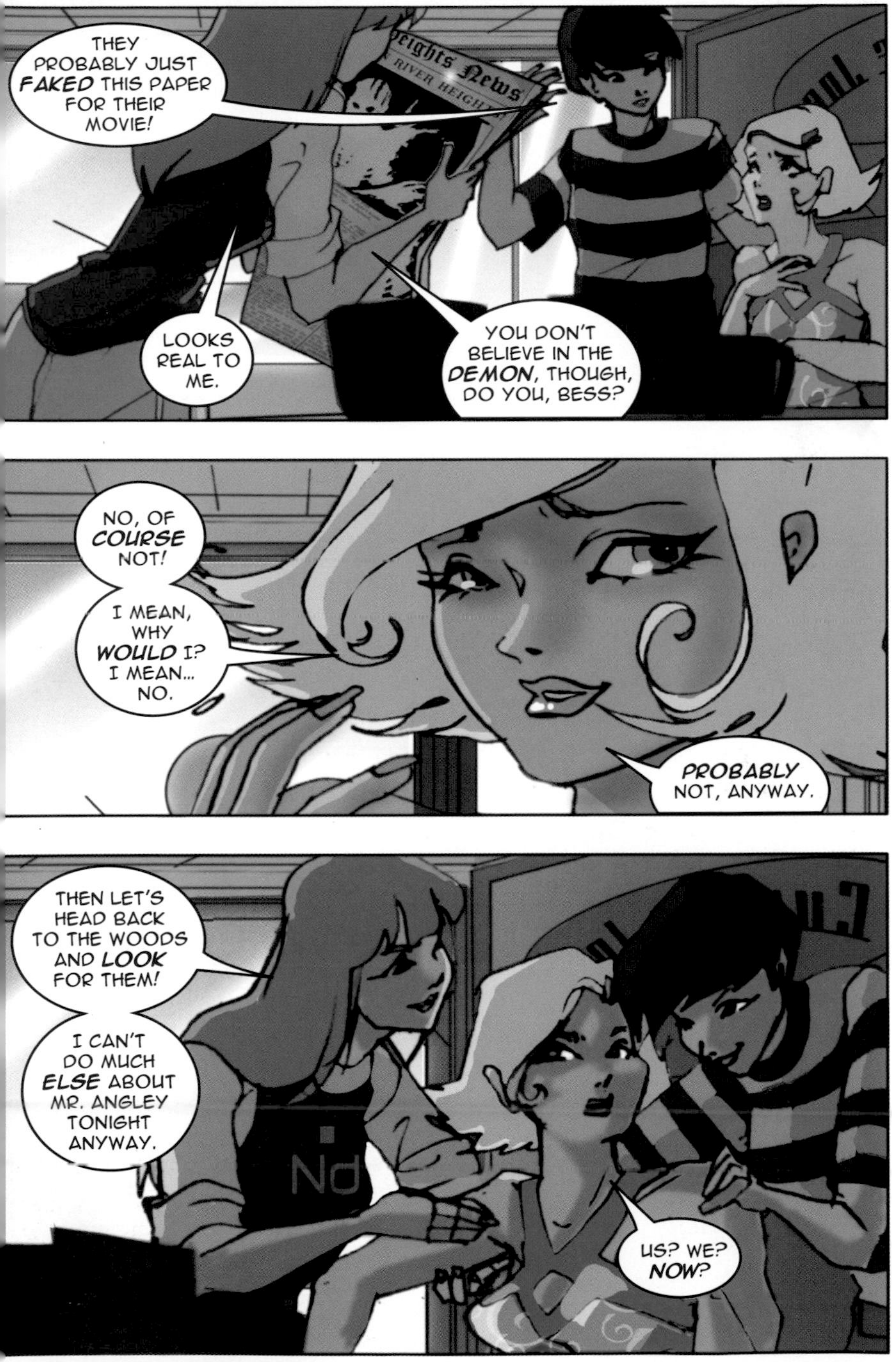
THEY PROBABLY JUST FAKED THIS PAPER FOR THEIR MOVIE!
LOOKS REAL TO ME.
YOU DON'T BELIEVE IN THE DEMON, THOUGH, DO YOU, BESS?
NO, OF COURSE NOT!
I MEAN, WHY WOULD I? I MEAN... NO.
PROBABLY NOT, ANYWAY.
THEN LET'S HEAD BACK TO THE WOODS AND LOOK FOR THEM!
I CAN'T DO MUCH ELSE ABOUT MR. ANGLEY TONIGHT ANYWAY.
US? WE? NOW?

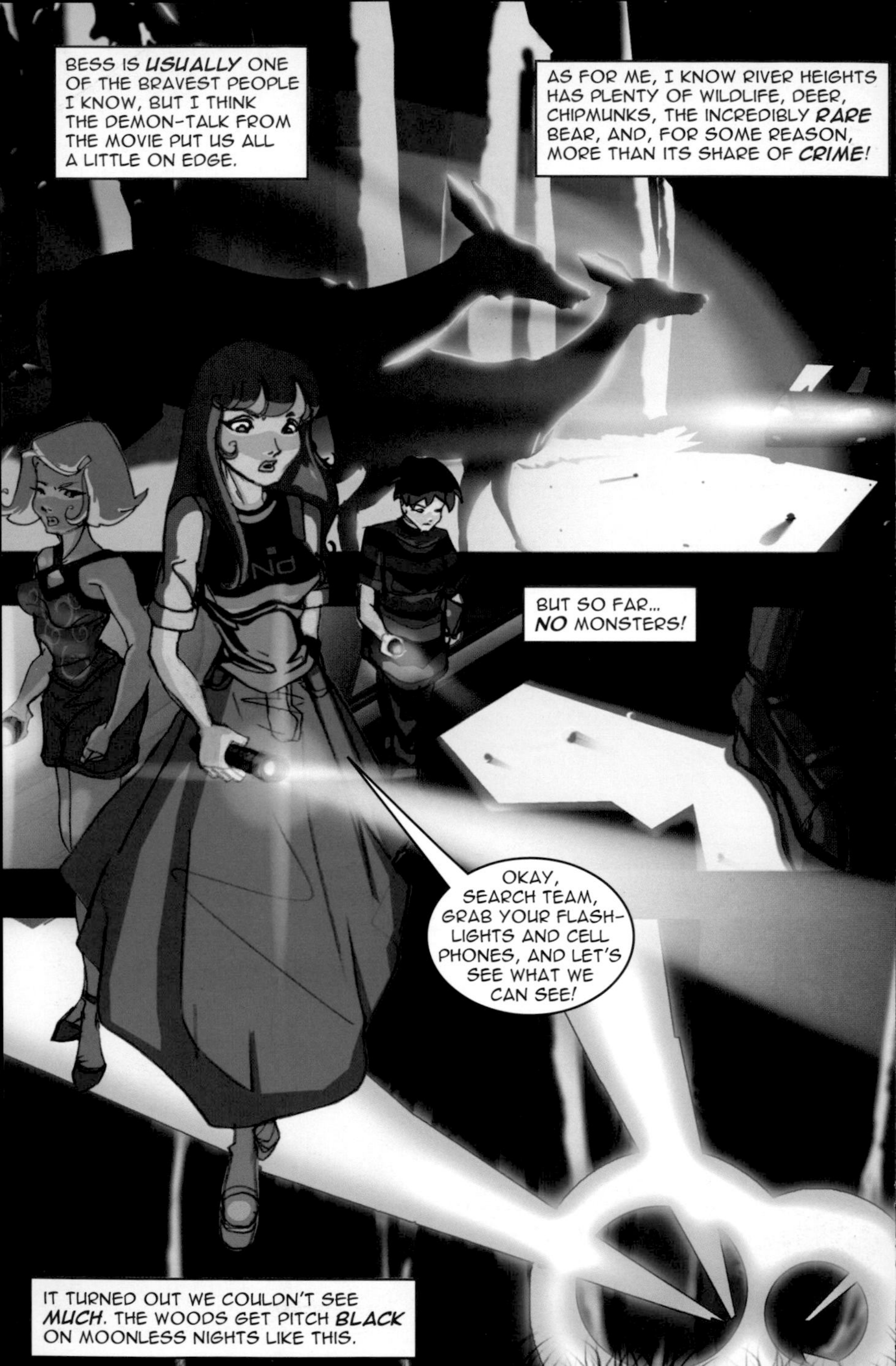
BESS IS USUALLY ONE OF THE BRAVEST PEOPLE I KNOW, BUT I THINK THE DEMON-TALK FROM THE MOVIE PUT US ALL A LITTLE ON EDGE.
AS FOR ME, I KNOW RIVER HEIGHTS HAS PLENTY OF WILDLIFE, DEER, CHIPMUNKS, THE INCREDIBLY RARE BEAR, AND, FOR SOME REASON, MORE THAN ITS SHARE OF CRIME!
BUT SO FAR... NO MONSTERS!
OKAY, SEARCH TEAM, GRAB YOUR FLASH-LIGHTS AND CELL PHONES, AND LET'S SEE WHAT WE CAN SEE!
IT TURNED OUT WE COULDN'T SEE MUCH. THE WOODS GET PITCH BLACK ON MOONLESS NIGHTS LIKE THIS.

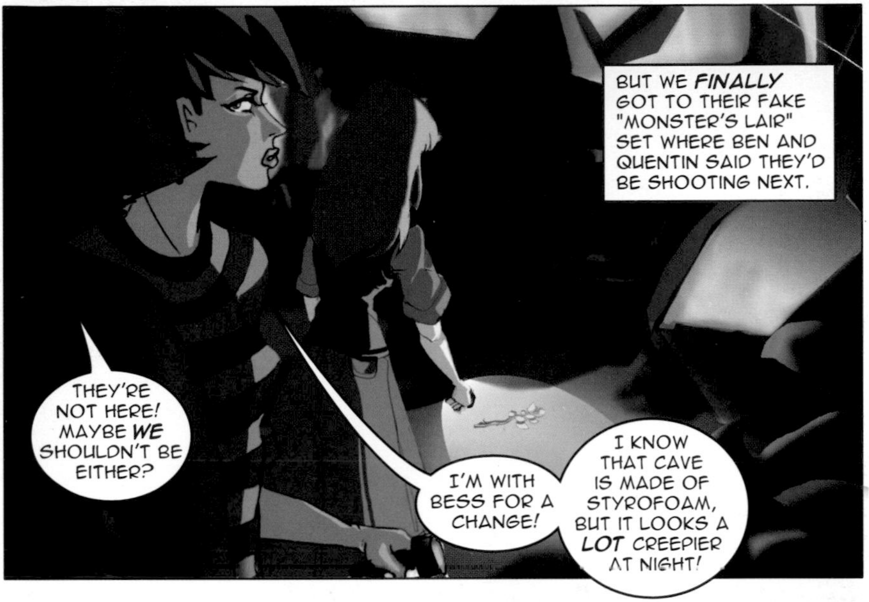
BUT WE *FINALLY* GOT TO THEIR FAKE "MONSTER'S LAIR" SET WHERE BEN AND QUENTIN SAID THEY'D BE SHOOTING NEXT.
THEY'RE NOT HERE! MAYBE *WE* SHOULDN'T BE EITHER?
I'M WITH BESS FOR A CHANGE!
I KNOW THAT CAVE IS MADE OF STYROFOAM, BUT IT LOOKS A *LOT* CREEPIER AT NIGHT!

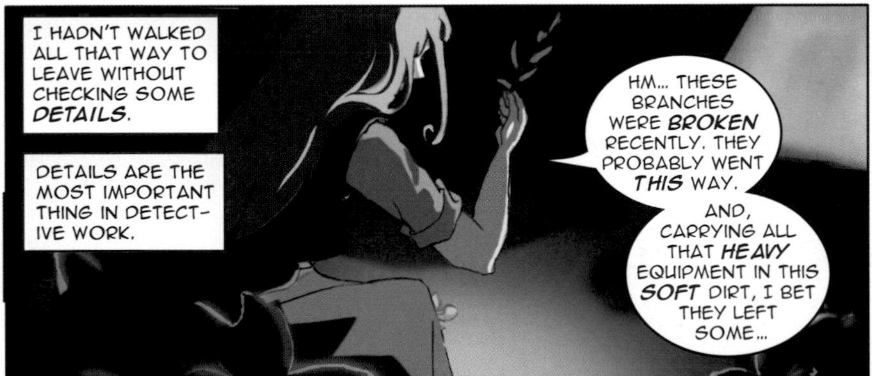
I HADN'T WALKED ALL THAT WAY TO LEAVE WITHOUT CHECKING SOME *DETAILS*.
DETAILS ARE THE MOST IMPORTANT THING IN DETECT-IVE WORK.
HM... THESE BRANCHES WERE *BROKEN* RECENTLY. THEY PROBABLY WENT *THIS* WAY.
AND, CARRYING ALL THAT *HEAVY* EQUIPMENT IN THIS *SOFT* DIRT, I BET THEY LEFT SOME...

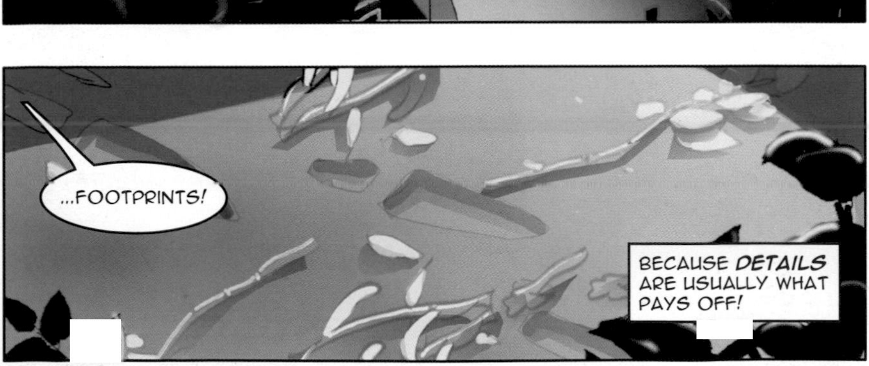
...FOOTPRINTS!
BECAUSE *DETAILS* ARE USUALLY WHAT PAYS OFF!

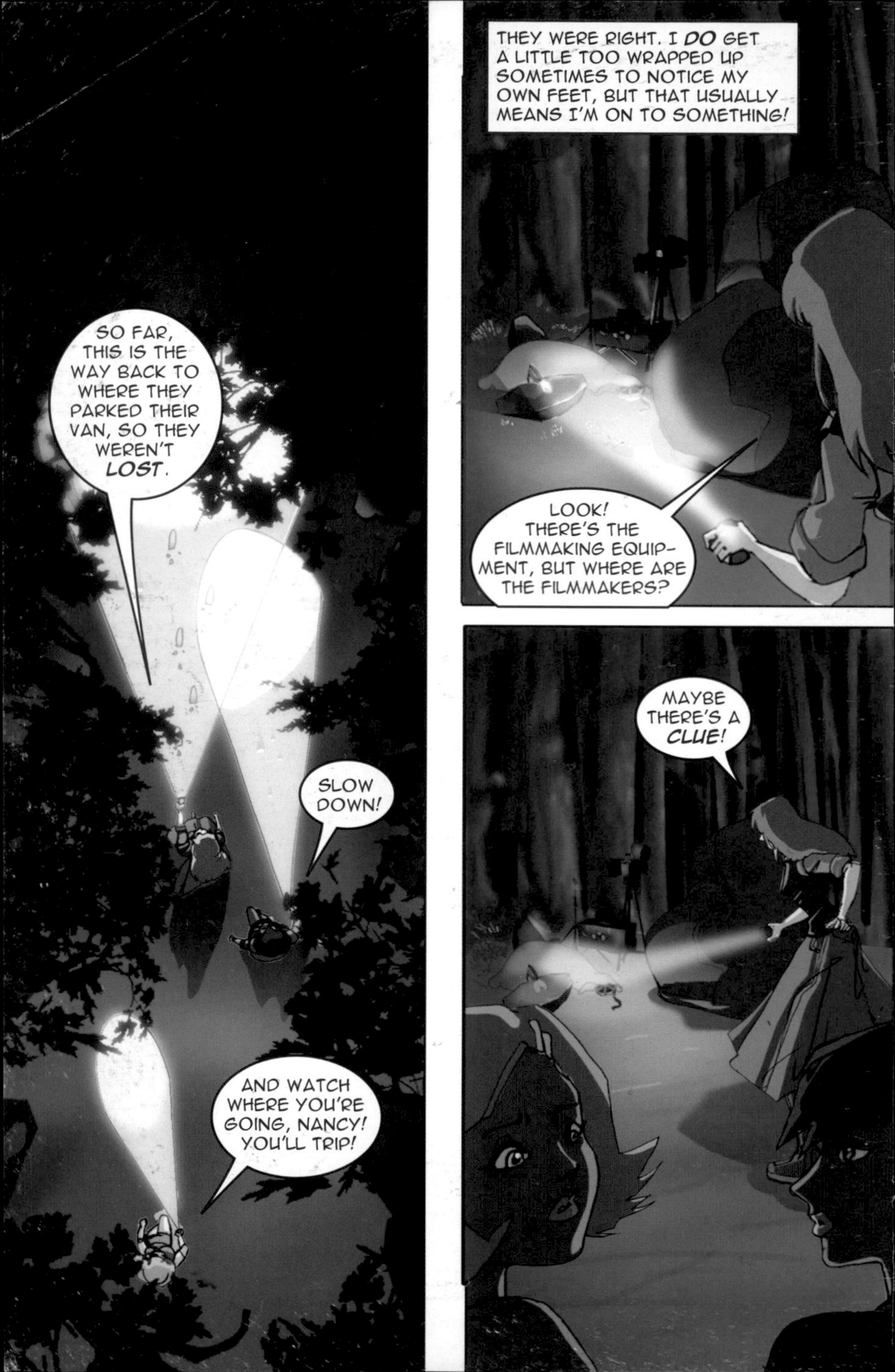
SO FAR, THIS IS THE WAY BACK TO WHERE THEY PARKED THEIR VAN, SO THEY WEREN'T LOST.
SLOW DOWN!
AND WATCH WHERE YOU'RE GOING, NANCY! YOU'LL TRIP!
THEY WERE RIGHT. I DO GET A LITTLE TOO WRAPPED UP SOMETIMES TO NOTICE MY OWN FEET, BUT THAT USUALLY MEANS I'M ON TO SOMETHING!
LOOK! THERE'S THE FILMMAKING EQUIPMENT, BUT WHERE ARE THE FILMMAKERS?
MAYBE THERE'S A CLUE!

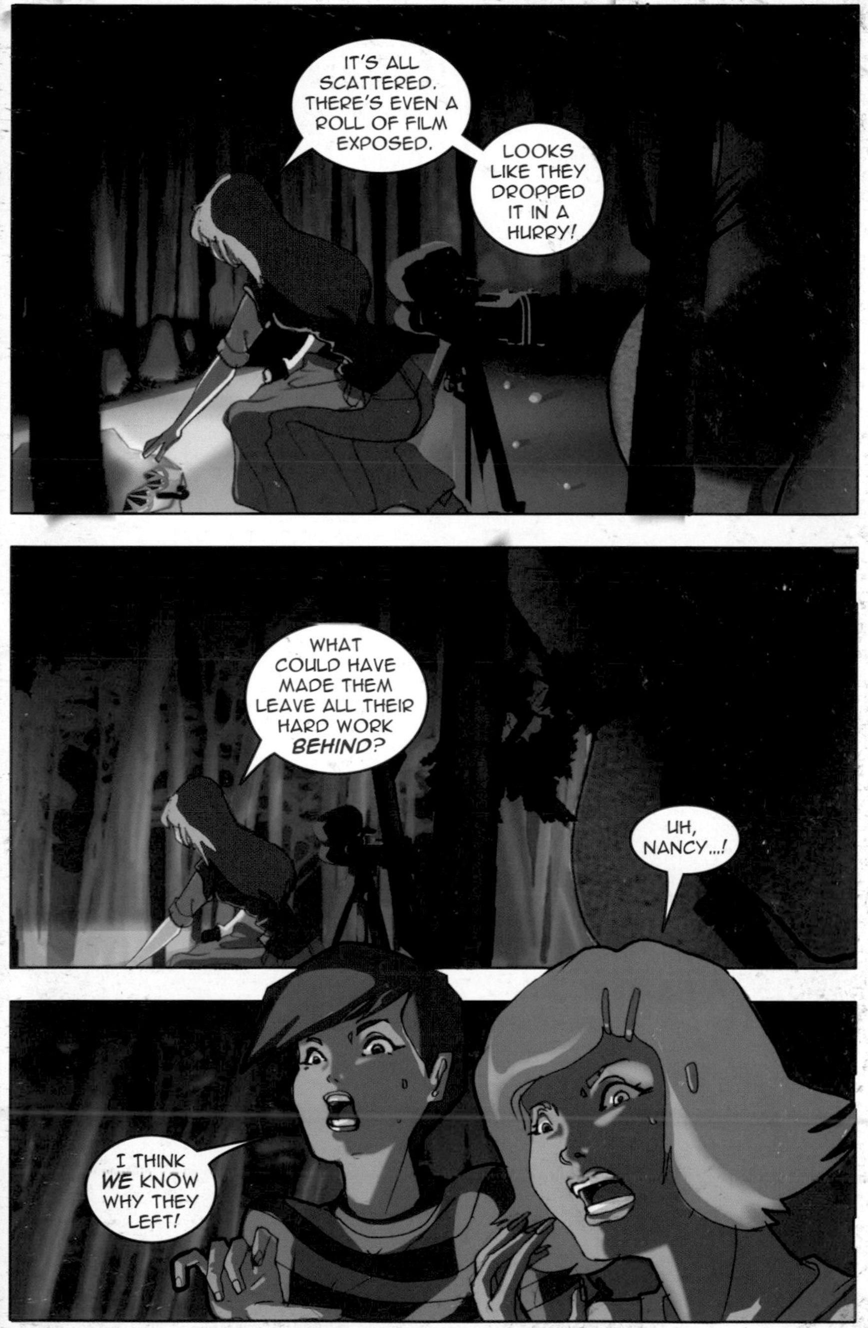
IT'S ALL SCATTERED. THERE'S EVEN A ROLL OF FILM EXPOSED.
LOOKS LIKE THEY DROPPED IT IN A HURRY!
WHAT COULD HAVE MADE THEM LEAVE ALL THEIR HARD WORK *BEHIND*?
UH, NANCY...!
I THINK *WE* KNOW WHY THEY LEFT!

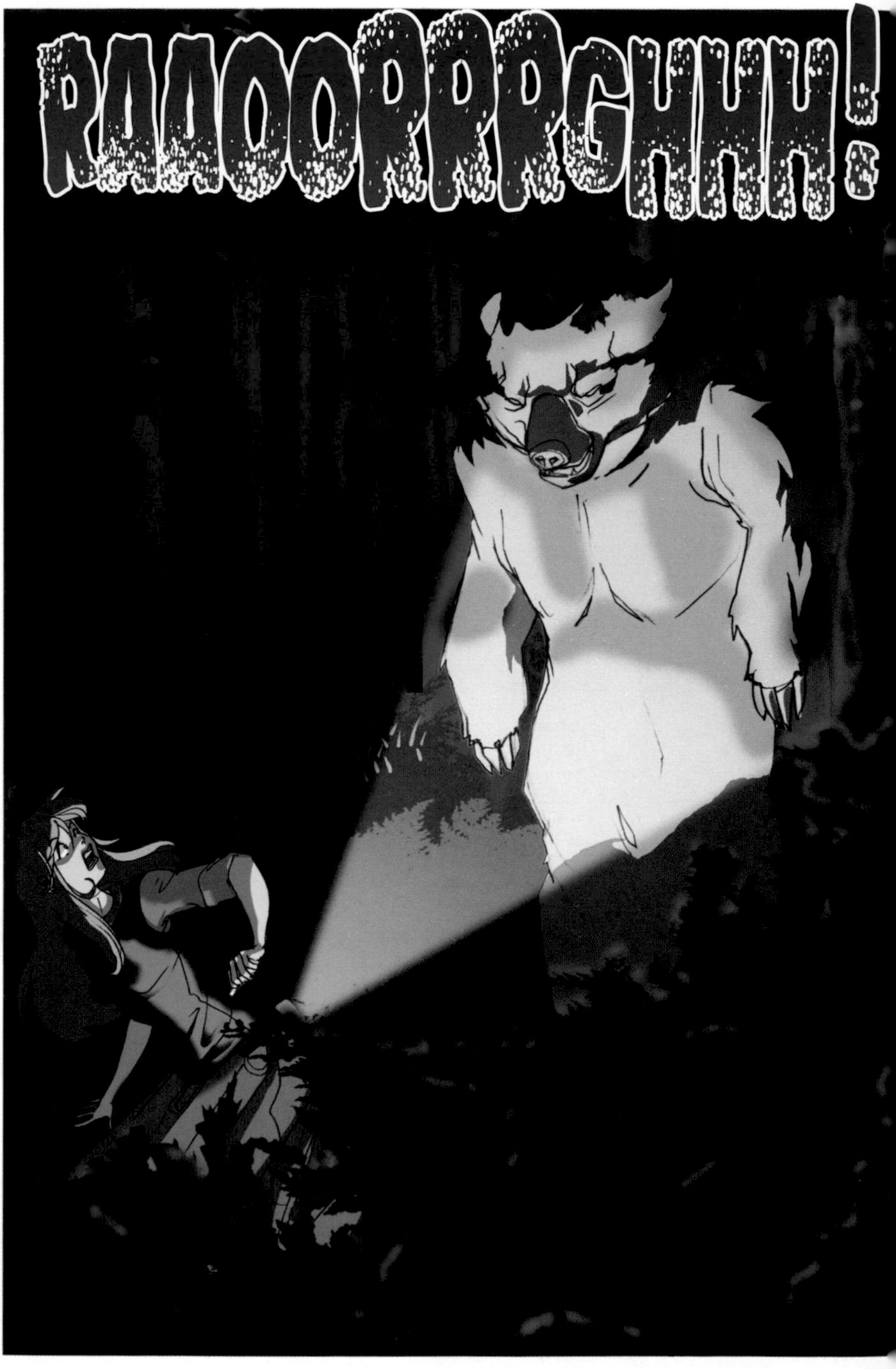
RAAOORRRGHHH!

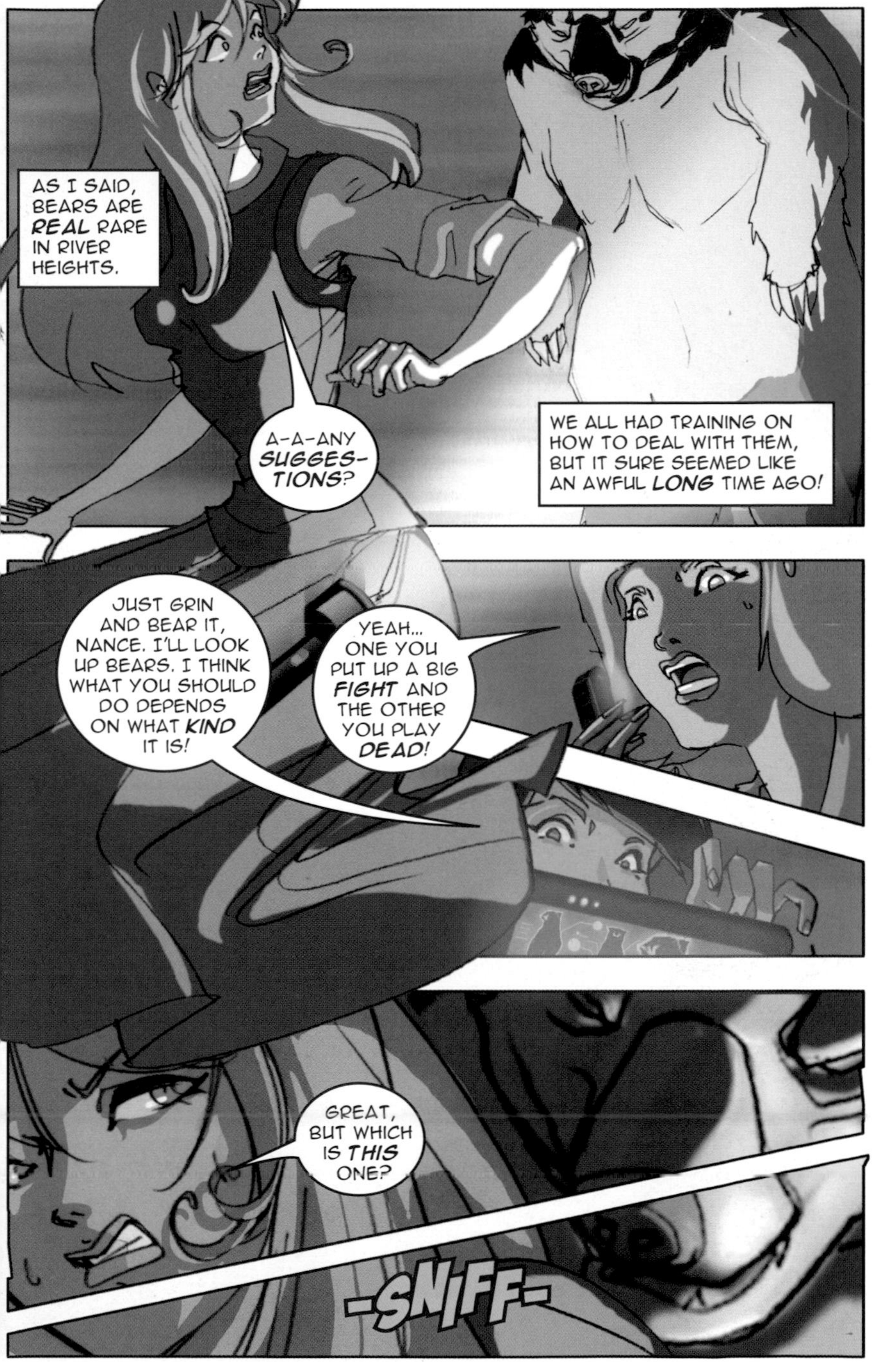

AS I SAID, BEARS ARE REAL RARE IN RIVER HEIGHTS.
A-A-ANY SUGGES-TIONS?
WE ALL HAD TRAINING ON HOW TO DEAL WITH THEM, BUT IT SURE SEEMED LIKE AN AWFUL LONG TIME AGO!
JUST GRIN AND BEAR IT, NANCE. I'LL LOOK UP BEARS. I THINK WHAT YOU SHOULD DO DEPENDS ON WHAT KIND IT IS!
YEAH... ONE YOU PUT UP A BIG FIGHT AND THE OTHER YOU PLAY DEAD!
GREAT, BUT WHICH IS THIS ONE?
-SNIFF-

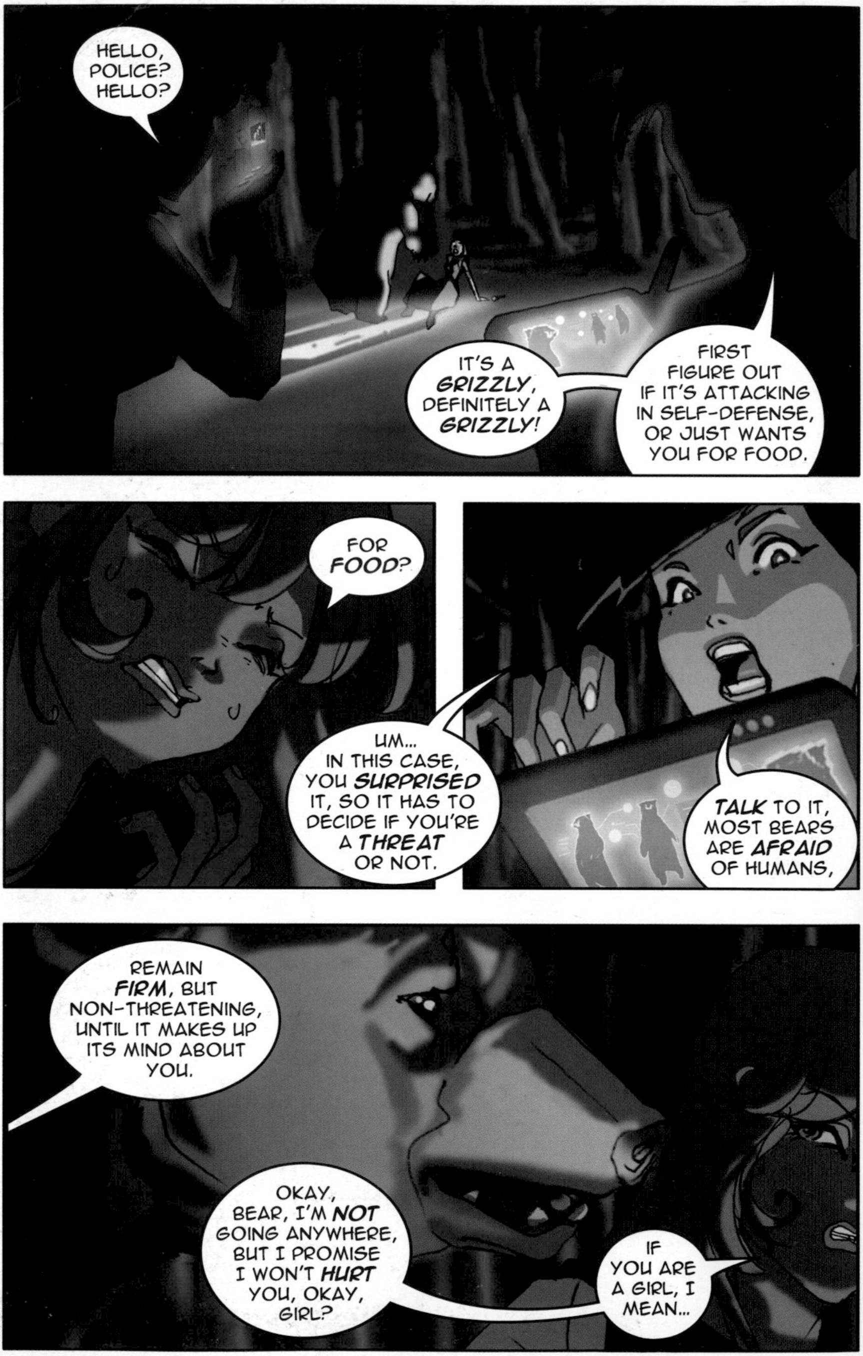
HELLO, POLICE? HELLO?
IT'S A GRIZZLY, DEFINITELY A GRIZZLY!
FIRST FIGURE OUT IF IT'S ATTACKING IN SELF-DEFENSE, OR JUST WANTS YOU FOR FOOD.
FOR FOOD?
TALK TO IT, MOST BEARS ARE AFRAID OF HUMANS,
UM... IN THIS CASE, YOU SURPRISED IT, SO IT HAS TO DECIDE IF YOU'RE A THREAT OR NOT.
REMAIN FIRM, BUT NON-THREATENING, UNTIL IT MAKES UP ITS MIND ABOUT YOU.
OKAY, BEAR, I'M NOT GOING ANYWHERE, BUT I PROMISE I WON'T HURT YOU, OKAY, GIRL?
IF YOU ARE A GIRL, I MEAN...

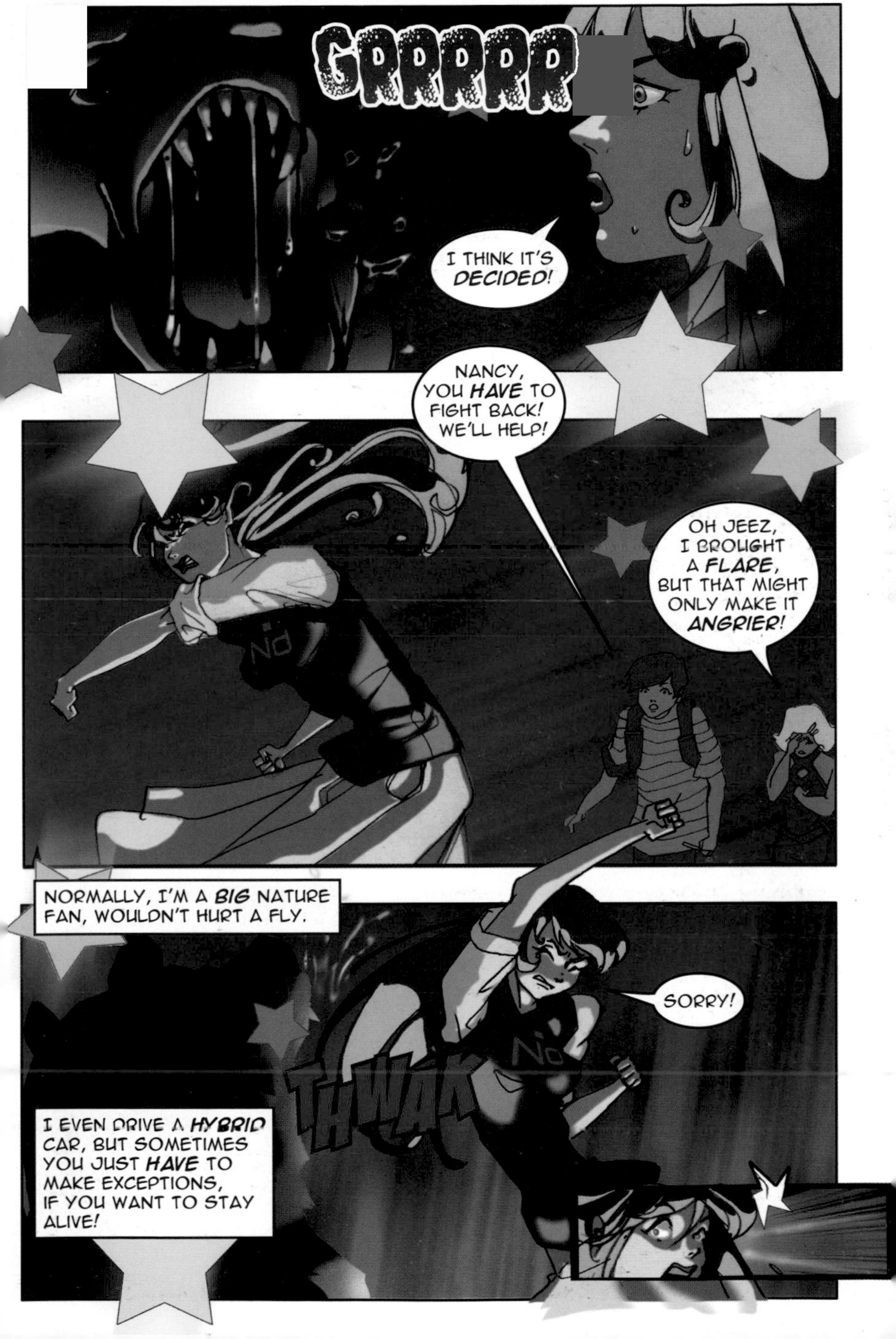
GRRRRR
I THINK IT'S DECIDED!
NANCY, YOU HAVE TO FIGHT BACK! WE'LL HELP!
OH JEEZ, I BROUGHT A FLARE, BUT THAT MIGHT ONLY MAKE IT ANGRIER!
NORMALLY, I'M A BIG NATURE FAN, WOULDN'T HURT A FLY.
SORRY!
THWAK
I EVEN DRIVE A HYBRID CAR, BUT SOMETIMES YOU JUST HAVE TO MAKE EXCEPTIONS, IF YOU WANT TO STAY ALIVE!

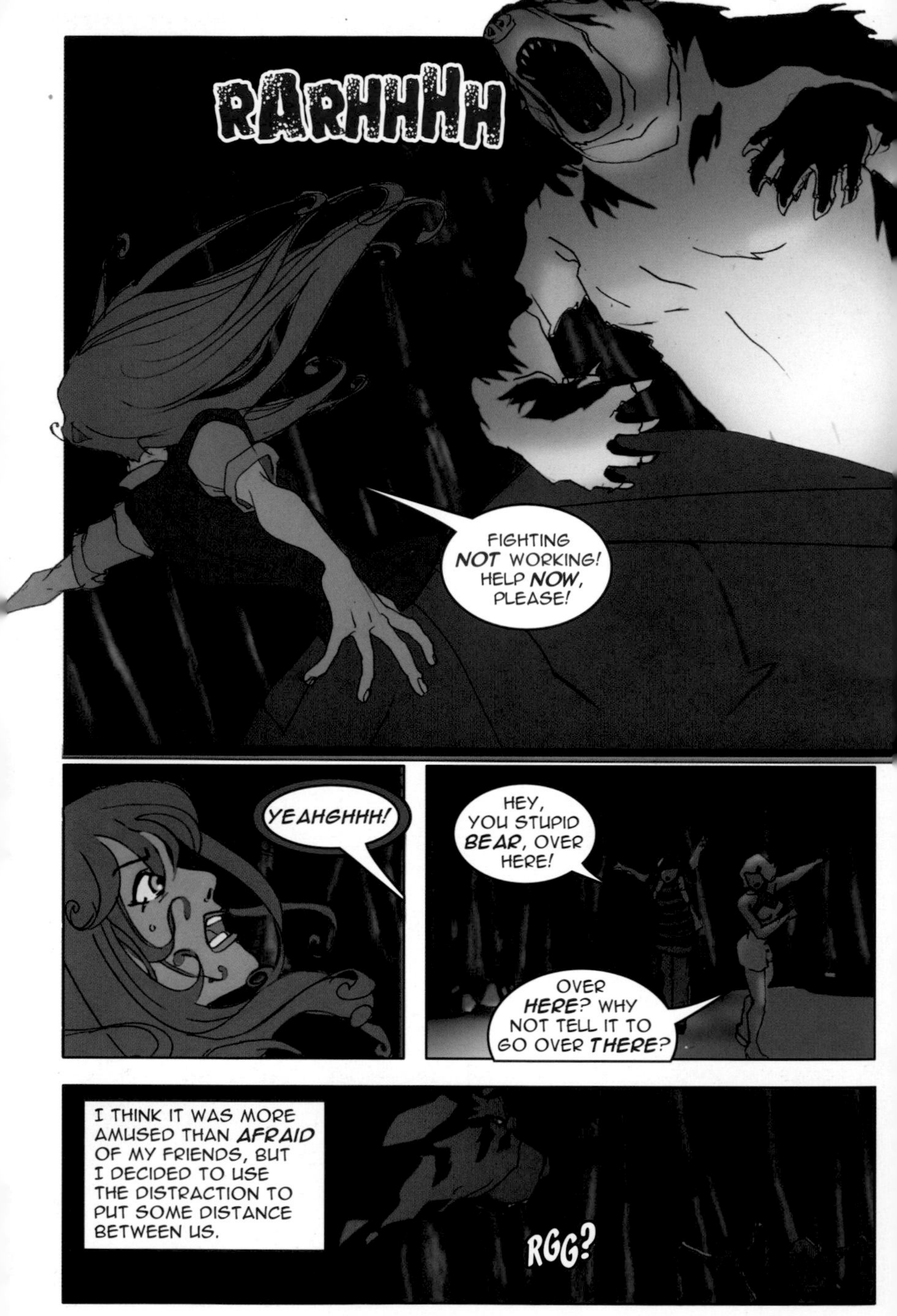
RARHHHH
FIGHTING NOT WORKING! HELP NOW, PLEASE!
YEAHGHHH!
HEY, YOU STUPID BEAR, OVER HERE!
OVER HERE? WHY NOT TELL IT TO GO OVER THERE?
I THINK IT WAS MORE AMUSED THAN AFRAID OF MY FRIENDS, BUT I DECIDED TO USE THE DISTRACTION TO PUT SOME DISTANCE BETWEEN US.
RGG?

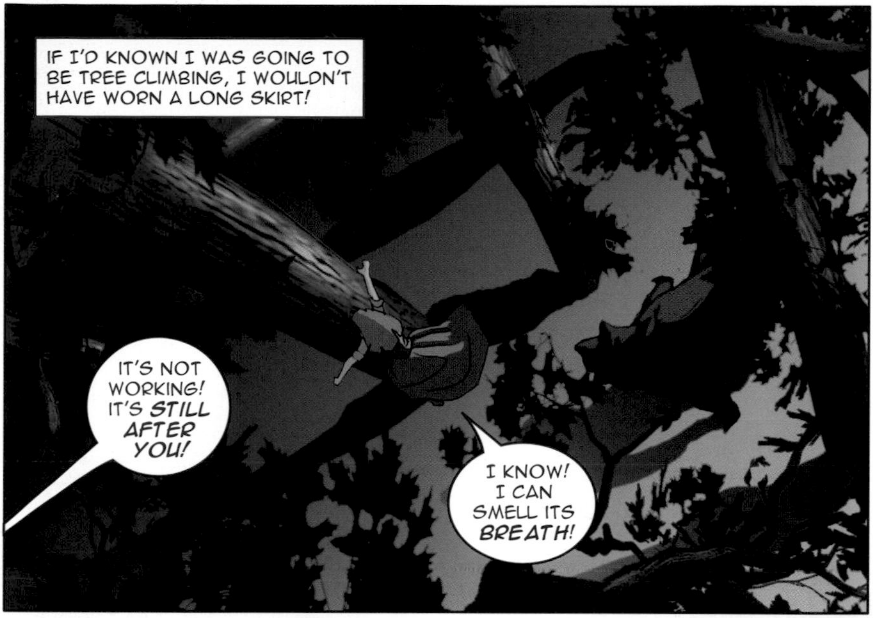
IF I'D KNOWN I WAS GOING TO BE TREE CLIMBING, I WOULDN'T HAVE WORN A LONG SKIRT!
IT'S NOT WORKING! IT'S STILL AFTER YOU!
I KNOW! I CAN SMELL ITS BREATH!

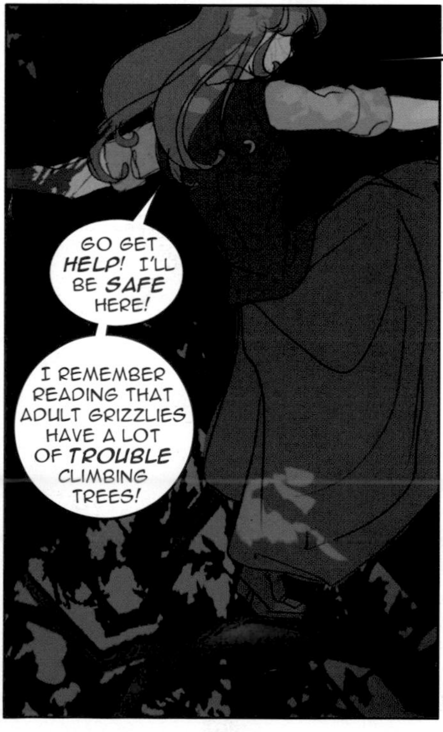
GO GET HELP! I'LL BE SAFE HERE!
I REMEMBER READING THAT ADULT GRIZZLIES HAVE A LOT OF TROUBLE CLIMBING TREES!

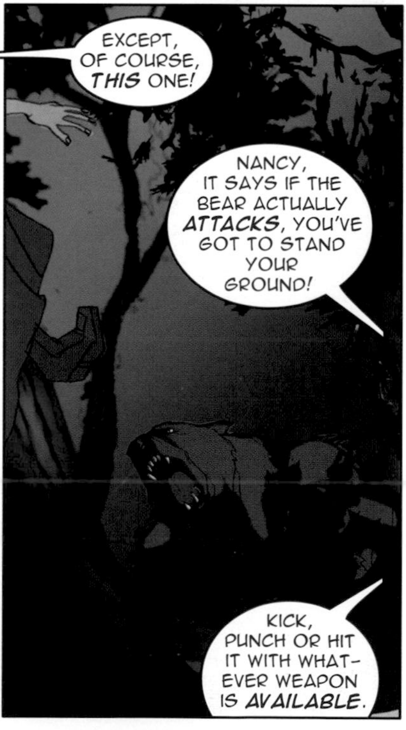
EXCEPT, OF COURSE, THIS ONE!
NANCY, IT SAYS IF THE BEAR ACTUALLY ATTACKS, YOU'VE GOT TO STAND YOUR GROUND!
KICK, PUNCH OR HIT IT WITH WHAT-EVER WEAPON IS AVAILABLE.

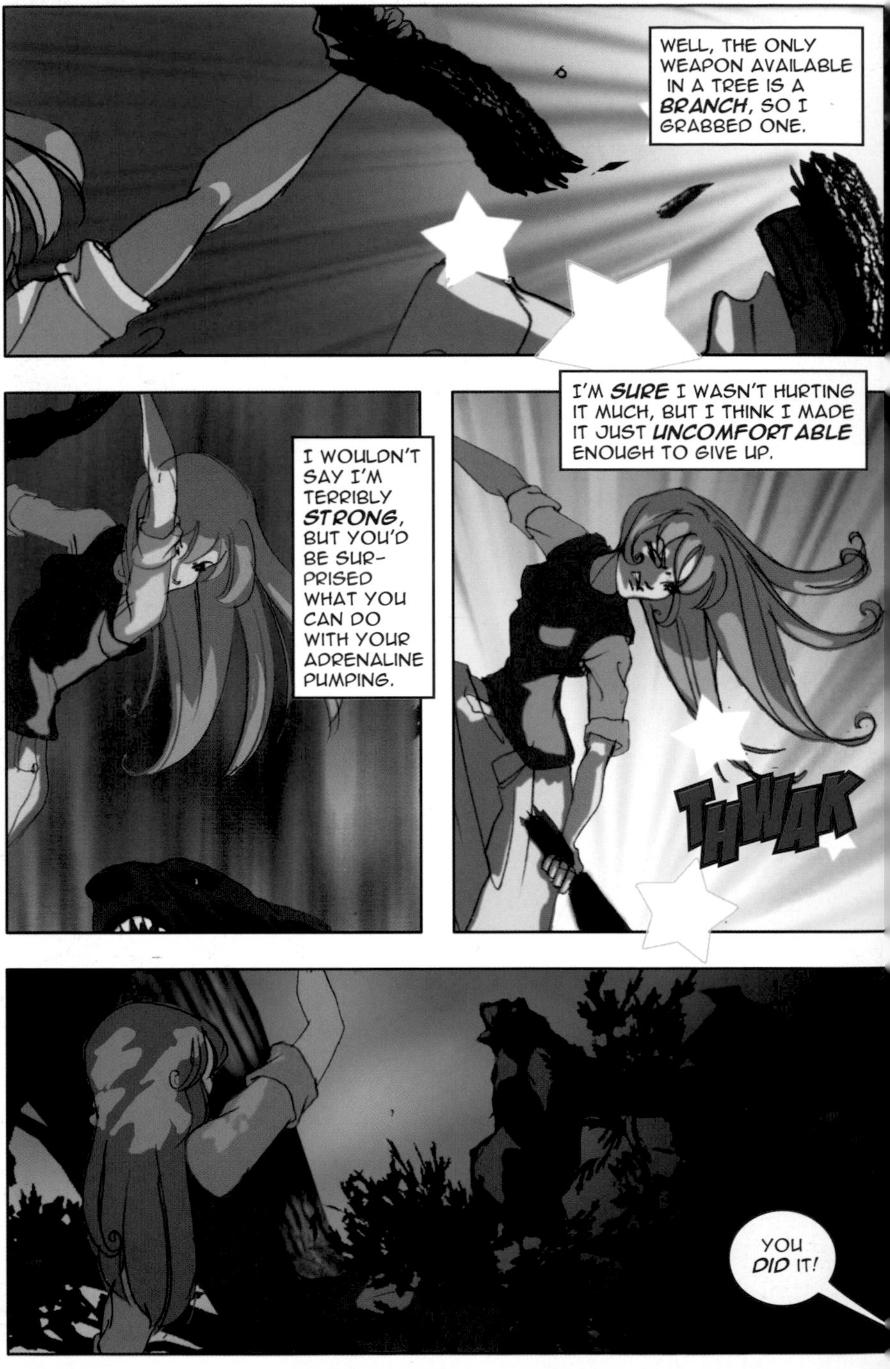
WELL, THE ONLY WEAPON AVAILABLE IN A TREE IS A BRANCH, SO I GRABBED ONE.
I WOULDN'T SAY I'M TERRIBLY STRONG, BUT YOU'D BE SUR-PRISED WHAT YOU CAN DO WITH YOUR ADRENALINE PUMPING.
I'M SURE I WASN'T HURTING IT MUCH, BUT I THINK I MADE IT JUST UNCOMFORTABLE ENOUGH TO GIVE UP.
THWAK
YOU DID IT!

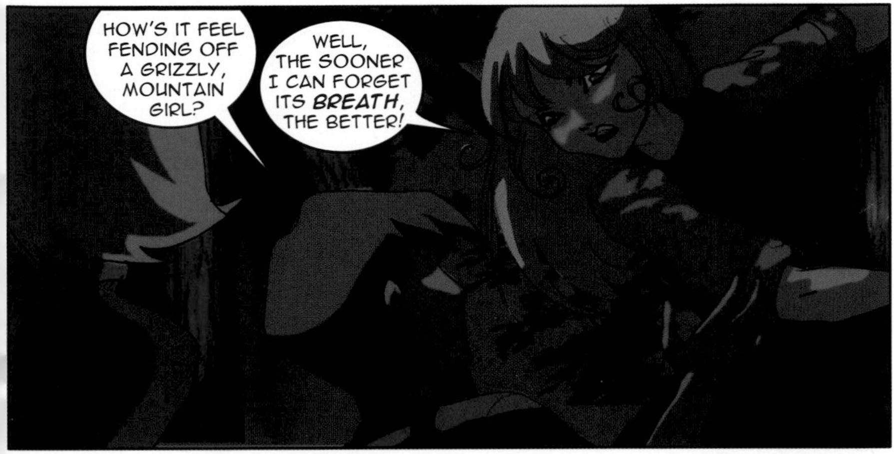
HOW'S IT FEEL FENDING OFF A GRIZZLY, MOUNTAIN GIRL?
WELL, THE SOONER I CAN FORGET ITS BREATH, THE BETTER!

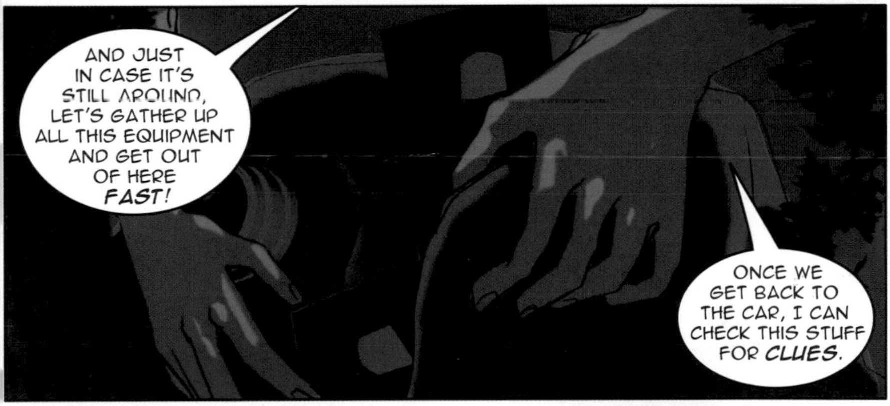
AND JUST IN CASE IT'S STILL AROUND, LET'S GATHER UP ALL THIS EQUIPMENT AND GET OUT OF HERE FAST!
ONCE WE GET BACK TO THE CAR, I CAN CHECK THIS STUFF FOR CLUES.

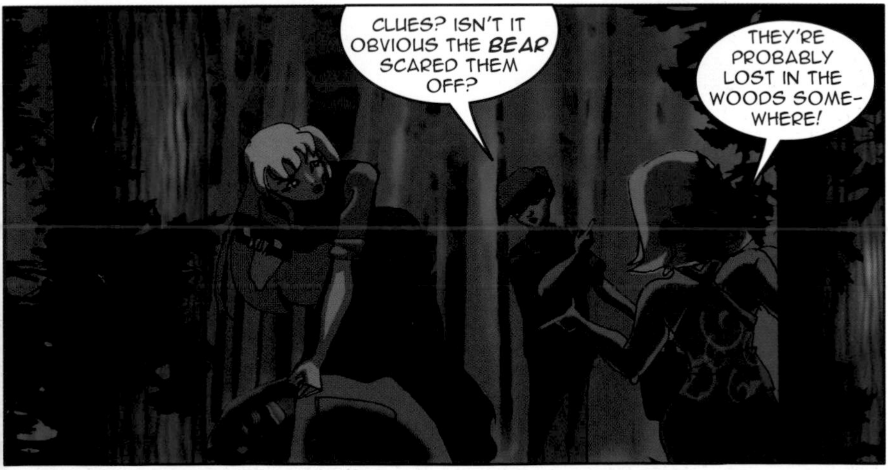
CLUES? ISN'T IT OBVIOUS THE BEAR SCARED THEM OFF?
THEY'RE PROBABLY LOST IN THE WOODS SOME-WHERE!

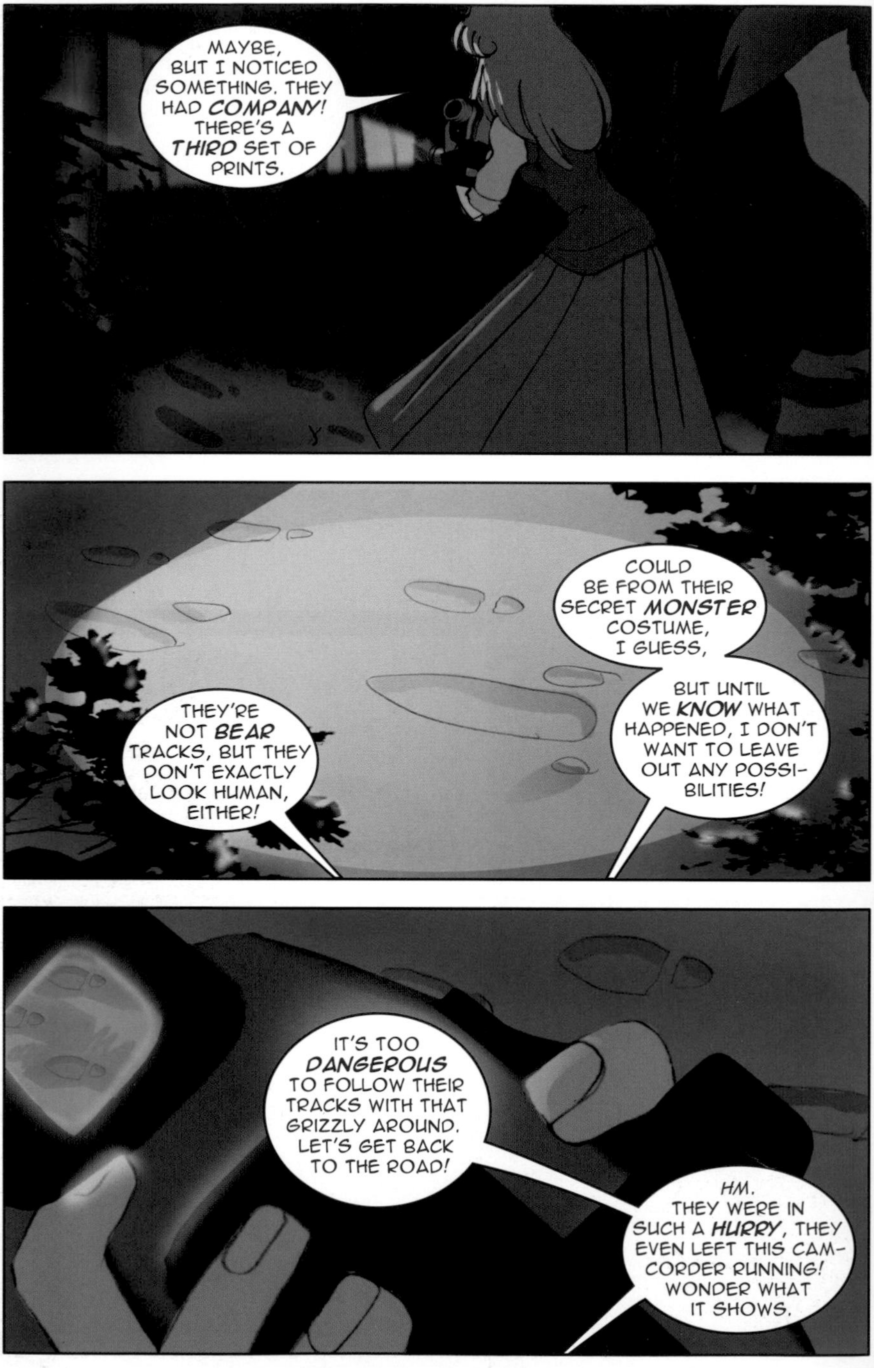
MAYBE, BUT I NOTICED SOMETHING. THEY HAD COMPANY! THERE'S A THIRD SET OF PRINTS.
THEY'RE NOT BEAR TRACKS, BUT THEY DON'T EXACTLY LOOK HUMAN, EITHER!
COULD BE FROM THEIR SECRET MONSTER COSTUME, I GUESS,
BUT UNTIL WE KNOW WHAT HAPPENED, I DON'T WANT TO LEAVE OUT ANY POSSI-BILITIES!
IT'S TOO DANGEROUS TO FOLLOW THEIR TRACKS WITH THAT GRIZZLY AROUND. LET'S GET BACK TO THE ROAD!
HM. THEY WERE IN SUCH A HURRY, THEY EVEN LEFT THIS CAM-CORDER RUNNING! WONDER WHAT IT SHOWS.

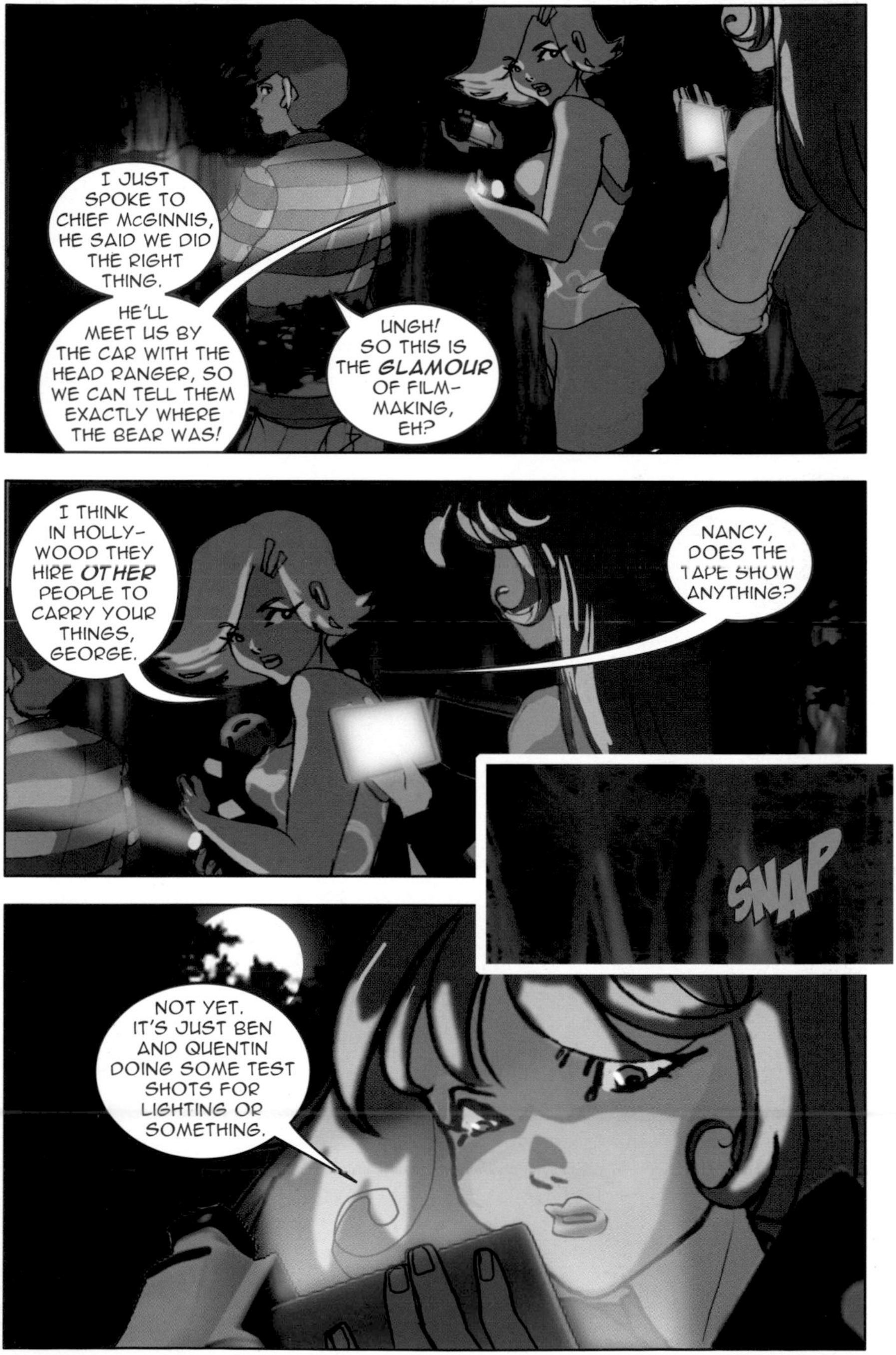
I JUST SPOKE TO CHIEF McGINNIS, HE SAID WE DID THE RIGHT THING.
HE'LL MEET US BY THE CAR WITH THE HEAD RANGER, SO WE CAN TELL THEM EXACTLY WHERE THE BEAR WAS!
UNGH! SO THIS IS THE *GLAMOUR* OF FILM-MAKING, EH?
I THINK IN HOLLY-WOOD THEY HIRE *OTHER* PEOPLE TO CARRY YOUR THINGS, GEORGE.
NANCY, DOES THE TAPE SHOW ANYTHING?
SNAP
NOT YET. IT'S JUST BEN AND QUENTIN DOING SOME TEST SHOTS FOR LIGHTING OR SOMETHING.

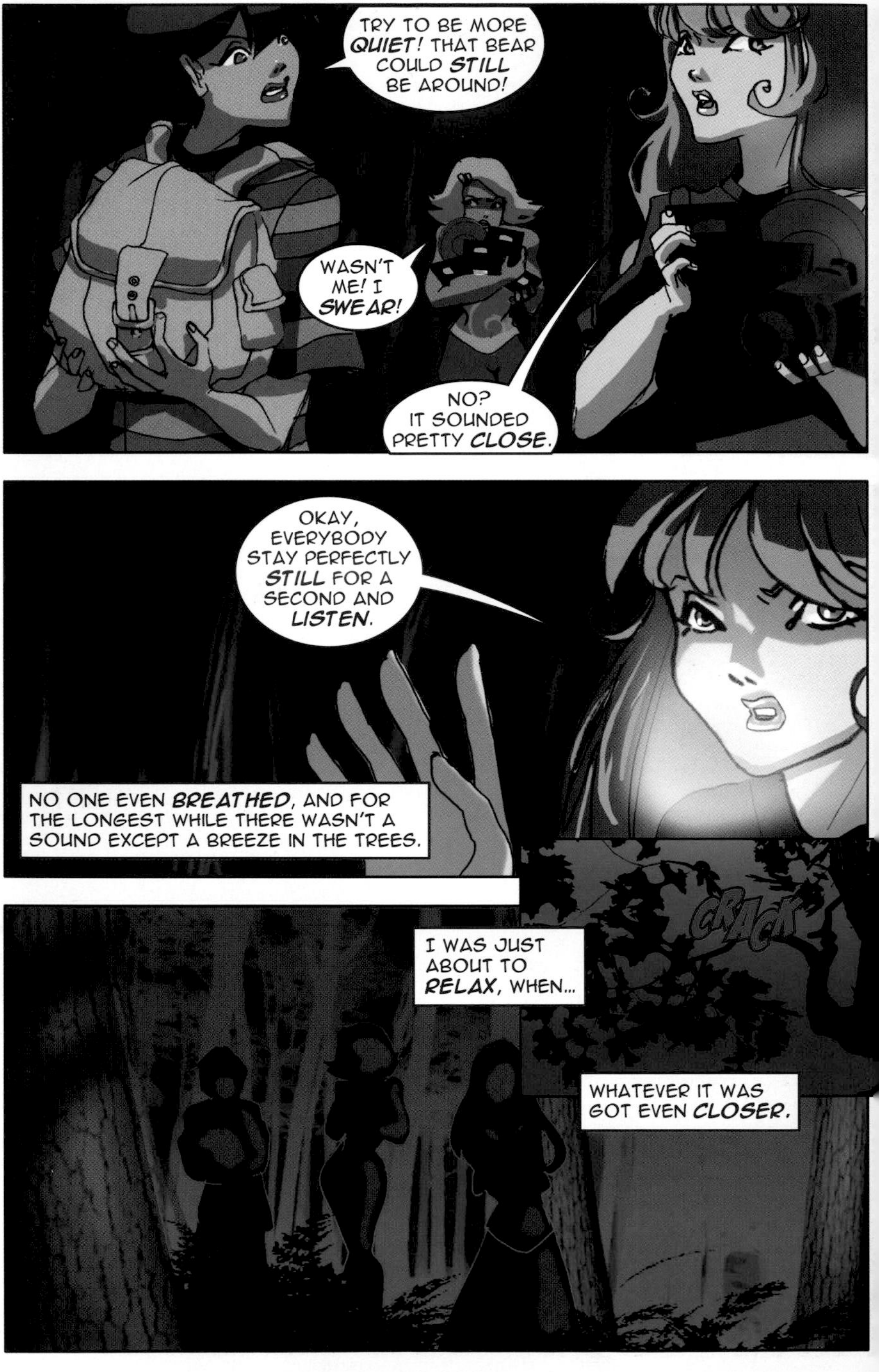
TRY TO BE MORE QUIET! THAT BEAR COULD STILL BE AROUND!
WASN'T ME! I SWEAR!
NO? IT SOUNDED PRETTY CLOSE.
OKAY, EVERYBODY STAY PERFECTLY STILL FOR A SECOND AND LISTEN.
NO ONE EVEN BREATHED, AND FOR THE LONGEST WHILE THERE WASN'T A SOUND EXCEPT A BREEZE IN THE TREES.
I WAS JUST ABOUT TO RELAX, WHEN...
CRACK
WHATEVER IT WAS GOT EVEN CLOSER.

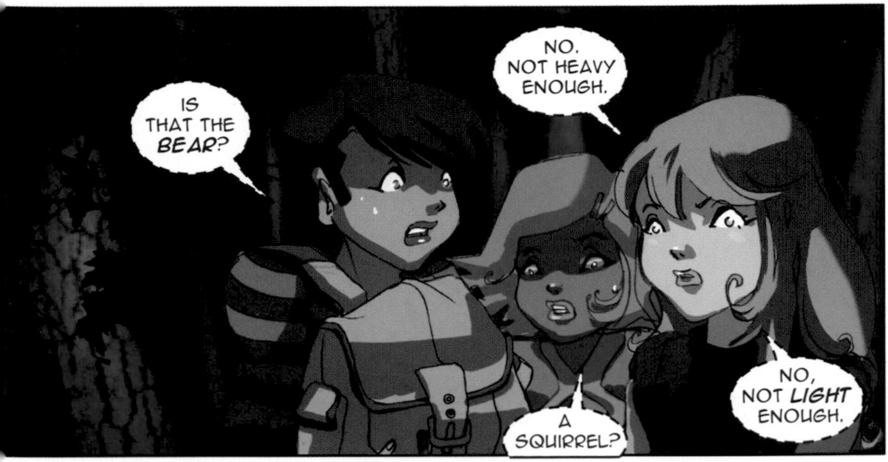
IS THAT THE BEAR?
NO. NOT HEAVY ENOUGH.
A SQUIRREL?
NO, NOT LIGHT ENOUGH.

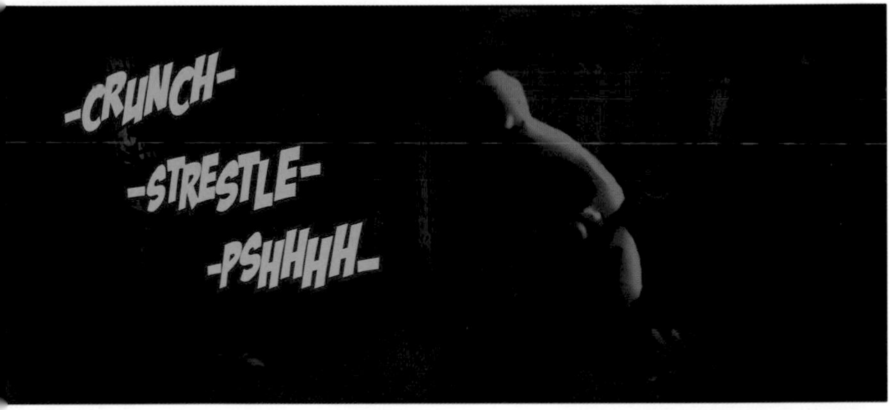
-CRUNCH-
-STRESTLE-
-PSHHHH-

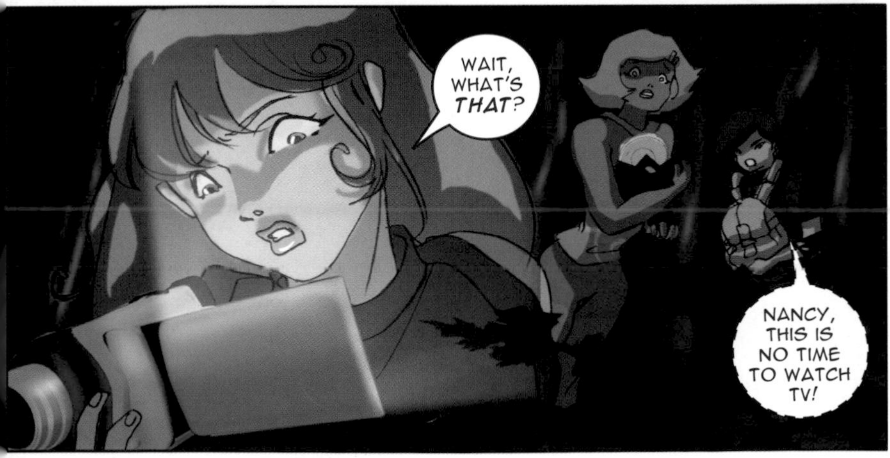
WAIT, WHAT'S THAT?
NANCY, THIS IS NO TIME TO WATCH TV!

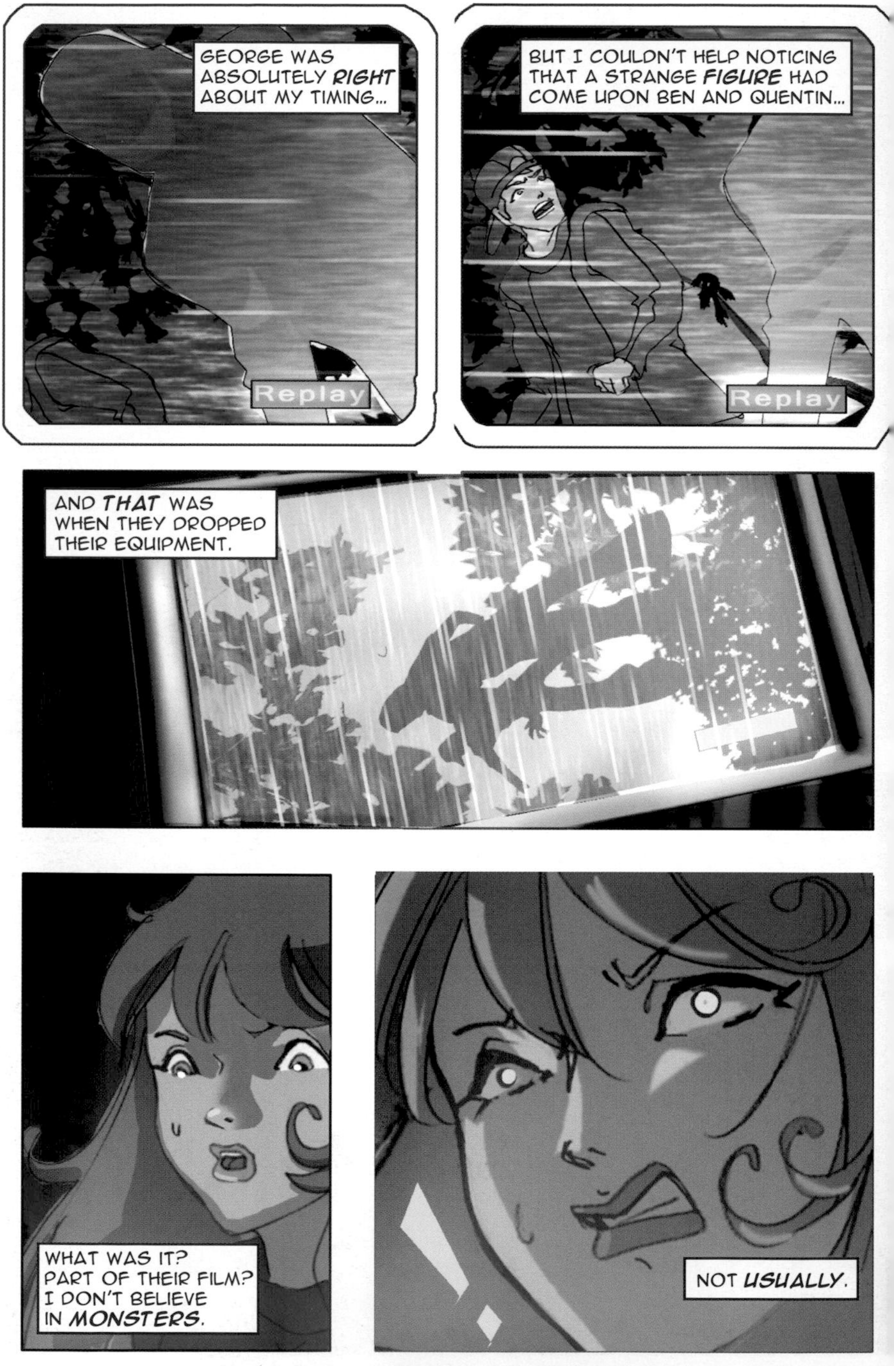
GEORGE WAS ABSOLUTELY RIGHT ABOUT MY TIMING...
Replay
BUT I COULDN'T HELP NOTICING THAT A STRANGE FIGURE HAD COME UPON BEN AND QUENTIN...
Replay
AND THAT WAS WHEN THEY DROPPED THEIR EQUIPMENT.
WHAT WAS IT? PART OF THEIR FILM? I DON'T BELIEVE IN MONSTERS.
NOT USUALLY.

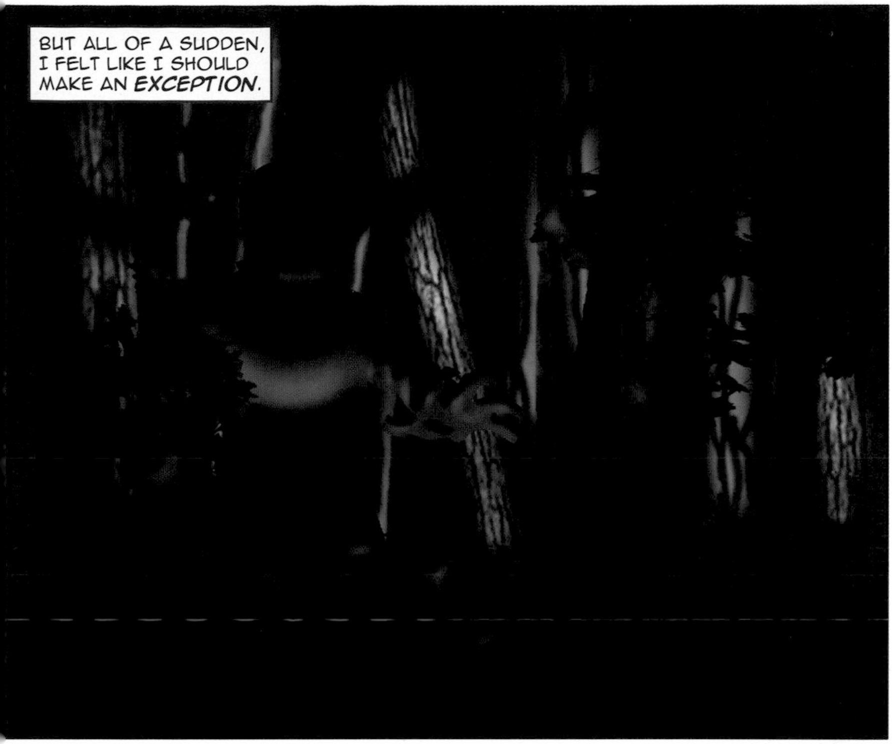
BUT ALL OF A SUDDEN, I FELT LIKE I SHOULD MAKE AN *EXCEPTION*.

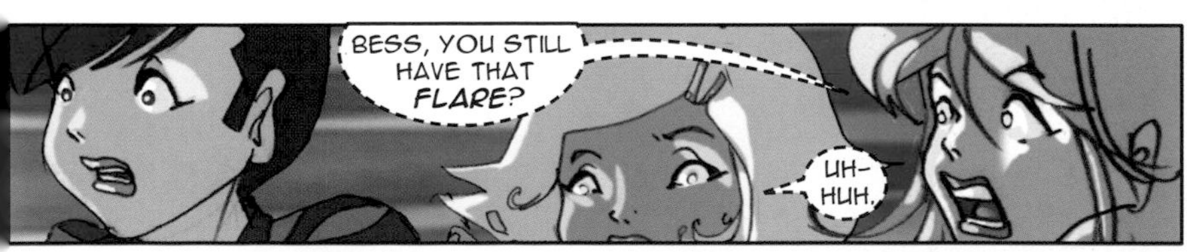
BESS, YOU STILL HAVE THAT *FLARE*?
UH-HUH.

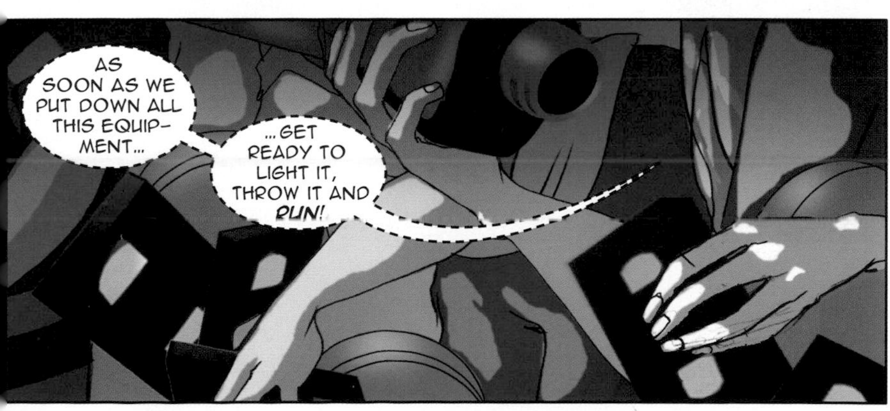
AS SOON AS WE PUT DOWN ALL THIS EQUIP-MENT...
...GET READY TO LIGHT IT, THROW IT AND *RUN*!

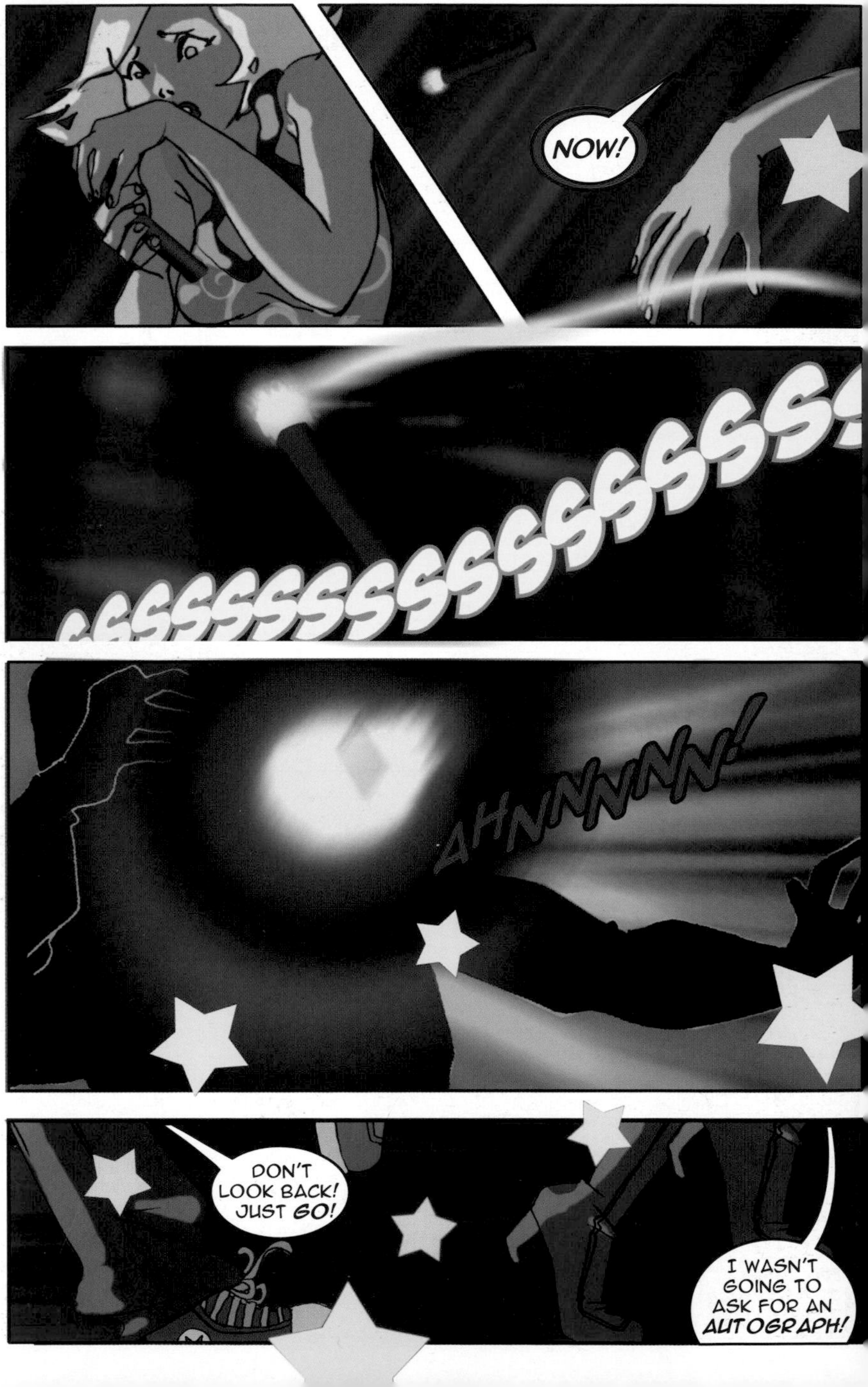
NOW!
SSSSSSSSSSSSSSSSSSSSSSS
AHNNNNNN!
DON'T LOOK BACK! JUST GO!
I WASN'T GOING TO ASK FOR AN AUTOGRAPH!

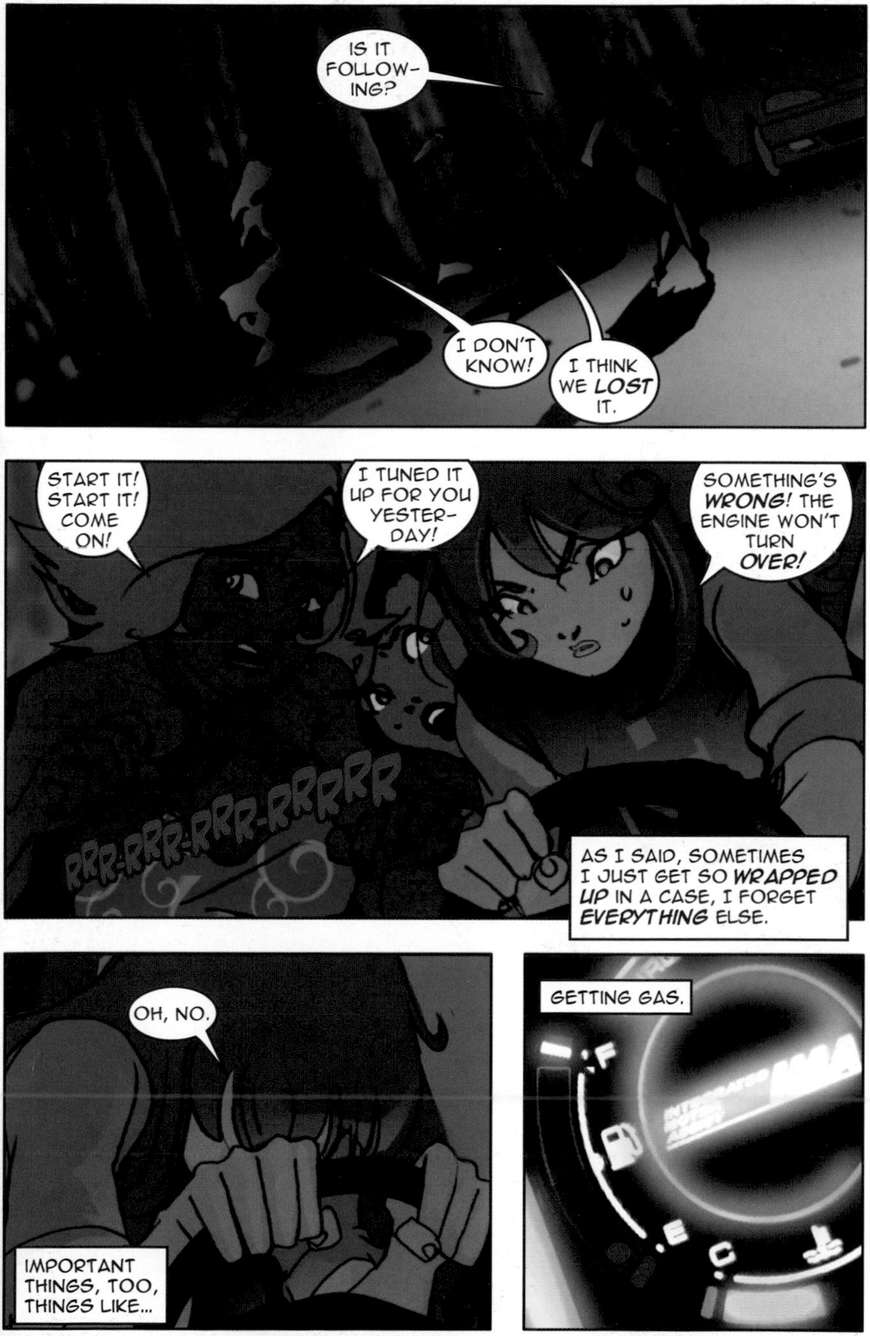
IS IT FOLLOW-ING?
I DON'T KNOW!
I THINK WE LOST IT.
START IT! START IT! COME ON!
I TUNED IT UP FOR YOU YESTER-DAY!
SOMETHING'S WRONG! THE ENGINE WON'T TURN OVER!
RRR-RRR-RRR-RRRRR
AS I SAID, SOMETIMES I JUST GET SO WRAPPED UP IN A CASE, I FORGET EVERYTHING ELSE.
OH, NO.
IMPORTANT THINGS, TOO, THINGS LIKE...
GETTING GAS.
F
E
C

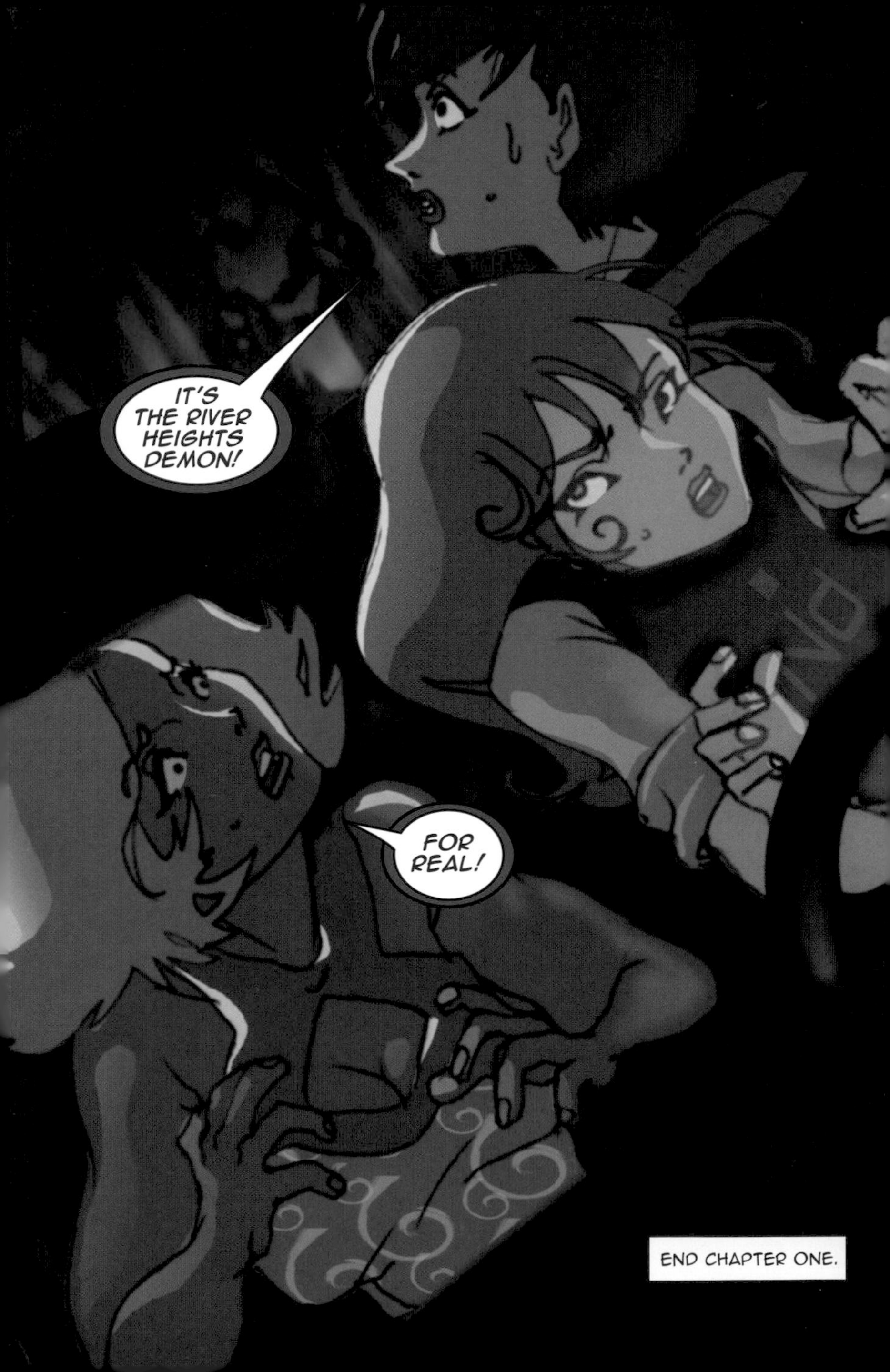
IT'S THE RIVER HEIGHTS DEMON!
FOR REAL!
END CHAPTER ONE.

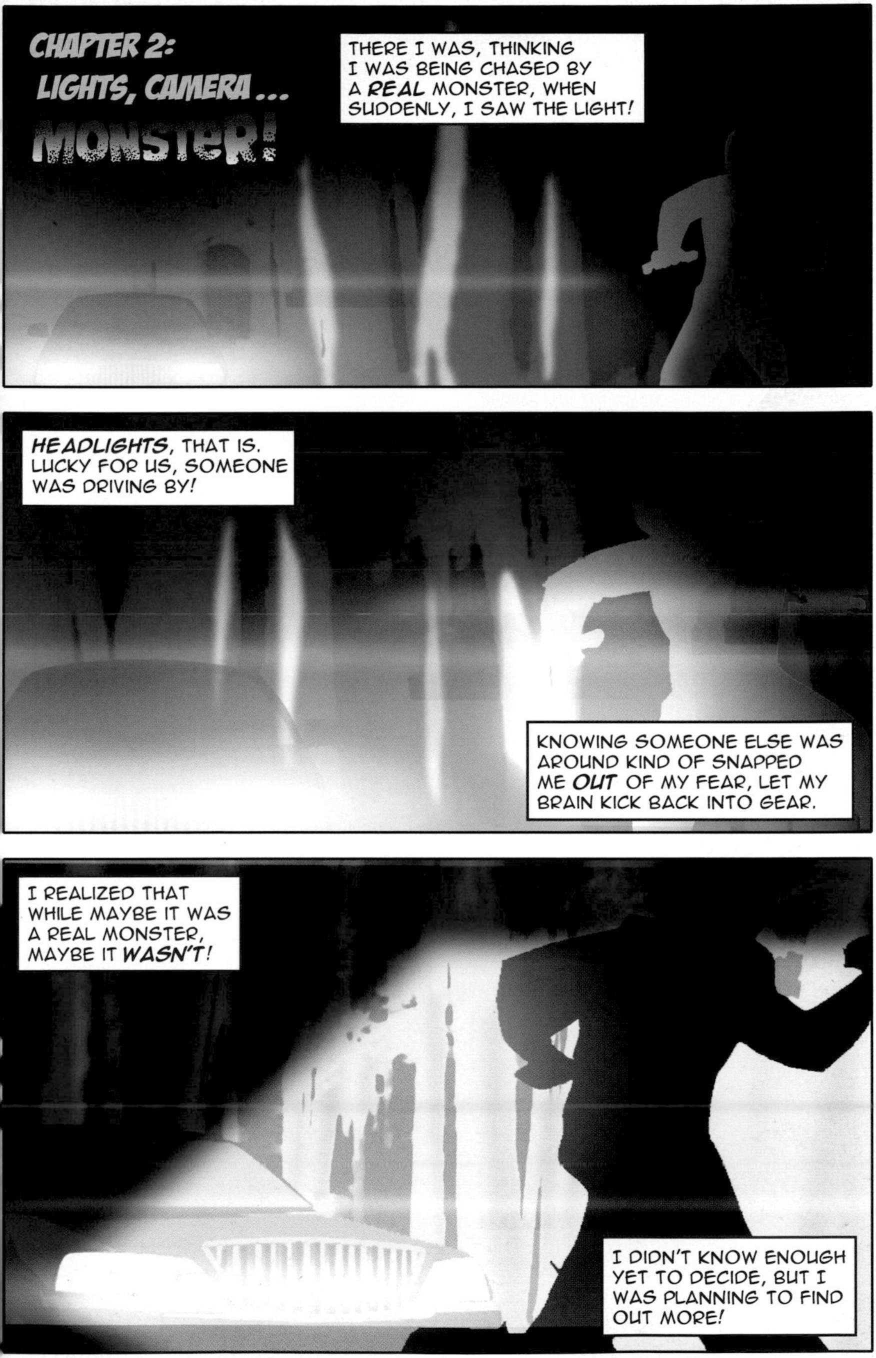
CHAPTER 2:
LIGHTS, CAMERA ...
MONSTER!
THERE I WAS, THINKING I WAS BEING CHASED BY A REAL MONSTER, WHEN SUDDENLY, I SAW THE LIGHT!
HEADLIGHTS, THAT IS. LUCKY FOR US, SOMEONE WAS DRIVING BY!
KNOWING SOMEONE ELSE WAS AROUND KIND OF SNAPPED ME OUT OF MY FEAR, LET MY BRAIN KICK BACK INTO GEAR.
I REALIZED THAT WHILE MAYBE IT WAS A REAL MONSTER, MAYBE IT WASN'T!
I DIDN'T KNOW ENOUGH YET TO DECIDE, BUT I WAS PLANNING TO FIND OUT MORE!

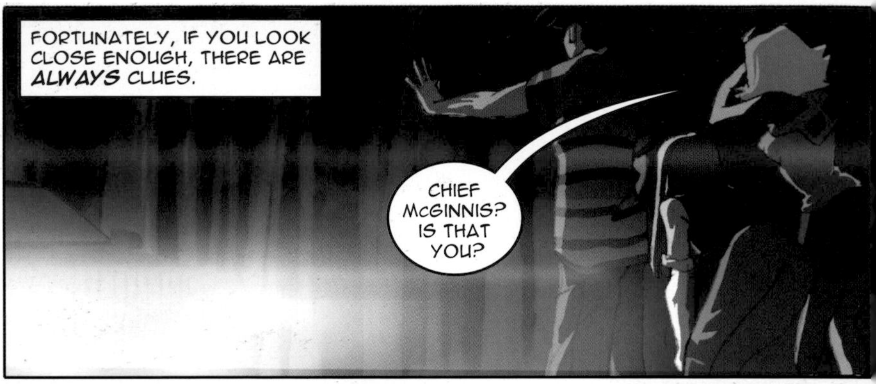
FORTUNATELY, IF YOU LOOK CLOSE ENOUGH, THERE ARE *ALWAYS* CLUES.
CHIEF McGINNIS? IS THAT YOU?

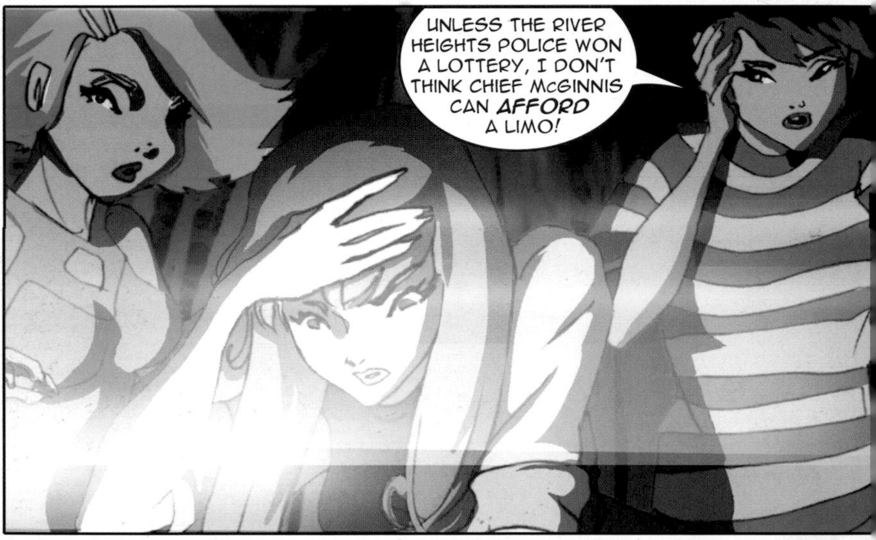
UNLESS THE RIVER HEIGHTS POLICE WON A LOTTERY, I DON'T THINK CHIEF McGINNIS CAN *AFFORD* A LIMO!

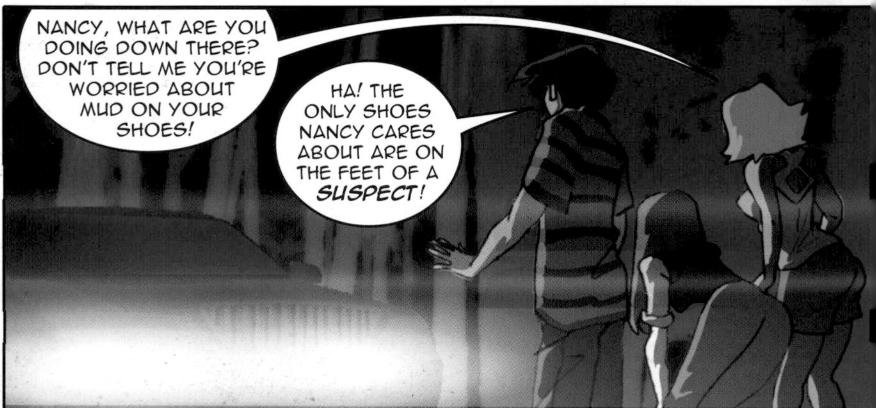
NANCY, WHAT ARE YOU DOING DOWN THERE? DON'T TELL ME YOU'RE WORRIED ABOUT MUD ON YOUR SHOES!
HA! THE ONLY SHOES NANCY CARES ABOUT ARE ON THE FEET OF A *SUSPECT*!

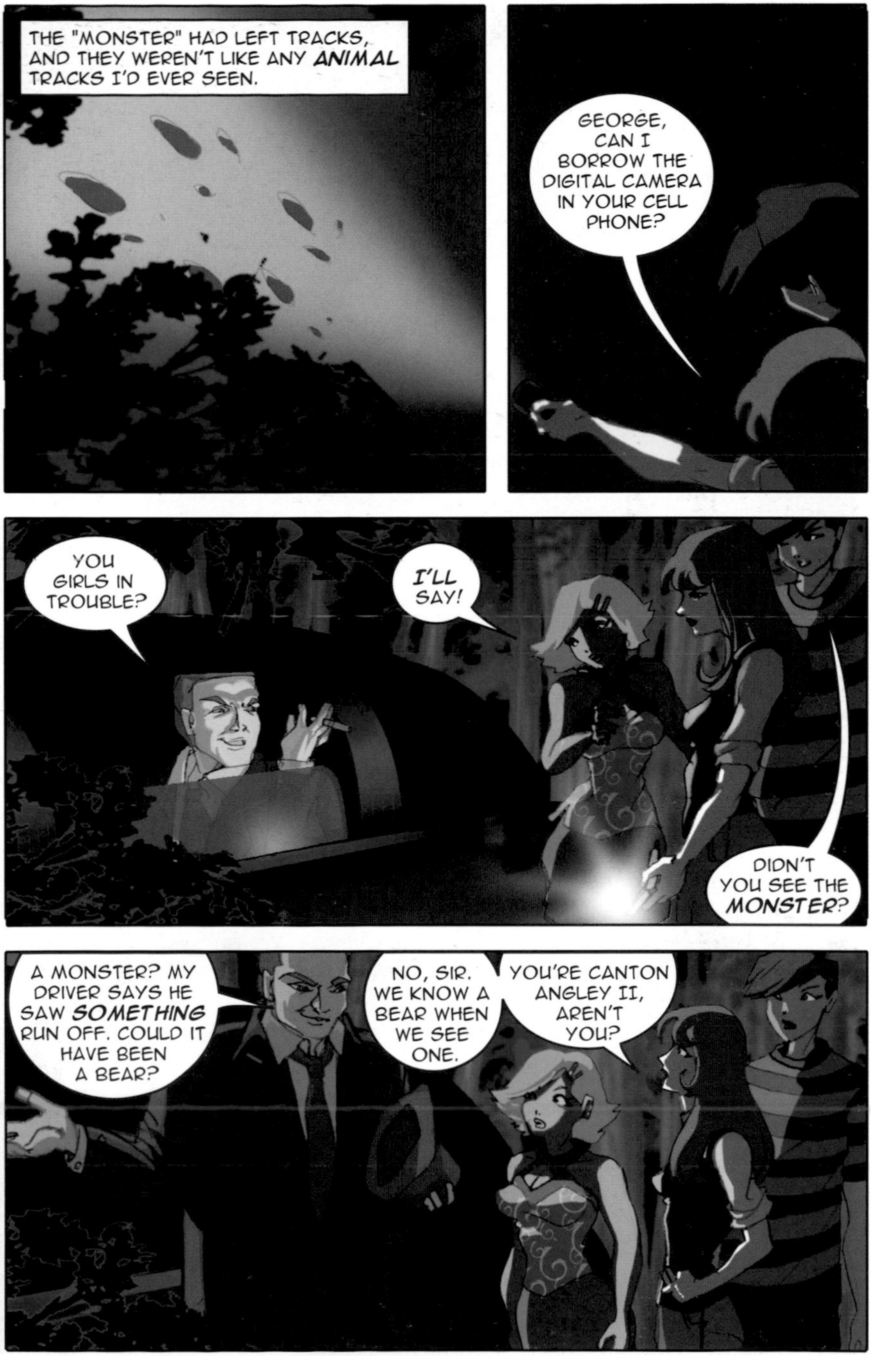
THE "MONSTER" HAD LEFT TRACKS, AND THEY WEREN'T LIKE ANY ANIMAL TRACKS I'D EVER SEEN.
GEORGE, CAN I BORROW THE DIGITAL CAMERA IN YOUR CELL PHONE?
YOU GIRLS IN TROUBLE?
I'LL SAY!
DIDN'T YOU SEE THE MONSTER?
A MONSTER? MY DRIVER SAYS HE SAW SOMETHING RUN OFF. COULD IT HAVE BEEN A BEAR?
NO, SIR. WE KNOW A BEAR WHEN WE SEE ONE.
YOU'RE CANTON ANGLEY II, AREN'T YOU?

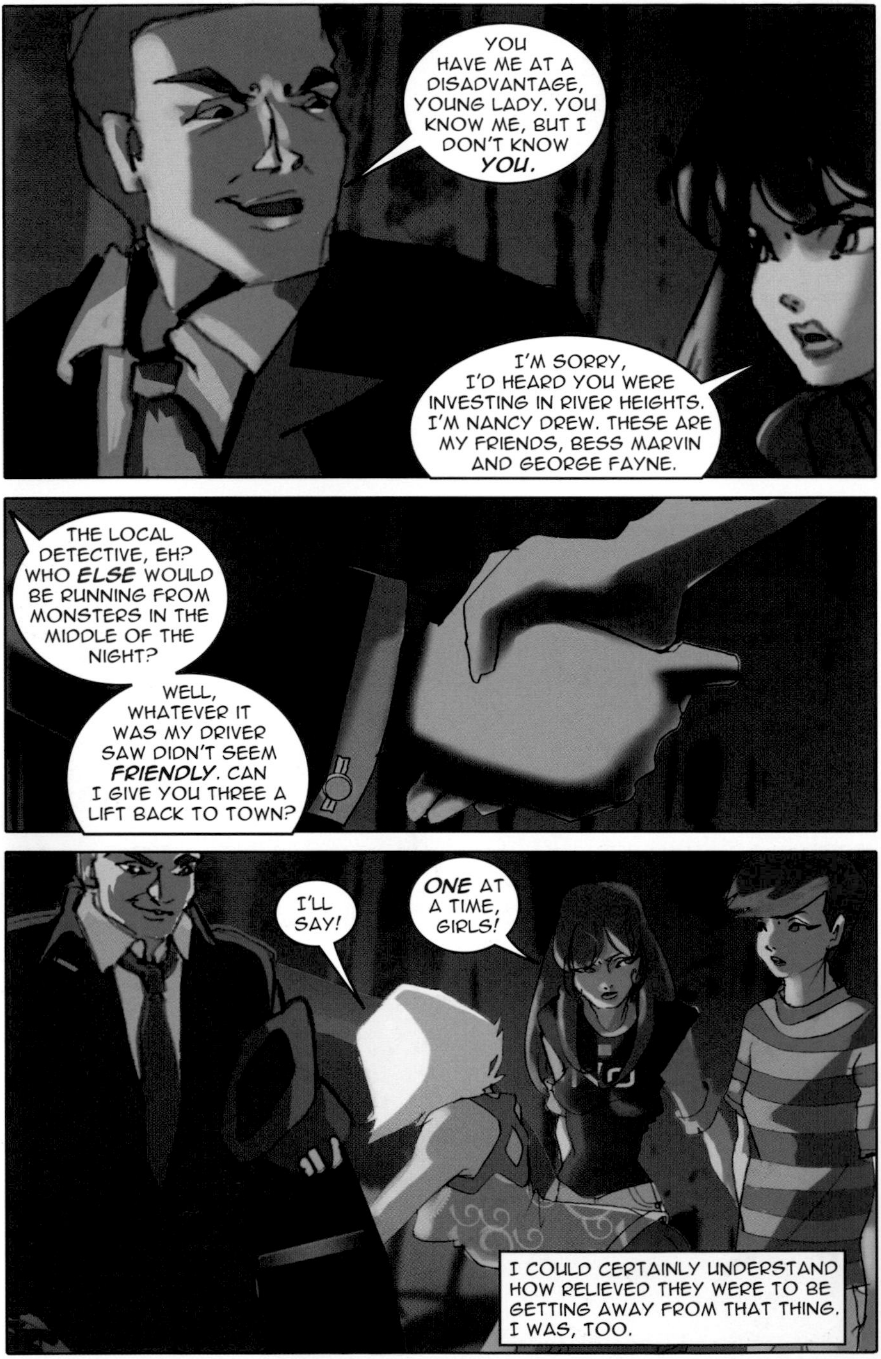
YOU HAVE ME AT A DISADVANTAGE, YOUNG LADY. YOU KNOW ME, BUT I DON'T KNOW ***YOU.***
I'M SORRY, I'D HEARD YOU WERE INVESTING IN RIVER HEIGHTS. I'M NANCY DREW. THESE ARE MY FRIENDS, BESS MARVIN AND GEORGE FAYNE.
THE LOCAL DETECTIVE, EH? WHO ***ELSE*** WOULD BE RUNNING FROM MONSTERS IN THE MIDDLE OF THE NIGHT?
WELL, WHATEVER IT WAS MY DRIVER SAW DIDN'T SEEM ***FRIENDLY***. CAN I GIVE YOU THREE A LIFT BACK TO TOWN?
I'LL SAY!
ONE AT A TIME, GIRLS!
I COULD CERTAINLY UNDERSTAND HOW RELIEVED THEY WERE TO BE GETTING AWAY FROM THAT THING. I WAS, TOO.

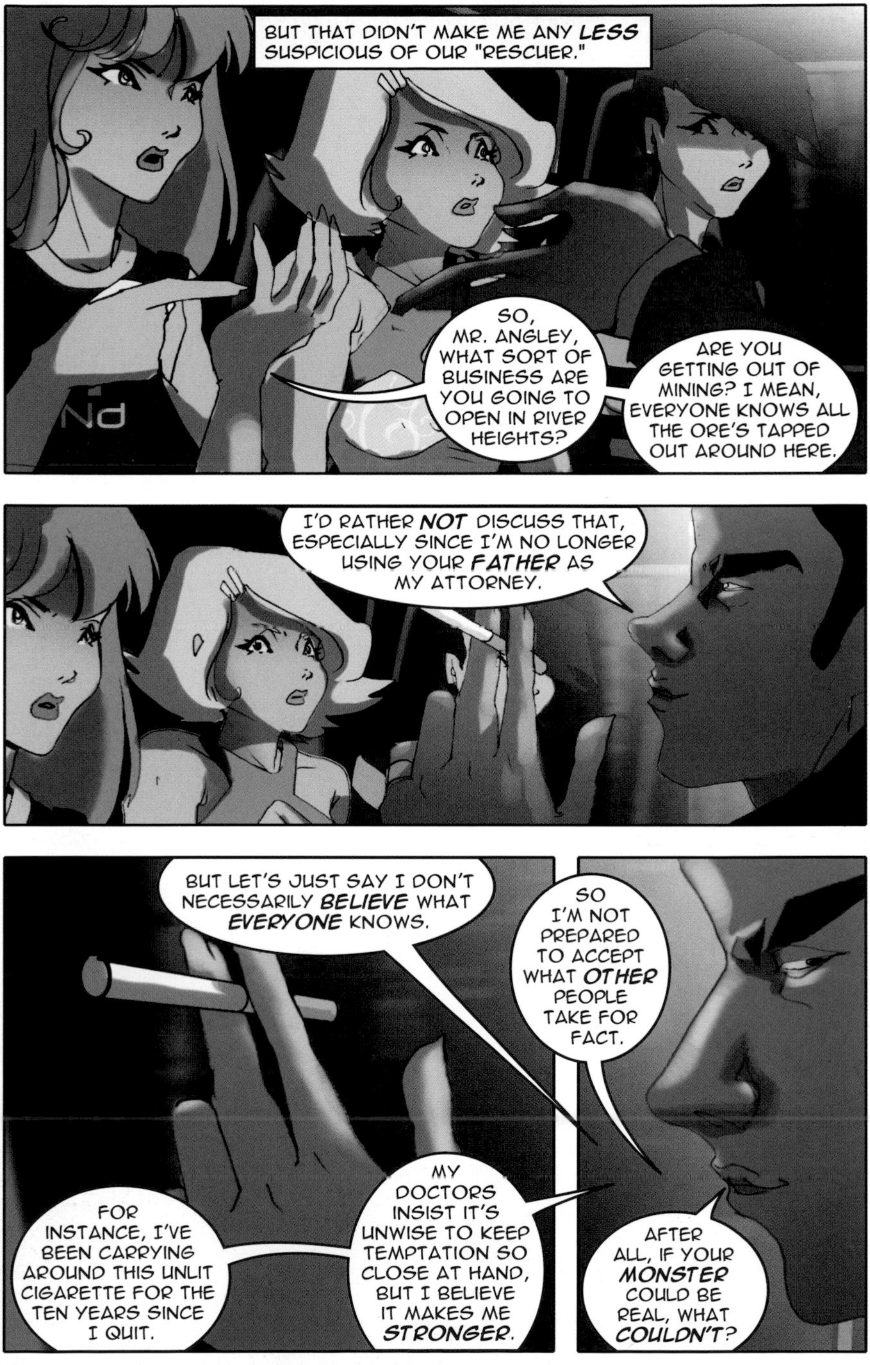
BUT THAT DIDN'T MAKE ME ANY LESS SUSPICIOUS OF OUR "RESCUER."
SO, MR. ANGLEY, WHAT SORT OF BUSINESS ARE YOU GOING TO OPEN IN RIVER HEIGHTS?
ARE YOU GETTING OUT OF MINING? I MEAN, EVERYONE KNOWS ALL THE ORE'S TAPPED OUT AROUND HERE.
I'D RATHER NOT DISCUSS THAT, ESPECIALLY SINCE I'M NO LONGER USING YOUR FATHER AS MY ATTORNEY.
BUT LET'S JUST SAY I DON'T NECESSARILY BELIEVE WHAT EVERYONE KNOWS.
FOR INSTANCE, I'VE BEEN CARRYING AROUND THIS UNLIT CIGARETTE FOR THE TEN YEARS SINCE I QUIT.
MY DOCTORS INSIST IT'S UNWISE TO KEEP TEMPTATION SO CLOSE AT HAND, BUT I BELIEVE IT MAKES ME STRONGER.
SO I'M NOT PREPARED TO ACCEPT WHAT OTHER PEOPLE TAKE FOR FACT.
AFTER ALL, IF YOUR MONSTER COULD BE REAL, WHAT COULDN'T?

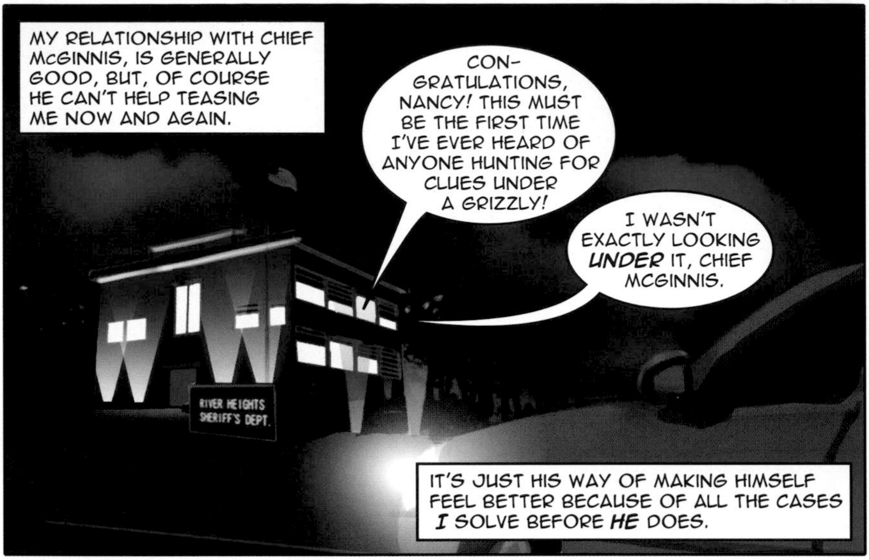
MY RELATIONSHIP WITH CHIEF McGINNIS, IS GENERALLY GOOD, BUT, OF COURSE HE CAN'T HELP TEASING ME NOW AND AGAIN.
CON-GRATULATIONS, NANCY! THIS MUST BE THE FIRST TIME I'VE EVER HEARD OF ANYONE HUNTING FOR CLUES UNDER A GRIZZLY!
I WASN'T EXACTLY LOOKING ***UNDER*** IT, CHIEF MCGINNIS.
RIVER HEIGHTS SHERIFF'S DEPT.
IT'S JUST HIS WAY OF MAKING HIMSELF FEEL BETTER BECAUSE OF ALL THE CASES ***I*** SOLVE BEFORE ***HE*** DOES.

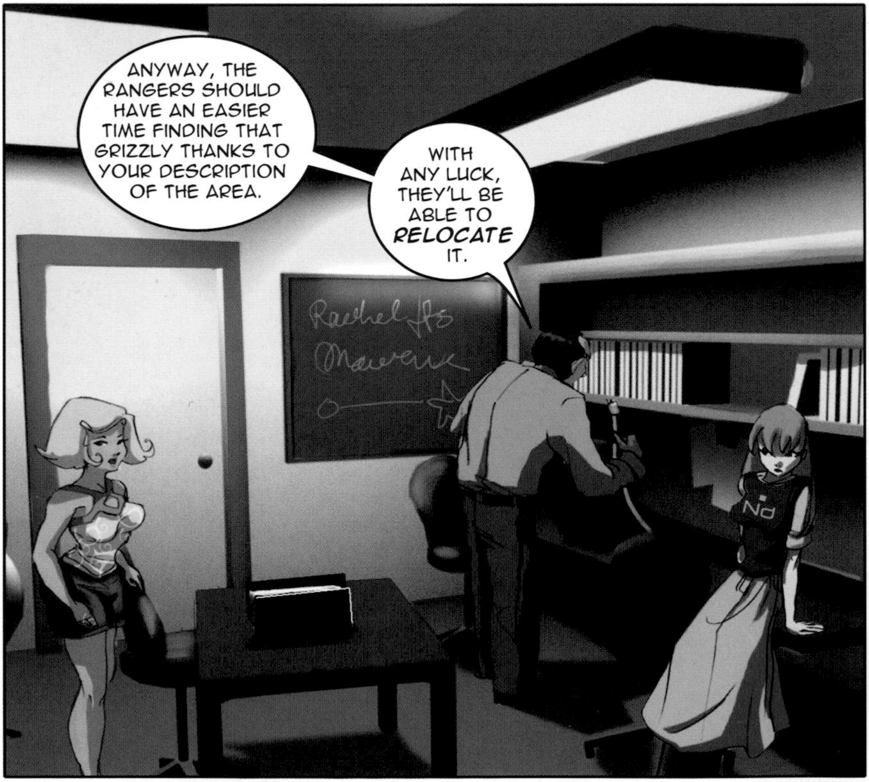
ANYWAY, THE RANGERS SHOULD HAVE AN EASIER TIME FINDING THAT GRIZZLY THANKS TO YOUR DESCRIPTION OF THE AREA.
WITH ANY LUCK, THEY'LL BE ABLE TO ***RELOCATE*** IT.

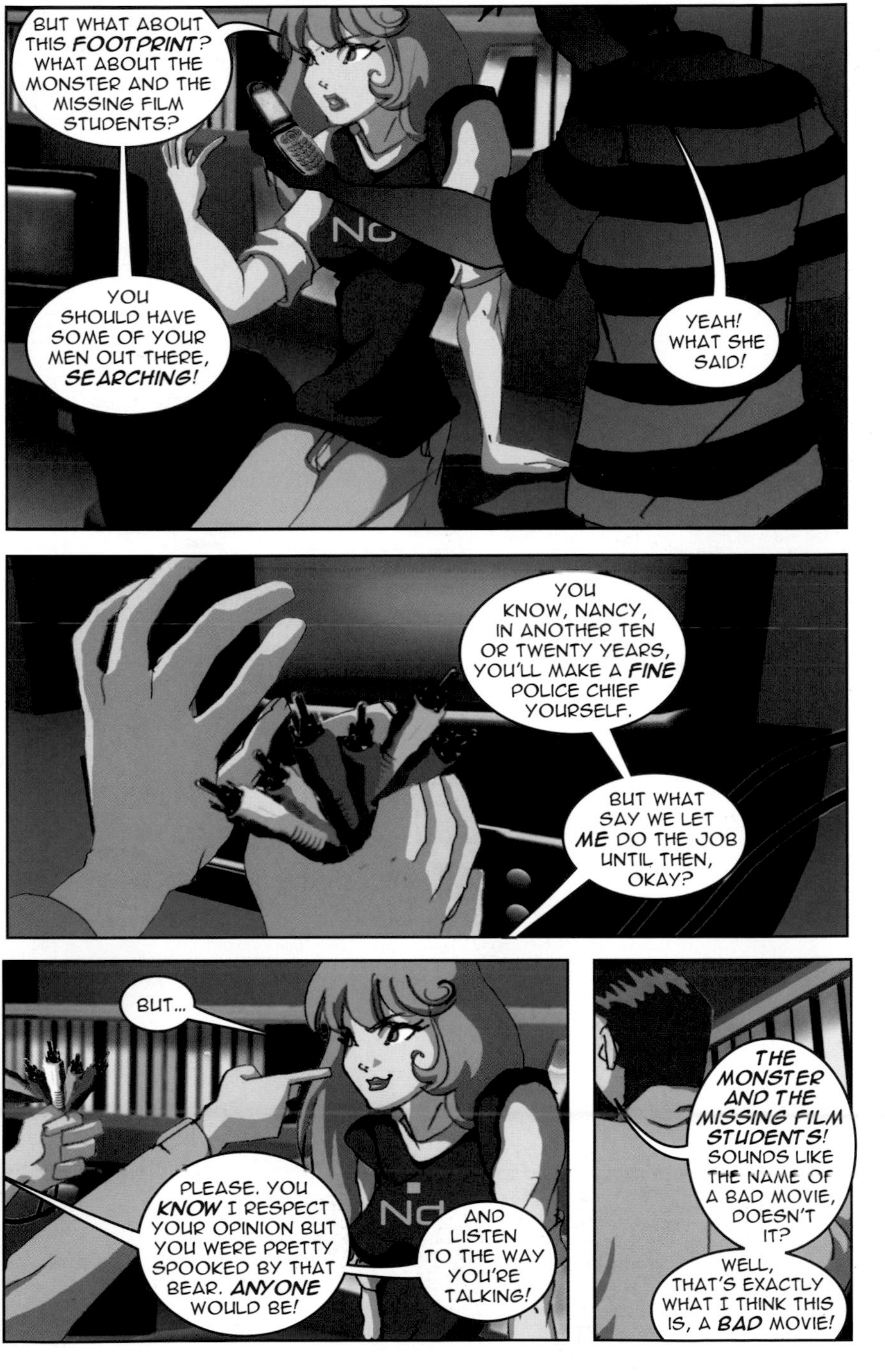
BUT WHAT ABOUT THIS **FOOTPRINT**? WHAT ABOUT THE MONSTER AND THE MISSING FILM STUDENTS?
YOU SHOULD HAVE SOME OF YOUR MEN OUT THERE, **SEARCHING**!
YEAH! WHAT SHE SAID!
YOU KNOW, NANCY, IN ANOTHER TEN OR TWENTY YEARS, YOU'LL MAKE A **FINE** POLICE CHIEF YOURSELF.
BUT WHAT SAY WE LET **ME** DO THE JOB UNTIL THEN, OKAY?
BUT...
PLEASE. YOU **KNOW** I RESPECT YOUR OPINION BUT YOU WERE PRETTY SPOOKED BY THAT BEAR. **ANYONE** WOULD BE!
AND LISTEN TO THE WAY YOU'RE TALKING!
THE MONSTER AND THE MISSING FILM STUDENTS! SOUNDS LIKE THE NAME OF A BAD MOVIE, DOESN'T IT?
WELL, THAT'S EXACTLY WHAT I THINK THIS IS, A **BAD** MOVIE!

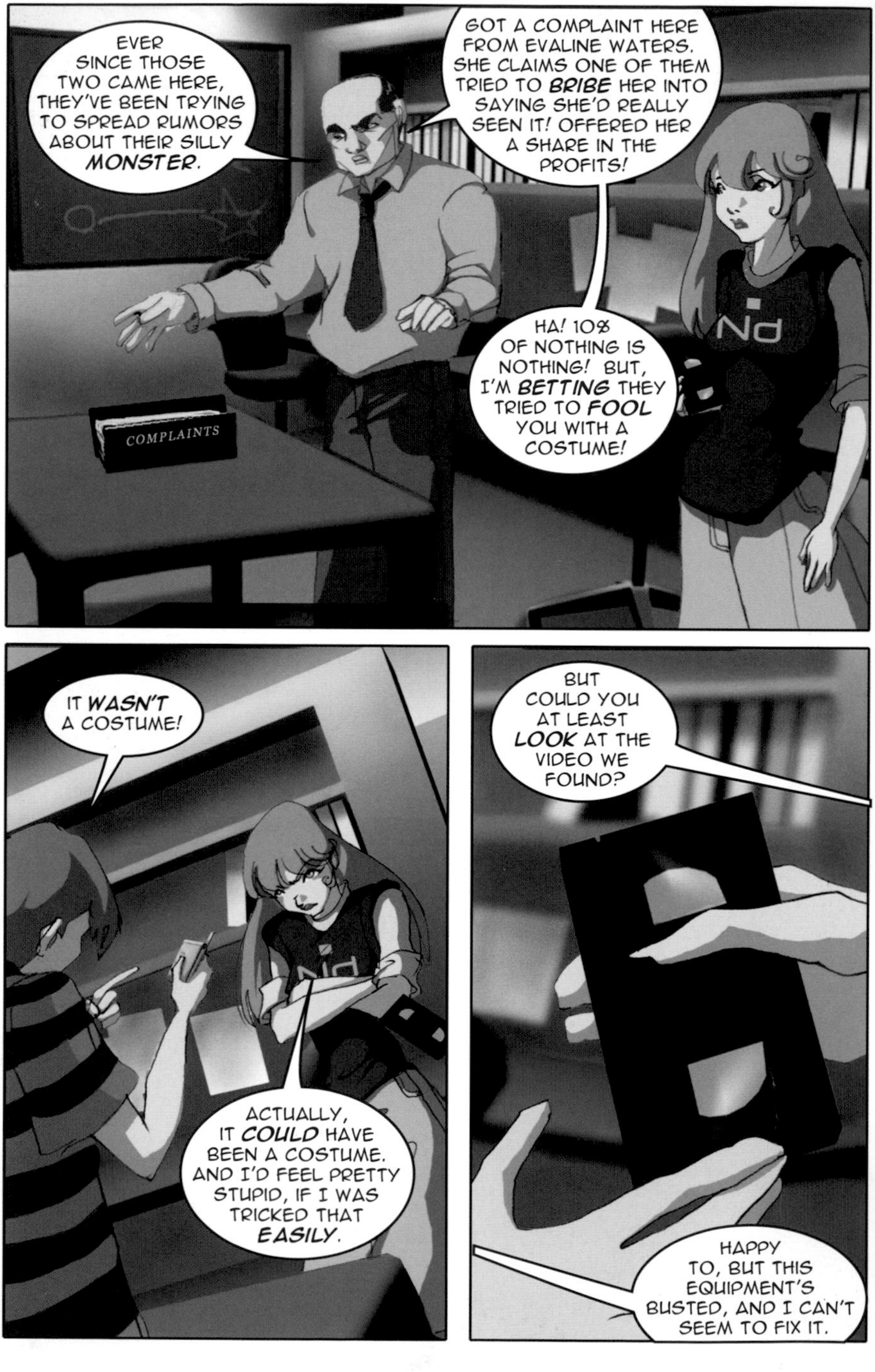
EVER SINCE THOSE TWO CAME HERE, THEY'VE BEEN TRYING TO SPREAD RUMORS ABOUT THEIR SILLY MONSTER.
GOT A COMPLAINT HERE FROM EVALINE WATERS. SHE CLAIMS ONE OF THEM TRIED TO BRIBE HER INTO SAYING SHE'D REALLY SEEN IT! OFFERED HER A SHARE IN THE PROFITS!
HA! 10% OF NOTHING IS NOTHING! BUT, I'M BETTING THEY TRIED TO FOOL YOU WITH A COSTUME!
COMPLAINTS
Nd
IT WASN'T A COSTUME!
ACTUALLY, IT COULD HAVE BEEN A COSTUME. AND I'D FEEL PRETTY STUPID, IF I WAS TRICKED THAT EASILY.
BUT COULD YOU AT LEAST LOOK AT THE VIDEO WE FOUND?
HAPPY TO, BUT THIS EQUIPMENT'S BUSTED, AND I CAN'T SEEM TO FIX IT.

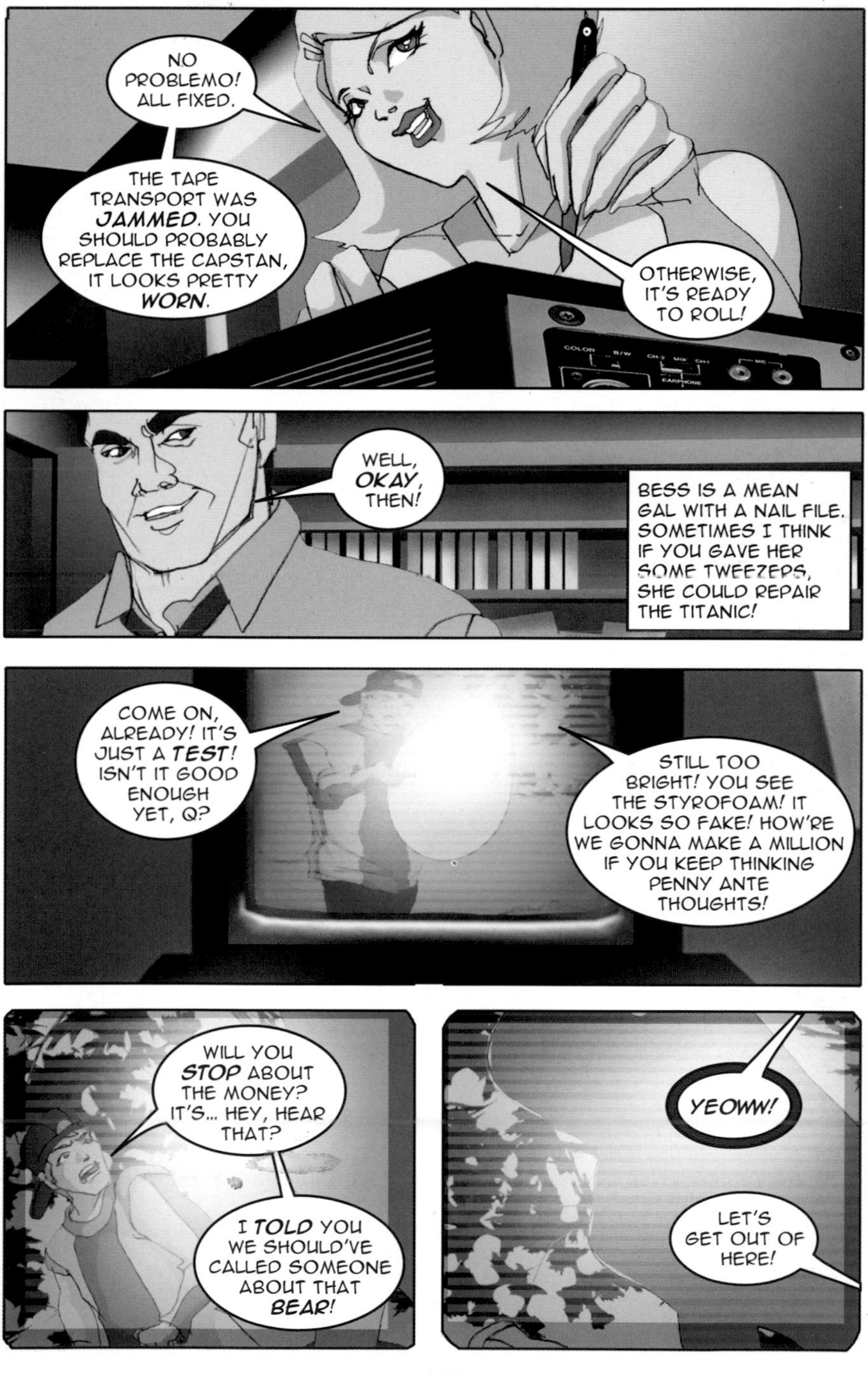
NO PROBLEMO! ALL FIXED.
THE TAPE TRANSPORT WAS JAMMED. YOU SHOULD PROBABLY REPLACE THE CAPSTAN, IT LOOKS PRETTY WORN.
OTHERWISE, IT'S READY TO ROLL!
COLOR B/W CH-2 MIX CH-1 MIC EARPHONE
WELL, OKAY, THEN!
BESS IS A MEAN GAL WITH A NAIL FILE. SOMETIMES I THINK IF YOU GAVE HER SOME TWEEZERS, SHE COULD REPAIR THE TITANIC!
COME ON, ALREADY! IT'S JUST A TEST! ISN'T IT GOOD ENOUGH YET, Q?
STILL TOO BRIGHT! YOU SEE THE STYROFOAM! IT LOOKS SO FAKE! HOW'RE WE GONNA MAKE A MILLION IF YOU KEEP THINKING PENNY ANTE THOUGHTS!
WILL YOU STOP ABOUT THE MONEY? IT'S... HEY, HEAR THAT?
I TOLD YOU WE SHOULD'VE CALLED SOMEONE ABOUT THAT BEAR!
YEOWW!
LET'S GET OUT OF HERE!

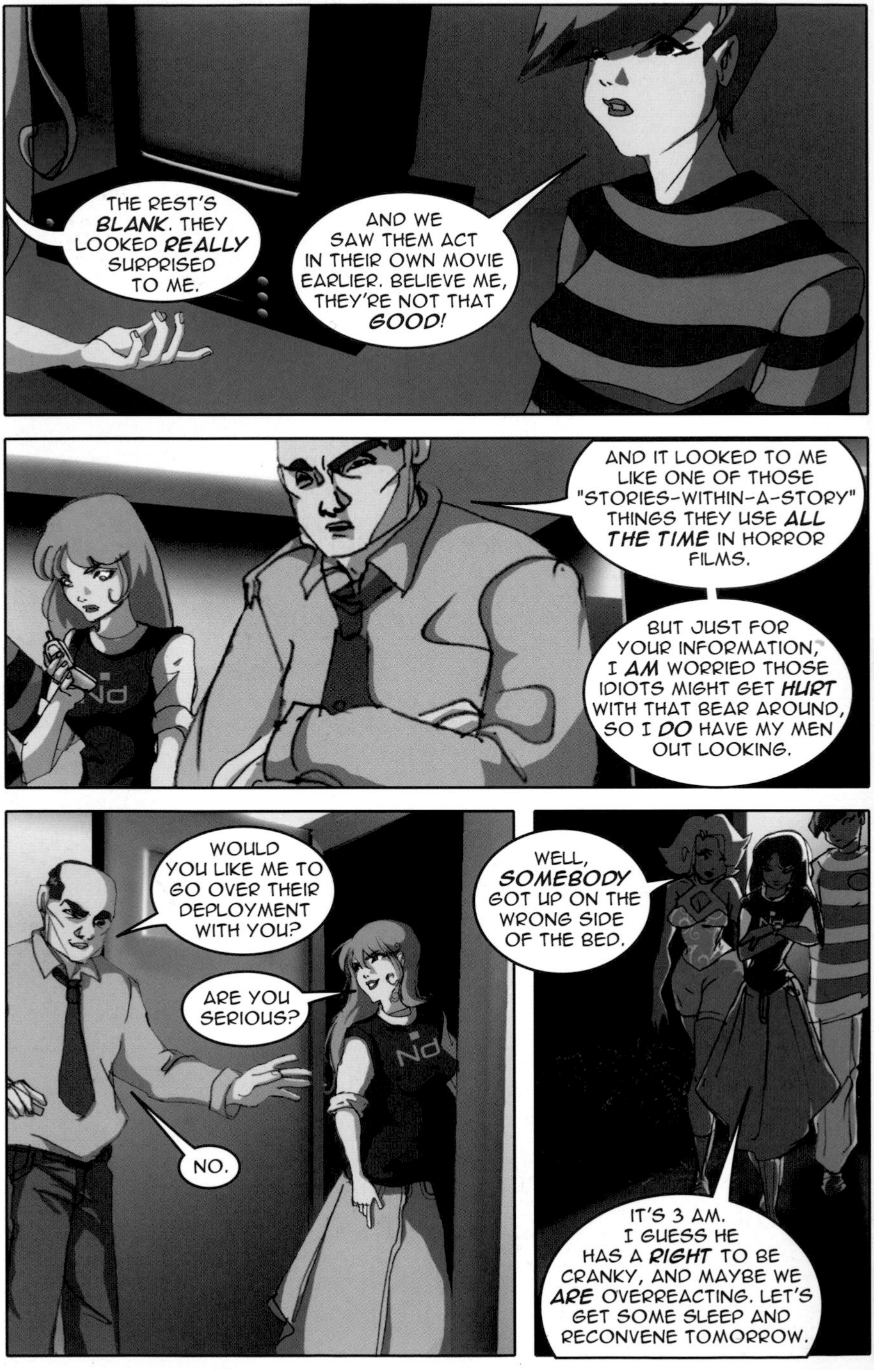
THE REST'S BLANK. THEY LOOKED REALLY SURPRISED TO ME.
AND WE SAW THEM ACT IN THEIR OWN MOVIE EARLIER. BELIEVE ME, THEY'RE NOT THAT GOOD!
AND IT LOOKED TO ME LIKE ONE OF THOSE "STORIES-WITHIN-A-STORY" THINGS THEY USE ALL THE TIME IN HORROR FILMS.
BUT JUST FOR YOUR INFORMATION, I AM WORRIED THOSE IDIOTS MIGHT GET HURT WITH THAT BEAR AROUND, SO I DO HAVE MY MEN OUT LOOKING.
WOULD YOU LIKE ME TO GO OVER THEIR DEPLOYMENT WITH YOU?
ARE YOU SERIOUS?
NO.
WELL, SOMEBODY GOT UP ON THE WRONG SIDE OF THE BED.
IT'S 3 AM. I GUESS HE HAS A RIGHT TO BE CRANKY, AND MAYBE WE ARE OVERREACTING. LET'S GET SOME SLEEP AND RECONVENE TOMORROW.

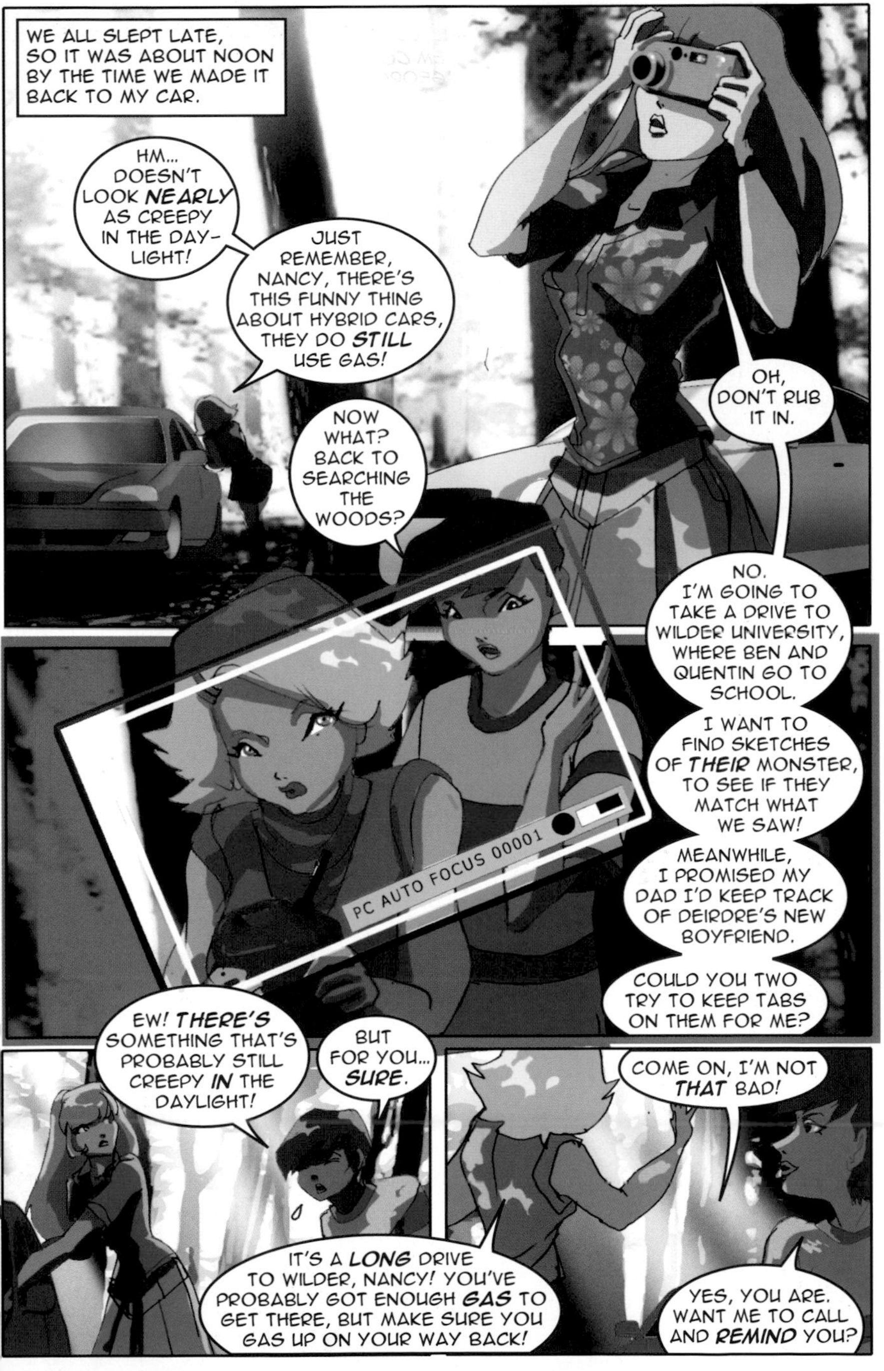

WE ALL SLEPT LATE, SO IT WAS ABOUT NOON BY THE TIME WE MADE IT BACK TO MY CAR.
HM... DOESN'T LOOK NEARLY AS CREEPY IN THE DAY-LIGHT!
JUST REMEMBER, NANCY, THERE'S THIS FUNNY THING ABOUT HYBRID CARS, THEY DO STILL USE GAS!
OH, DON'T RUB IT IN.
NOW WHAT? BACK TO SEARCHING THE WOODS?
NO. I'M GOING TO TAKE A DRIVE TO WILDER UNIVERSITY, WHERE BEN AND QUENTIN GO TO SCHOOL.
I WANT TO FIND SKETCHES OF THEIR MONSTER, TO SEE IF THEY MATCH WHAT WE SAW!
PC AUTO FOCUS 00001
MEANWHILE, I PROMISED MY DAD I'D KEEP TRACK OF DEIRDRE'S NEW BOYFRIEND.
COULD YOU TWO TRY TO KEEP TABS ON THEM FOR ME?
EW! THERE'S SOMETHING THAT'S PROBABLY STILL CREEPY IN THE DAYLIGHT!
BUT FOR YOU... SURE.
IT'S A LONG DRIVE TO WILDER, NANCY! YOU'VE PROBABLY GOT ENOUGH GAS TO GET THERE, BUT MAKE SURE YOU GAS UP ON YOUR WAY BACK!
COME ON, I'M NOT THAT BAD!
YES, YOU ARE. WANT ME TO CALL AND REMIND YOU?

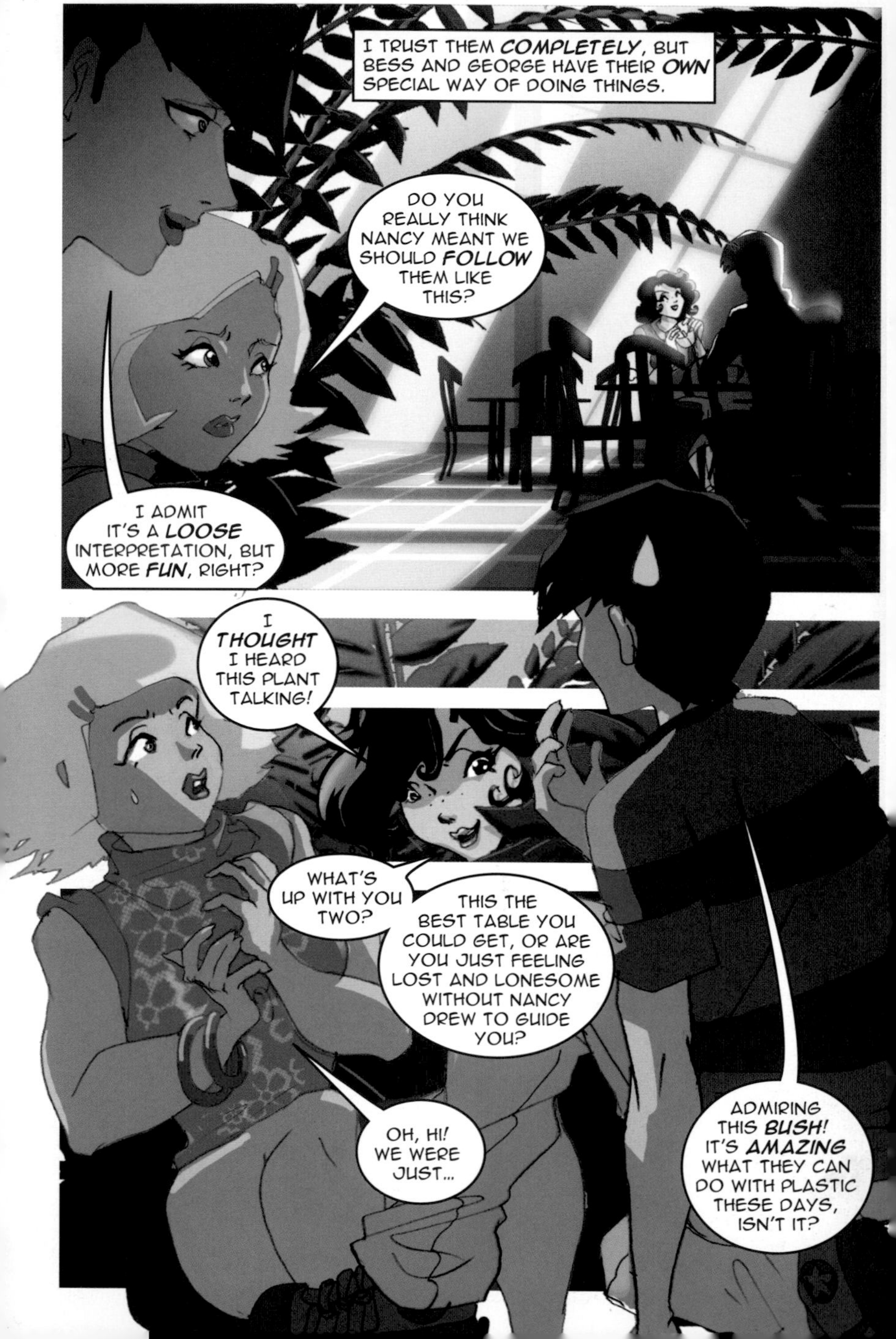
I TRUST THEM COMPLETELY, BUT BESS AND GEORGE HAVE THEIR OWN SPECIAL WAY OF DOING THINGS.
DO YOU REALLY THINK NANCY MEANT WE SHOULD FOLLOW THEM LIKE THIS?
I ADMIT IT'S A LOOSE INTERPRETATION, BUT MORE FUN, RIGHT?
I THOUGHT I HEARD THIS PLANT TALKING!
WHAT'S UP WITH YOU TWO?
THIS THE BEST TABLE YOU COULD GET, OR ARE YOU JUST FEELING LOST AND LONESOME WITHOUT NANCY DREW TO GUIDE YOU?
OH, HI! WE WERE JUST...
ADMIRING THIS BUSH! IT'S AMAZING WHAT THEY CAN DO WITH PLASTIC THESE DAYS, ISN'T IT?

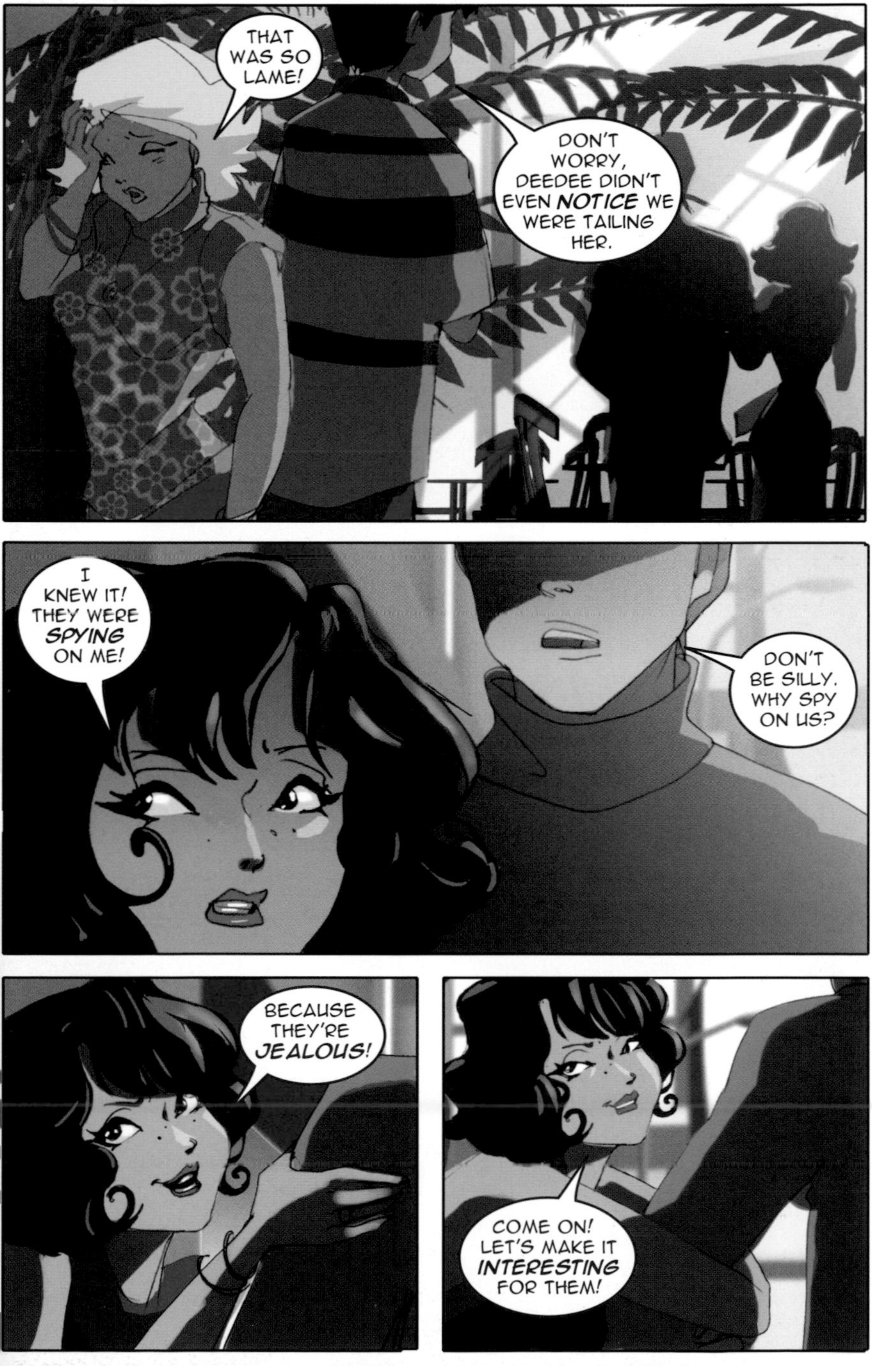
THAT WAS SO LAME!
DON'T WORRY, DEEDEE DIDN'T EVEN NOTICE WE WERE TAILING HER.
I KNEW IT! THEY WERE SPYING ON ME!
DON'T BE SILLY. WHY SPY ON US?
BECAUSE THEY'RE JEALOUS!
COME ON! LET'S MAKE IT INTERESTING FOR THEM!

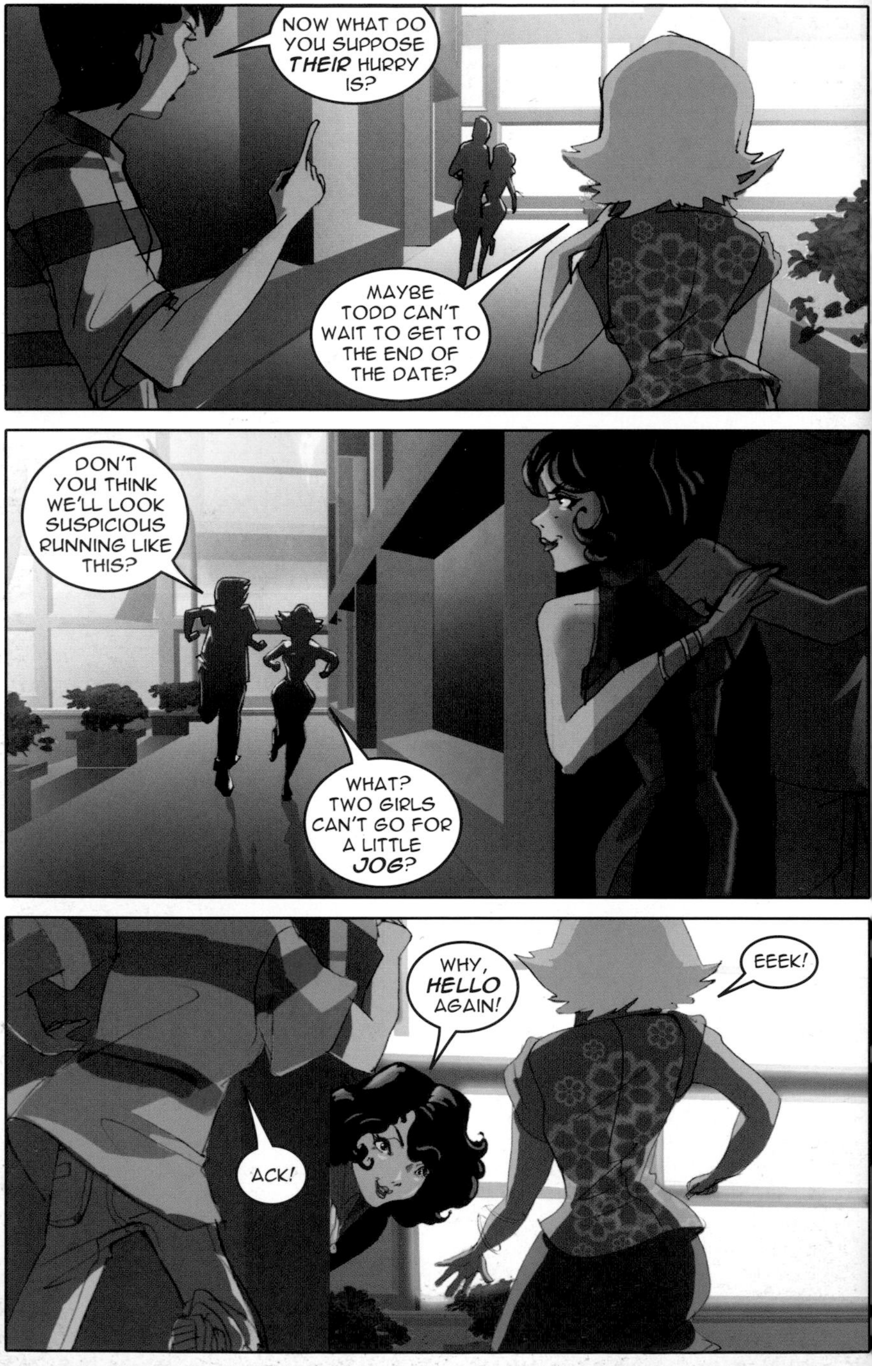
NOW WHAT DO YOU SUPPOSE THEIR HURRY IS?
MAYBE TODD CAN'T WAIT TO GET TO THE END OF THE DATE?
DON'T YOU THINK WE'LL LOOK SUSPICIOUS RUNNING LIKE THIS?
WHAT? TWO GIRLS CAN'T GO FOR A LITTLE JOG?
WHY, HELLO AGAIN!
EEEK!
ACK!

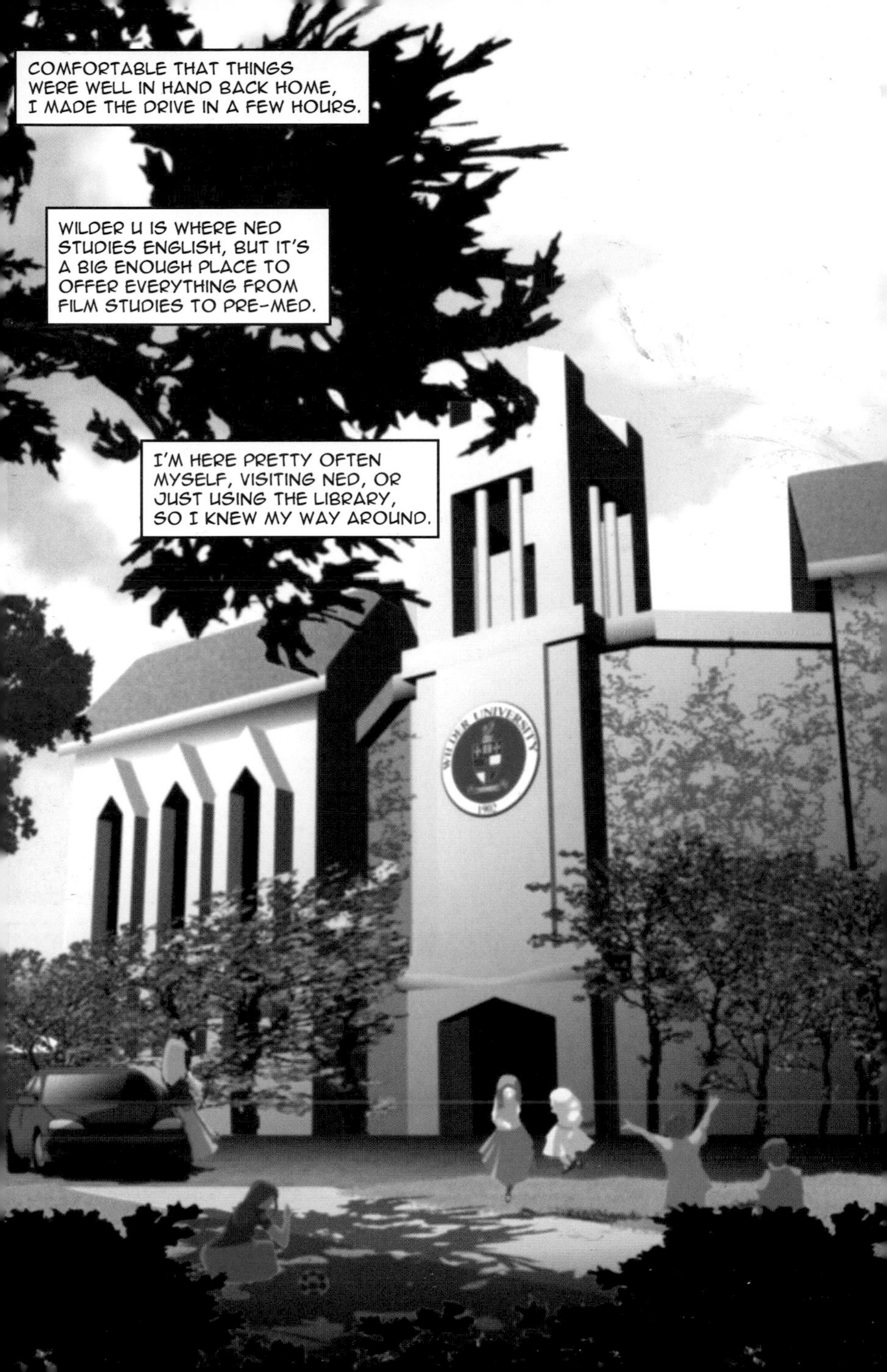
COMFORTABLE THAT THINGS WERE WELL IN HAND BACK HOME, I MADE THE DRIVE IN A FEW HOURS.
WILDER U IS WHERE NED STUDIES ENGLISH, BUT IT'S A BIG ENOUGH PLACE TO OFFER EVERYTHING FROM FILM STUDIES TO PRE-MED.
I'M HERE PRETTY OFTEN MYSELF, VISITING NED, OR JUST USING THE LIBRARY, SO I KNEW MY WAY AROUND.
WILDER UNIVERSITY

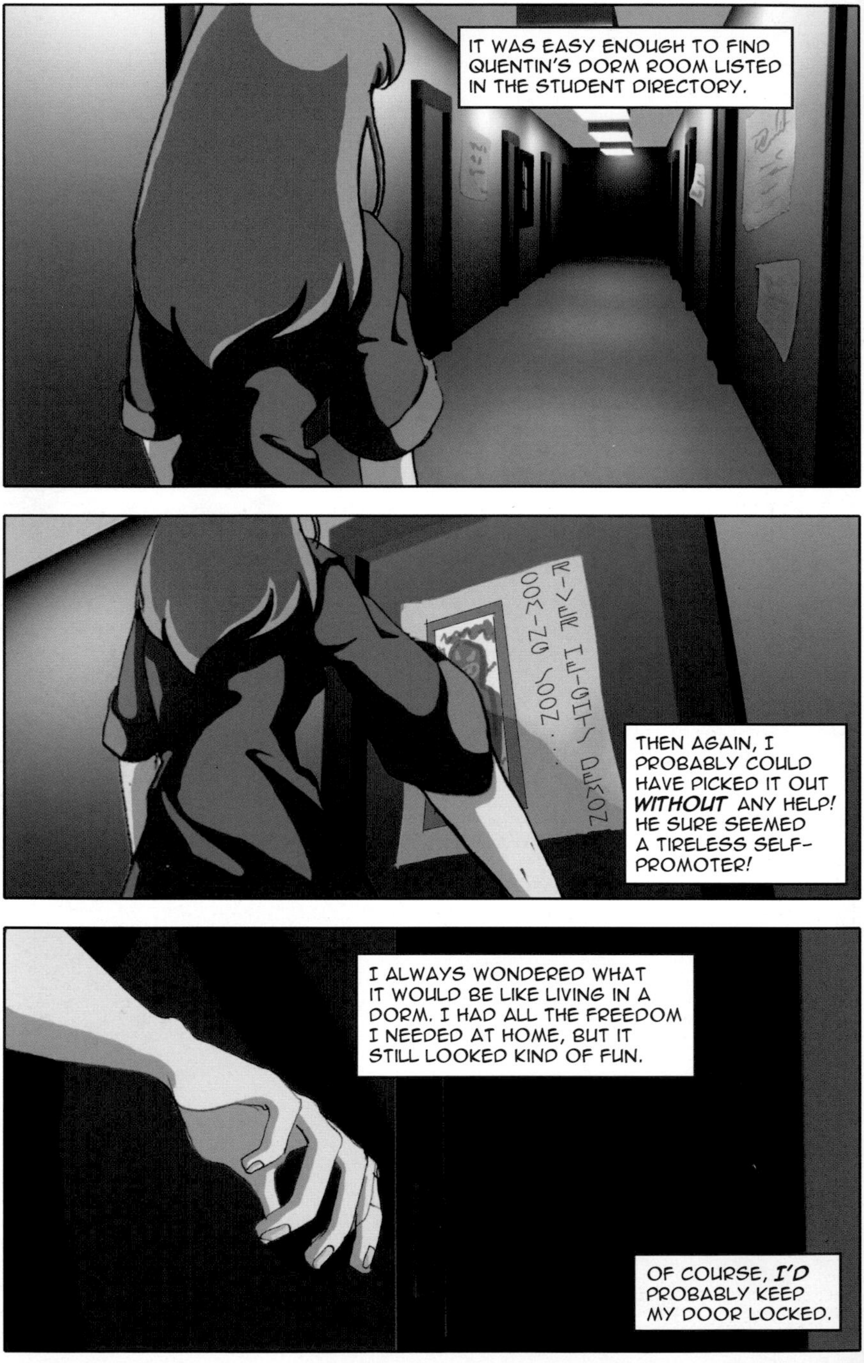
IT WAS EASY ENOUGH TO FIND QUENTIN'S DORM ROOM LISTED IN THE STUDENT DIRECTORY.
RIVER HEIGHTS DEMON
COMING SOON...
THEN AGAIN, I PROBABLY COULD HAVE PICKED IT OUT ***WITHOUT*** ANY HELP! HE SURE SEEMED A TIRELESS SELF-PROMOTER!
I ALWAYS WONDERED WHAT IT WOULD BE LIKE LIVING IN A DORM. I HAD ALL THE FREEDOM I NEEDED AT HOME, BUT IT STILL LOOKED KIND OF FUN.
OF COURSE, ***I'D*** PROBABLY KEEP MY DOOR LOCKED.

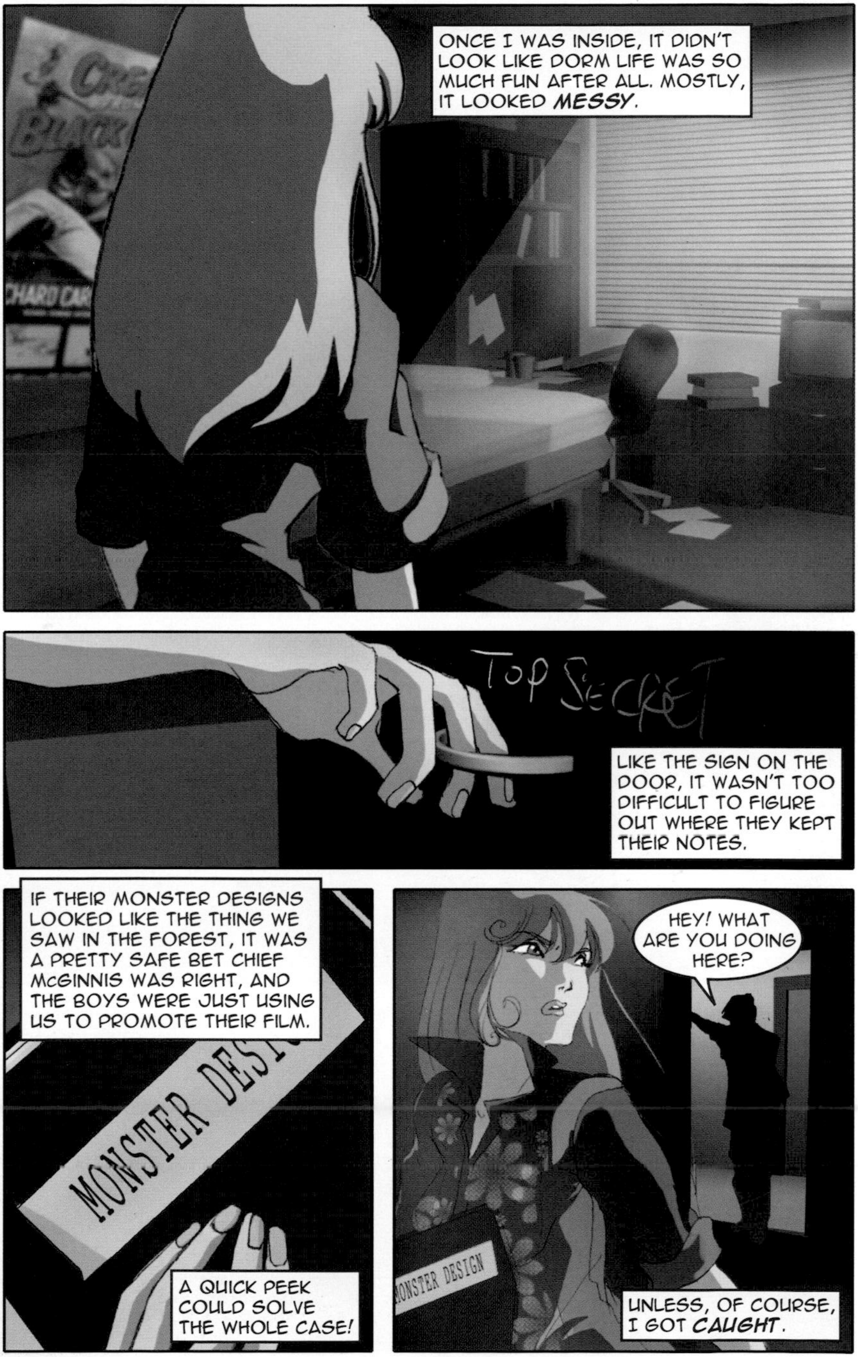
ONCE I WAS INSIDE, IT DIDN'T LOOK LIKE DORM LIFE WAS SO MUCH FUN AFTER ALL. MOSTLY, IT LOOKED ***MESSY***.
TOP SECRET
LIKE THE SIGN ON THE DOOR, IT WASN'T TOO DIFFICULT TO FIGURE OUT WHERE THEY KEPT THEIR NOTES.
IF THEIR MONSTER DESIGNS LOOKED LIKE THE THING WE SAW IN THE FOREST, IT WAS A PRETTY SAFE BET CHIEF McGINNIS WAS RIGHT, AND THE BOYS WERE JUST USING US TO PROMOTE THEIR FILM.
A QUICK PEEK COULD SOLVE THE WHOLE CASE!
HEY! WHAT ARE YOU DOING HERE?
MONSTER DESIGN
UNLESS, OF COURSE, I GOT ***CAUGHT***.

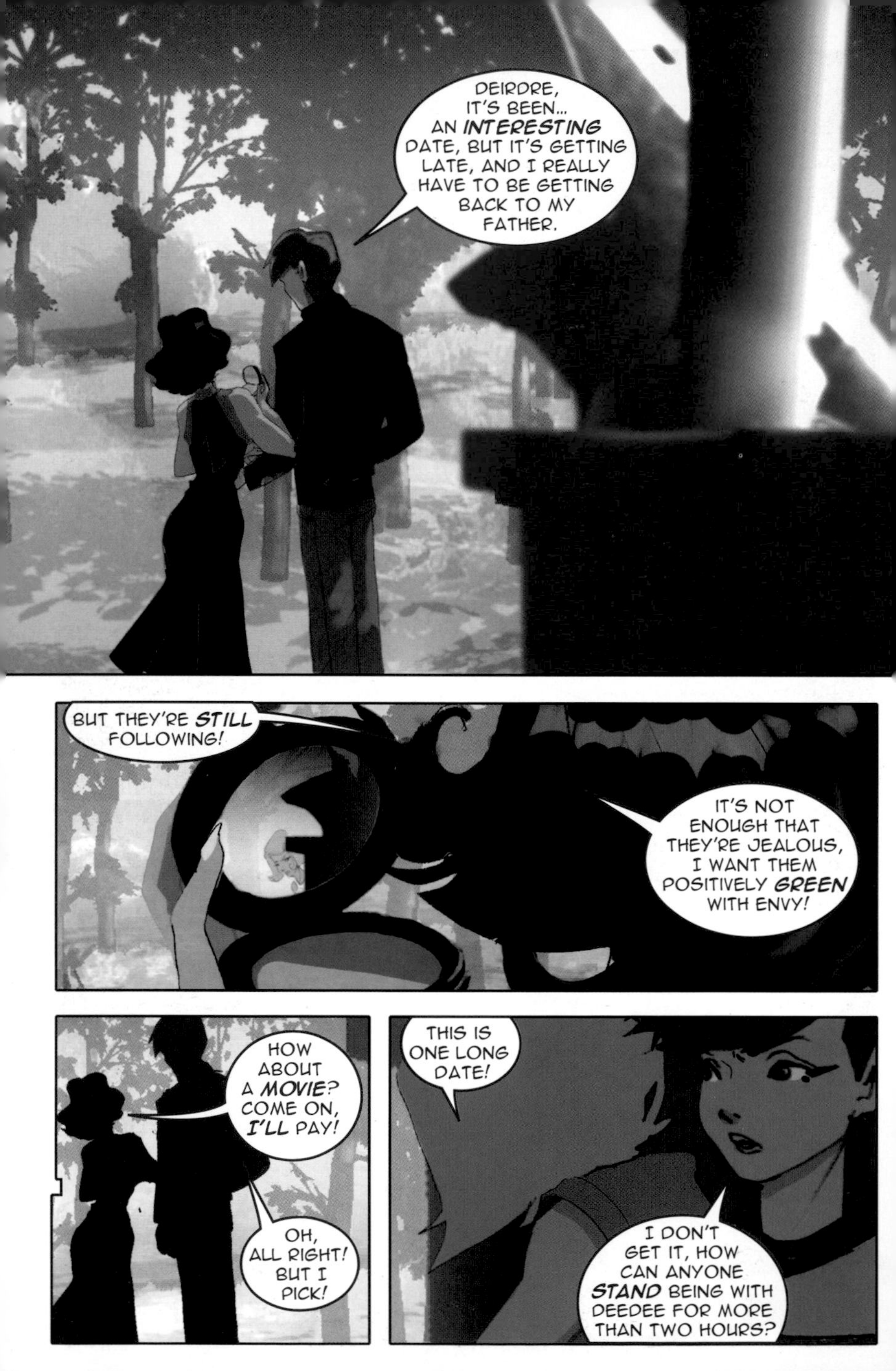
DEIRDRE, IT'S BEEN... AN INTERESTING DATE, BUT IT'S GETTING LATE, AND I REALLY HAVE TO BE GETTING BACK TO MY FATHER.
BUT THEY'RE STILL FOLLOWING!
IT'S NOT ENOUGH THAT THEY'RE JEALOUS, I WANT THEM POSITIVELY GREEN WITH ENVY!
HOW ABOUT A MOVIE? COME ON, I'LL PAY!
OH, ALL RIGHT! BUT I PICK!
THIS IS ONE LONG DATE!
I DON'T GET IT, HOW CAN ANYONE STAND BEING WITH DEEDEE FOR MORE THAN TWO HOURS?

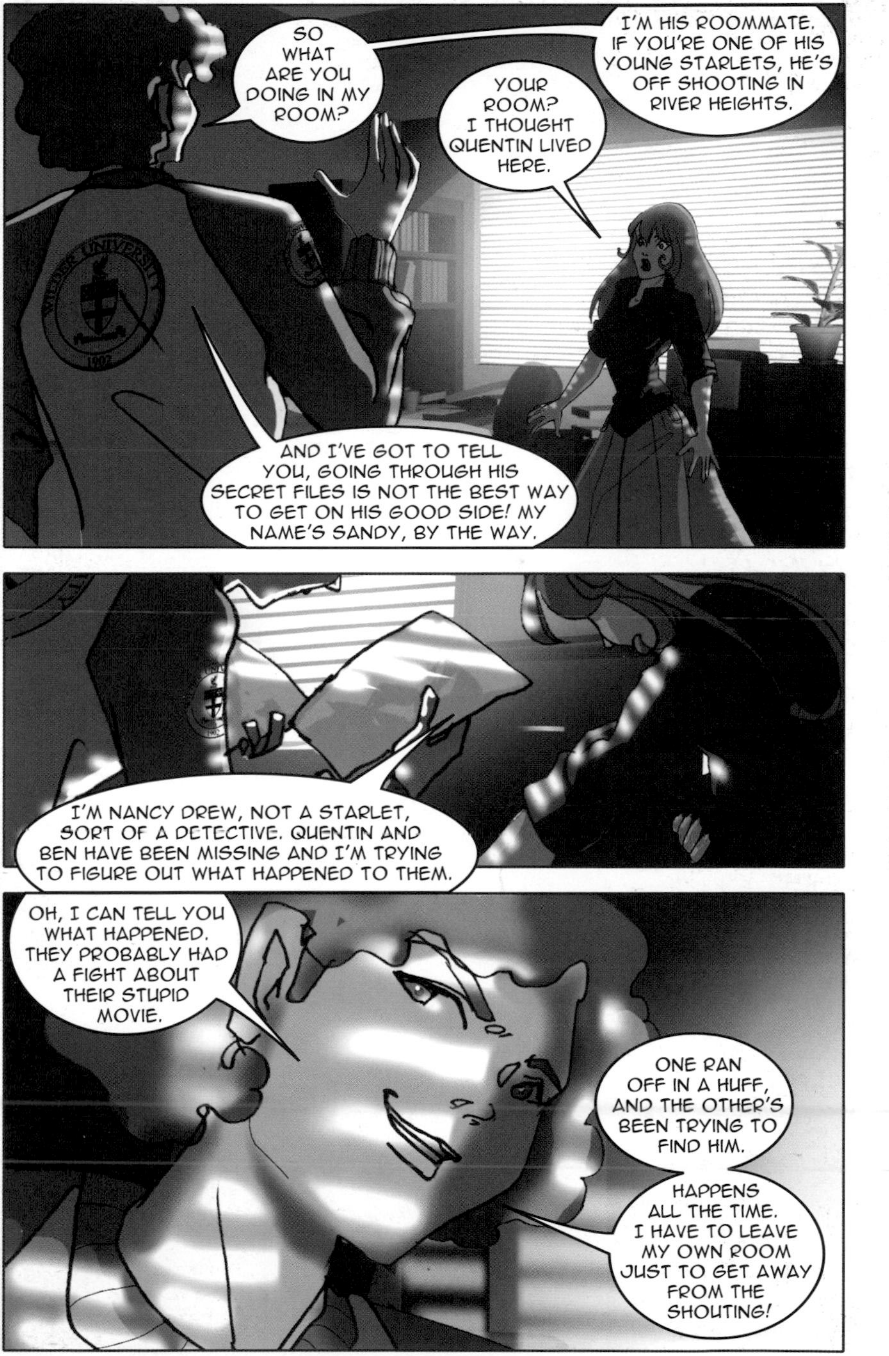
SO WHAT ARE YOU DOING IN MY ROOM?
YOUR ROOM? I THOUGHT QUENTIN LIVED HERE.
I'M HIS ROOMMATE. IF YOU'RE ONE OF HIS YOUNG STARLETS, HE'S OFF SHOOTING IN RIVER HEIGHTS.
AND I'VE GOT TO TELL YOU, GOING THROUGH HIS SECRET FILES IS NOT THE BEST WAY TO GET ON HIS GOOD SIDE! MY NAME'S SANDY, BY THE WAY.
I'M NANCY DREW, NOT A STARLET, SORT OF A DETECTIVE. QUENTIN AND BEN HAVE BEEN MISSING AND I'M TRYING TO FIGURE OUT WHAT HAPPENED TO THEM.
OH, I CAN TELL YOU WHAT HAPPENED. THEY PROBABLY HAD A FIGHT ABOUT THEIR STUPID MOVIE.
ONE RAN OFF IN A HUFF, AND THE OTHER'S BEEN TRYING TO FIND HIM.
HAPPENS ALL THE TIME. I HAVE TO LEAVE MY OWN ROOM JUST TO GET AWAY FROM THE SHOUTING!

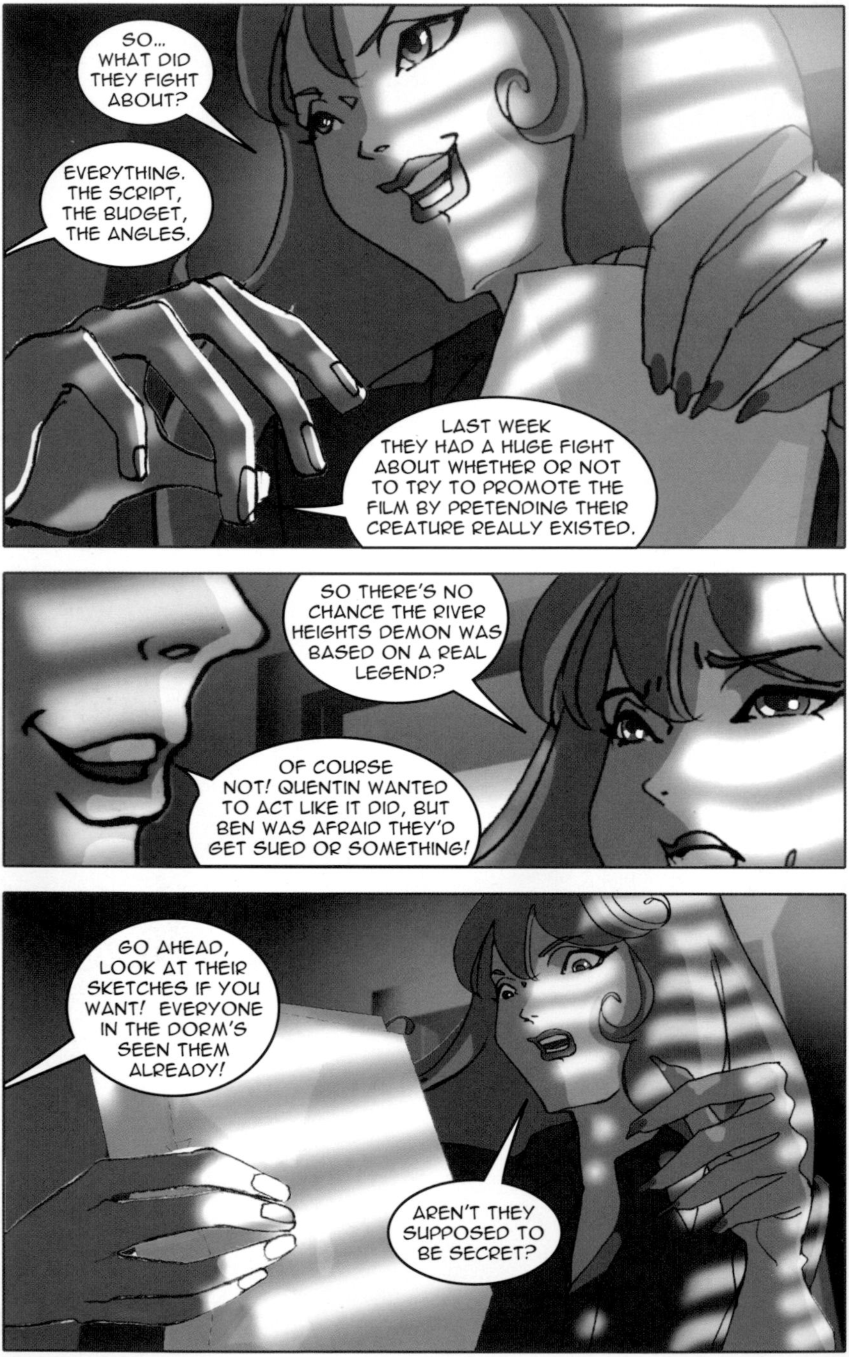
SO... WHAT DID THEY FIGHT ABOUT?
EVERYTHING. THE SCRIPT, THE BUDGET, THE ANGLES.
LAST WEEK THEY HAD A HUGE FIGHT ABOUT WHETHER OR NOT TO TRY TO PROMOTE THE FILM BY PRETENDING THEIR CREATURE REALLY EXISTED.
SO THERE'S NO CHANCE THE RIVER HEIGHTS DEMON WAS BASED ON A REAL LEGEND?
OF COURSE NOT! QUENTIN WANTED TO ACT LIKE IT DID, BUT BEN WAS AFRAID THEY'D GET SUED OR SOMETHING!
GO AHEAD, LOOK AT THEIR SKETCHES IF YOU WANT! EVERYONE IN THE DORM'S SEEN THEM ALREADY!
AREN'T THEY SUPPOSED TO BE SECRET?

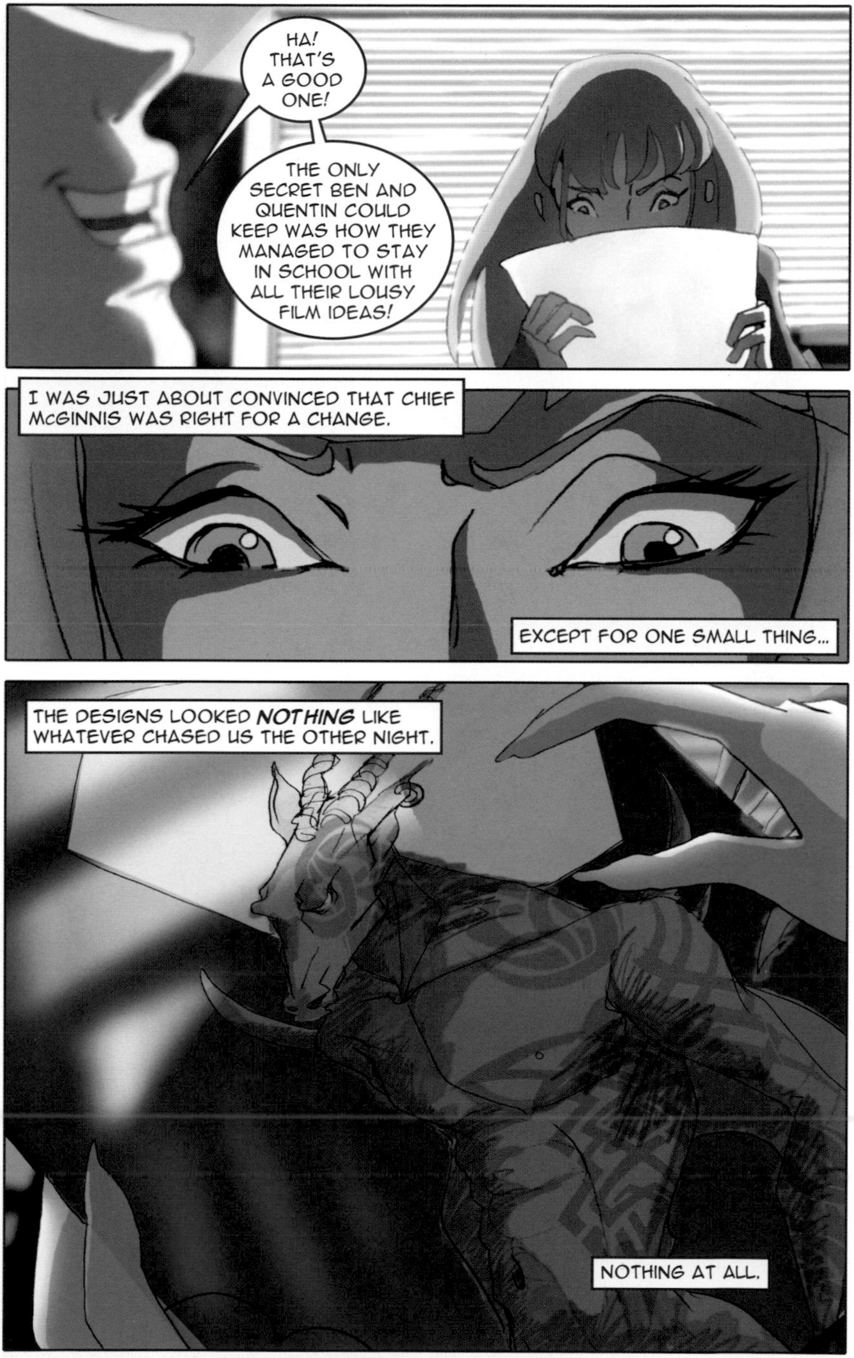
HA! THAT'S A GOOD ONE!
THE ONLY SECRET BEN AND QUENTIN COULD KEEP WAS HOW THEY MANAGED TO STAY IN SCHOOL WITH ALL THEIR LOUSY FILM IDEAS!
I WAS JUST ABOUT CONVINCED THAT CHIEF McGINNIS WAS RIGHT FOR A CHANGE.
EXCEPT FOR ONE SMALL THING...
THE DESIGNS LOOKED **NOTHING** LIKE WHATEVER CHASED US THE OTHER NIGHT.
NOTHING AT ALL.

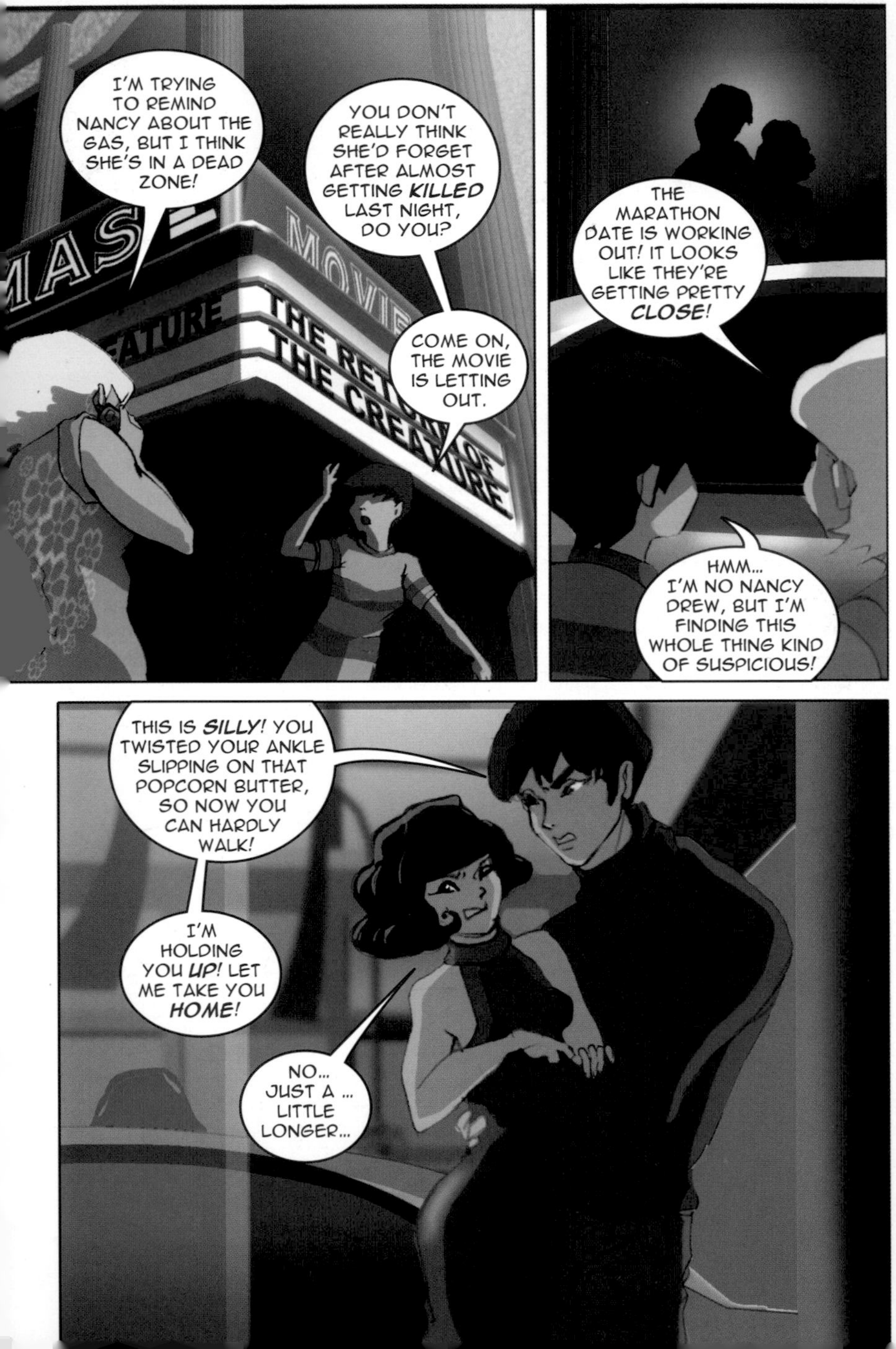
MAS
MOVIE
FEATURE
THE RETURN OF THE CREATURE
I'M TRYING TO REMIND NANCY ABOUT THE GAS, BUT I THINK SHE'S IN A DEAD ZONE!
YOU DON'T REALLY THINK SHE'D FORGET AFTER ALMOST GETTING *KILLED* LAST NIGHT, DO YOU?
COME ON, THE MOVIE IS LETTING OUT.
THE MARATHON DATE IS WORKING OUT! IT LOOKS LIKE THEY'RE GETTING PRETTY *CLOSE*!
HMM... I'M NO NANCY DREW, BUT I'M FINDING THIS WHOLE THING KIND OF SUSPICIOUS!
THIS IS *SILLY*! YOU TWISTED YOUR ANKLE SLIPPING ON THAT POPCORN BUTTER, SO NOW YOU CAN HARDLY WALK!
I'M HOLDING YOU *UP*! LET ME TAKE YOU *HOME*!
NO... JUST A ... LITTLE LONGER...

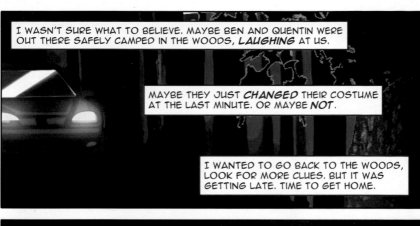

I WASN'T SURE WHAT TO BELIEVE. MAYBE BEN AND QUENTIN WERE OUT THERE SAFELY CAMPED IN THE WOODS, *LAUGHING* AT US.

MAYBE THEY JUST *CHANGED* THEIR COSTUME AT THE LAST MINUTE. OR MAYBE *NOT*.

I WANTED TO GO BACK TO THE WOODS, LOOK FOR MORE CLUES. BUT IT WAS GETTING LATE. TIME TO GET HOME.

OHHHH! OUT OF GAS *AGAIN*!

BESS IS GOING TO *KILL* ME! HECK, IF I WEREN'T ME, *I'D* KILL ME!

WRRR... WRRR... WRR...

OH WELL, NOT TOO LATE TO CALL MY AAA PAL, CHARLES ADAMS. HE SAYS HE KEEPS A CAN OF GAS BY HIS TRUCK WITH MY NAME ON IT!

CHARLIE? CAN YOU HEAR ME? I'M STUCK BY FOREST ROAD, NEAR THE...

NRGHTHY -CLICK- NANCY? PHSGHHRLLLL?

...BAD SIGNAL
...WHERE
DID YOU SAY...
-CRHSKLLL-

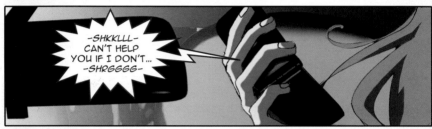

-SHKKLLL-
CAN'T HELP
YOU IF I DON'T...
-SHRGGGG-

IT WAS ALMOST LIKE *SUNLIGHT*, EXCEPT IT WAS COMING FROM THE *GROUND*, SOMEWHERE DOWN THAT HILL.

I FIGURED IT WAS THE BOYS, SHOOTING THEIR MOVIE. I WANTED TO GIVE THEM A PIECE OF MY MIND.

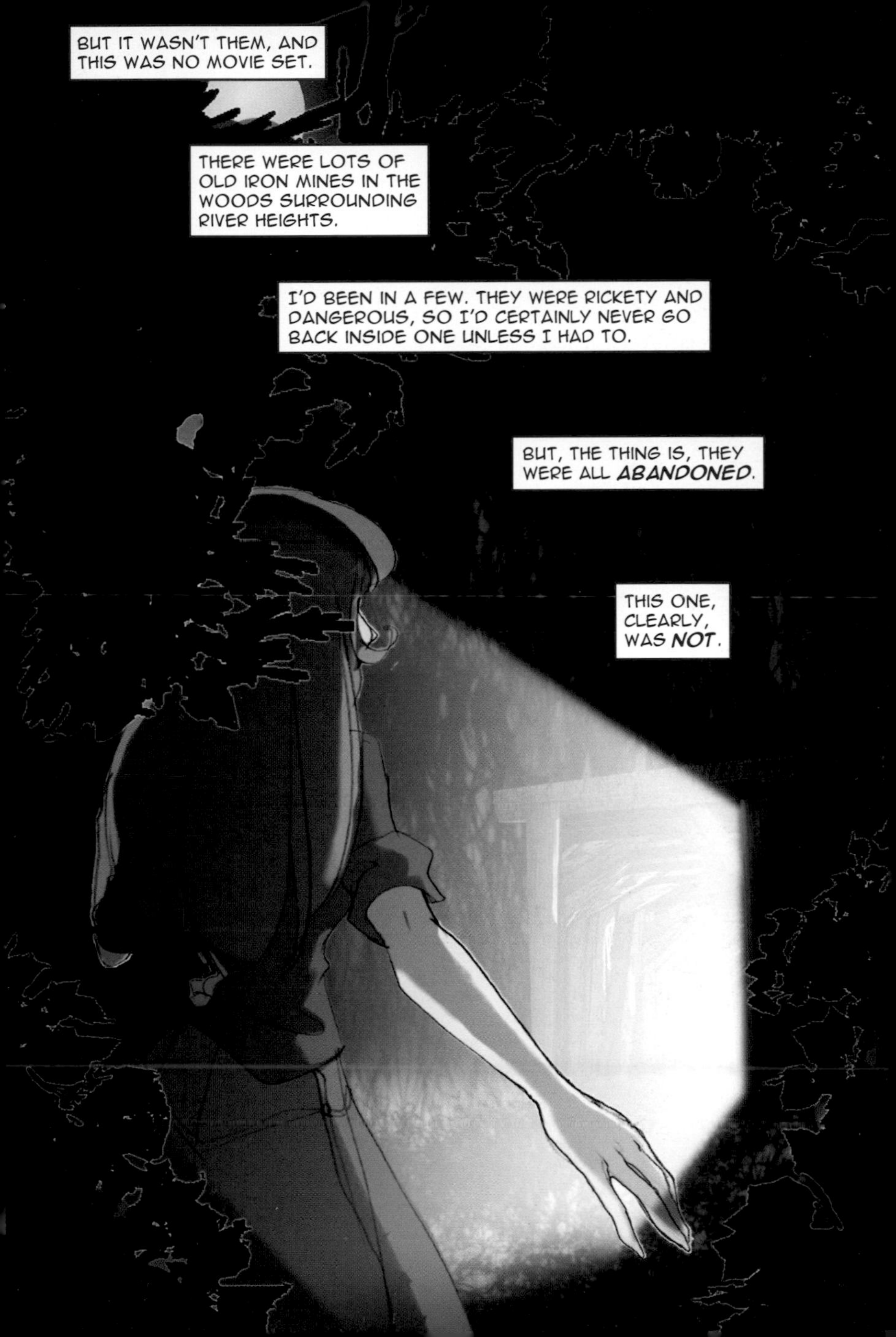
BUT IT WASN'T THEM, AND THIS WAS NO MOVIE SET.
THERE WERE LOTS OF OLD IRON MINES IN THE WOODS SURROUNDING RIVER HEIGHTS.
I'D BEEN IN A FEW. THEY WERE RICKETY AND DANGEROUS, SO I'D CERTAINLY NEVER GO BACK INSIDE ONE UNLESS I HAD TO.
BUT, THE THING IS, THEY WERE ALL *ABANDONED*.
THIS ONE, CLEARLY, WAS *NOT*.

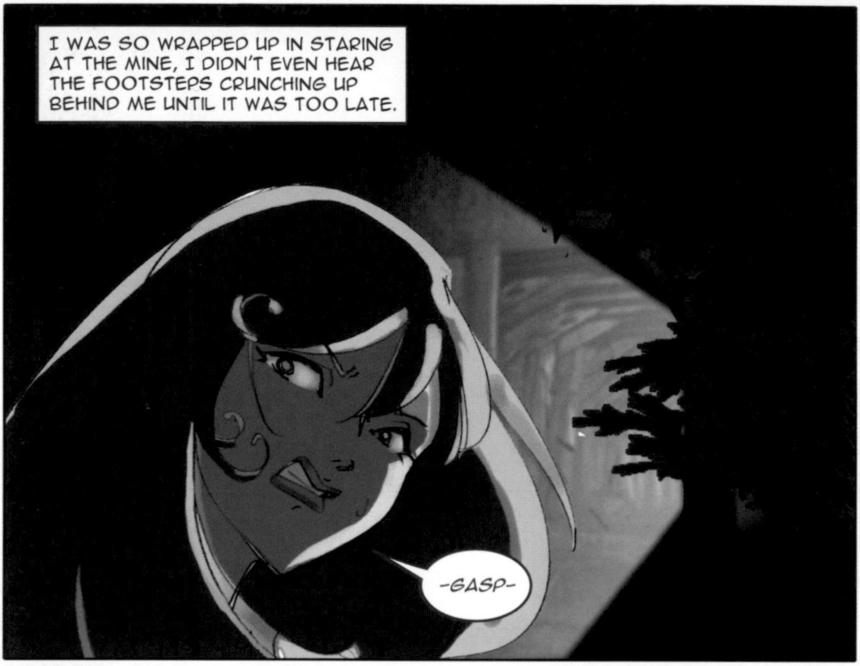
I WAS SO WRAPPED UP IN STARING AT THE MINE, I DIDN'T EVEN HEAR THE FOOTSTEPS CRUNCHING UP BEHIND ME UNTIL IT WAS TOO LATE.
-GASP-

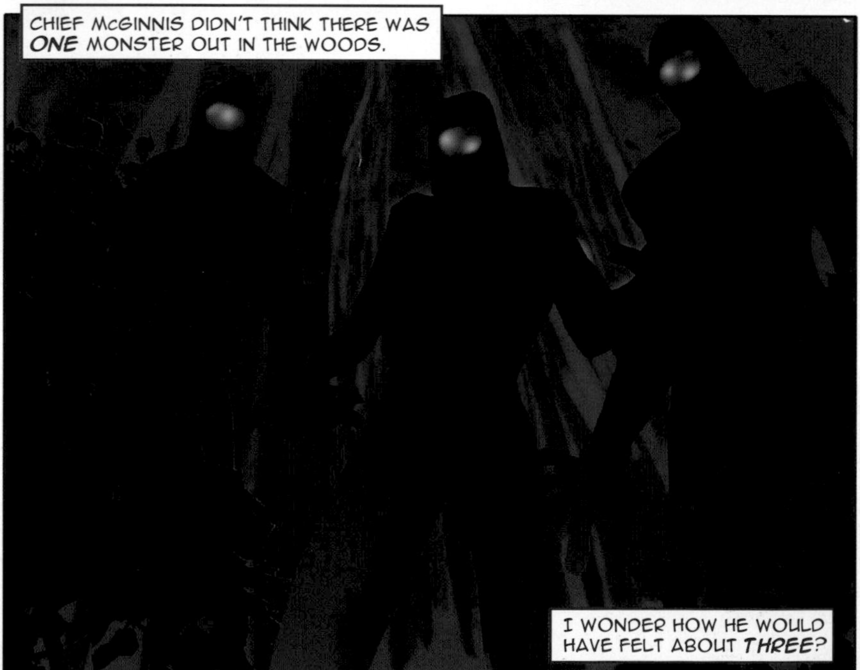
CHIEF McGINNIS DIDN'T THINK THERE WAS *ONE* MONSTER OUT IN THE WOODS.
I WONDER HOW HE WOULD HAVE FELT ABOUT *THREE*?

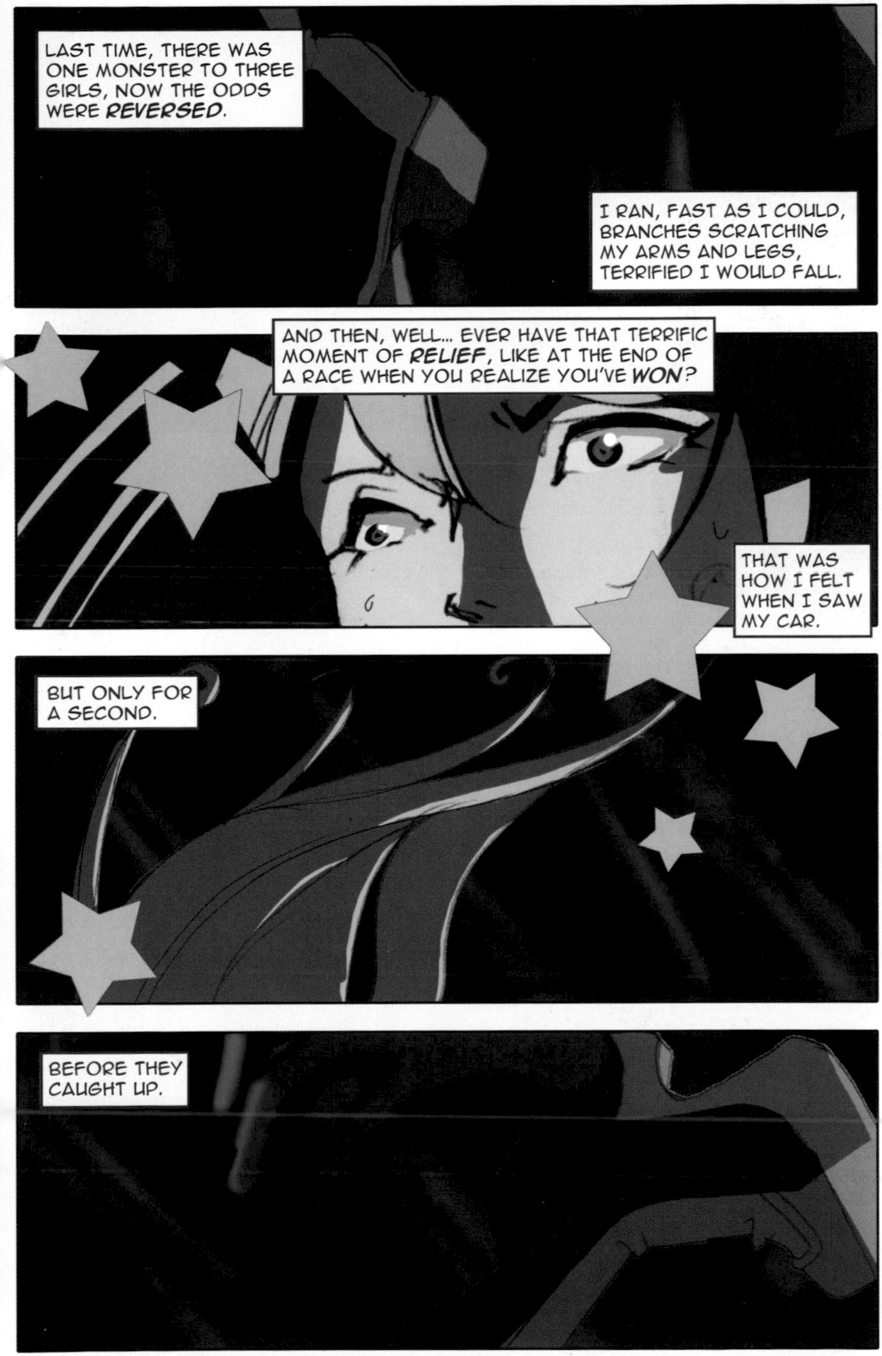
LAST TIME, THERE WAS ONE MONSTER TO THREE GIRLS, NOW THE ODDS WERE *REVERSED*.
I RAN, FAST AS I COULD, BRANCHES SCRATCHING MY ARMS AND LEGS, TERRIFIED I WOULD FALL.
AND THEN, WELL... EVER HAVE THAT TERRIFIC MOMENT OF *RELIEF*, LIKE AT THE END OF A RACE WHEN YOU REALIZE YOU'VE *WON*?
THAT WAS HOW I FELT WHEN I SAW MY CAR.
BUT ONLY FOR A SECOND.
BEFORE THEY CAUGHT UP.

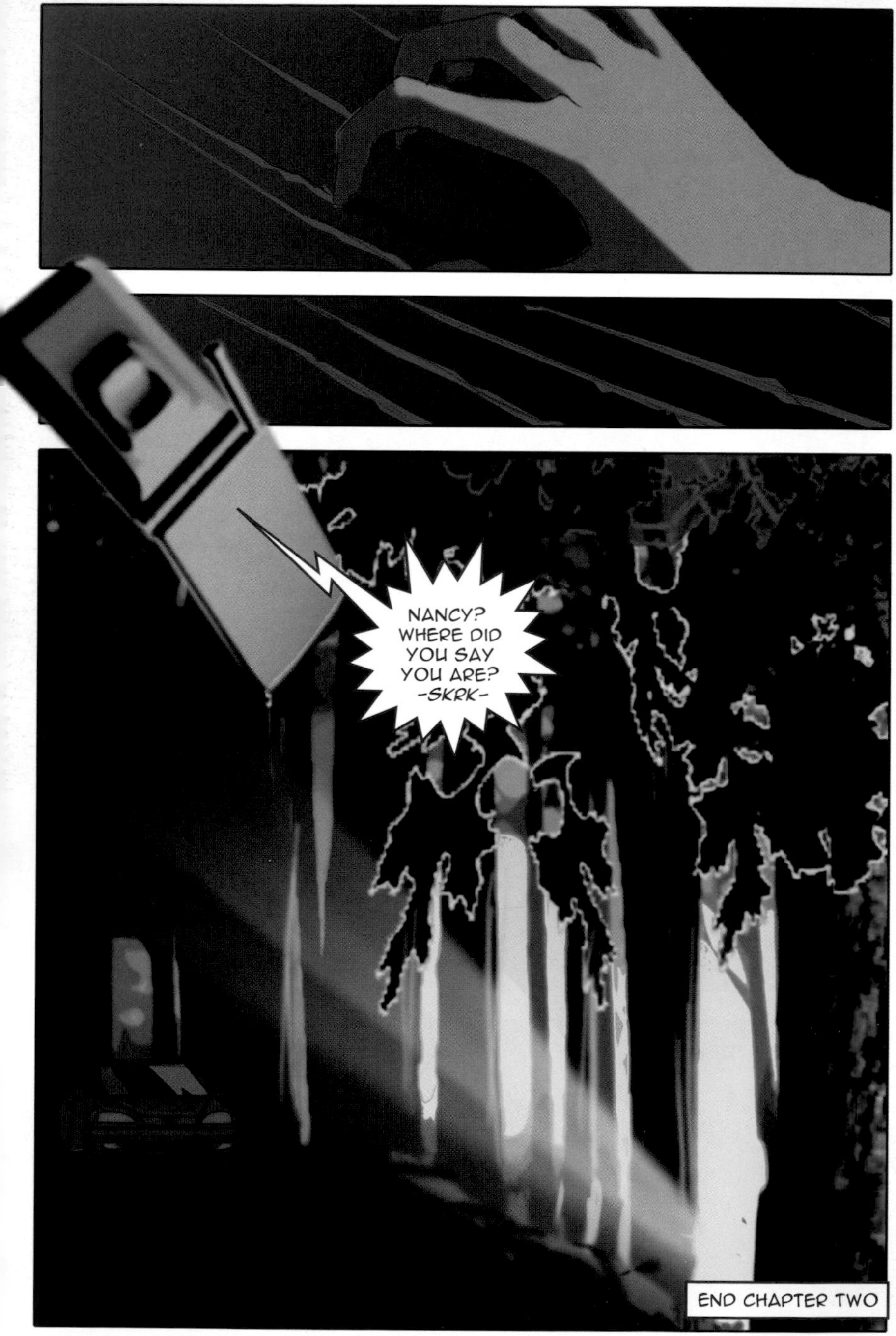
NANCY? WHERE DID YOU SAY YOU ARE? -SKRK-
END CHAPTER TWO

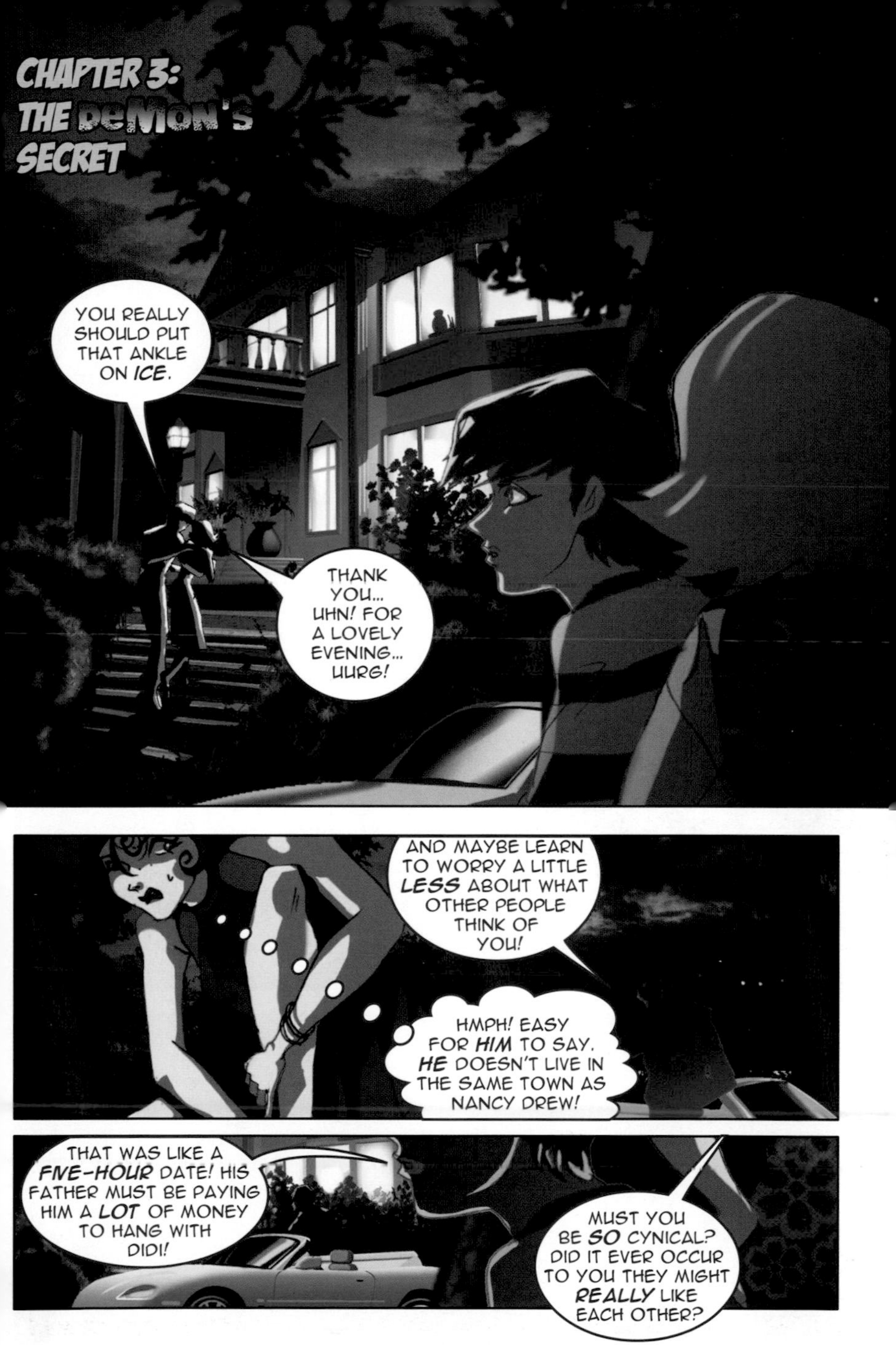
CHAPTER 3: THE DEMON'S SECRET
YOU REALLY SHOULD PUT THAT ANKLE ON ICE.
THANK YOU... UHN! FOR A LOVELY EVENING... UURG!
AND MAYBE LEARN TO WORRY A LITTLE LESS ABOUT WHAT OTHER PEOPLE THINK OF YOU!
HMPH! EASY FOR HIM TO SAY. HE DOESN'T LIVE IN THE SAME TOWN AS NANCY DREW!
THAT WAS LIKE A FIVE-HOUR DATE! HIS FATHER MUST BE PAYING HIM A LOT OF MONEY TO HANG WITH DIDI!
MUST YOU BE SO CYNICAL? DID IT EVER OCCUR TO YOU THEY MIGHT REALLY LIKE EACH OTHER?

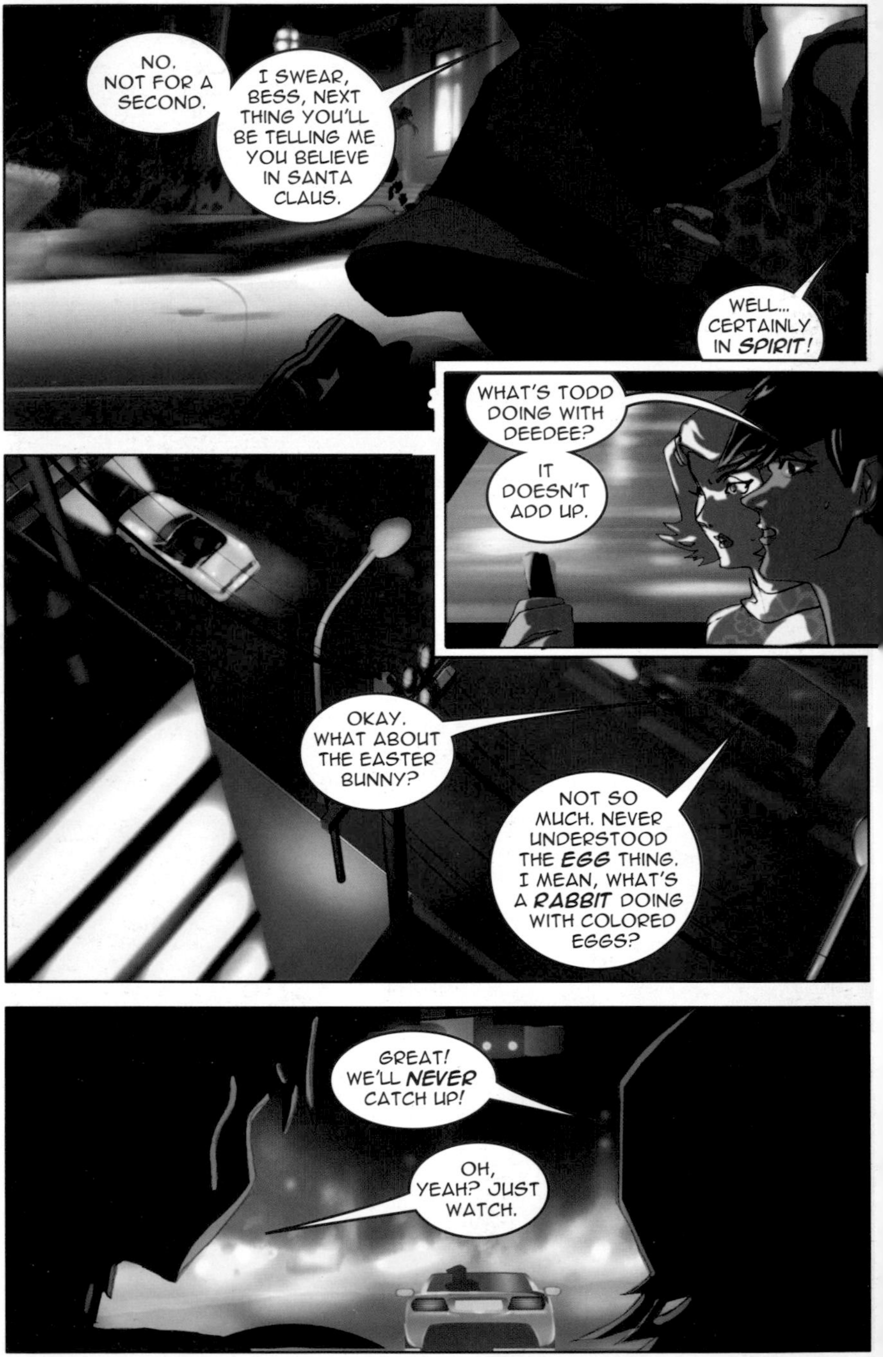
NO. NOT FOR A SECOND.
I SWEAR, BESS, NEXT THING YOU'LL BE TELLING ME YOU BELIEVE IN SANTA CLAUS.
WELL... CERTAINLY IN *SPIRIT*!
WHAT'S TODD DOING WITH DEEDEE?
IT DOESN'T ADD UP.
OKAY. WHAT ABOUT THE EASTER BUNNY?
NOT SO MUCH. NEVER UNDERSTOOD THE *EGG* THING. I MEAN, WHAT'S A *RABBIT* DOING WITH COLORED EGGS?
GREAT! WE'LL *NEVER* CATCH UP!
OH, YEAH? JUST WATCH.

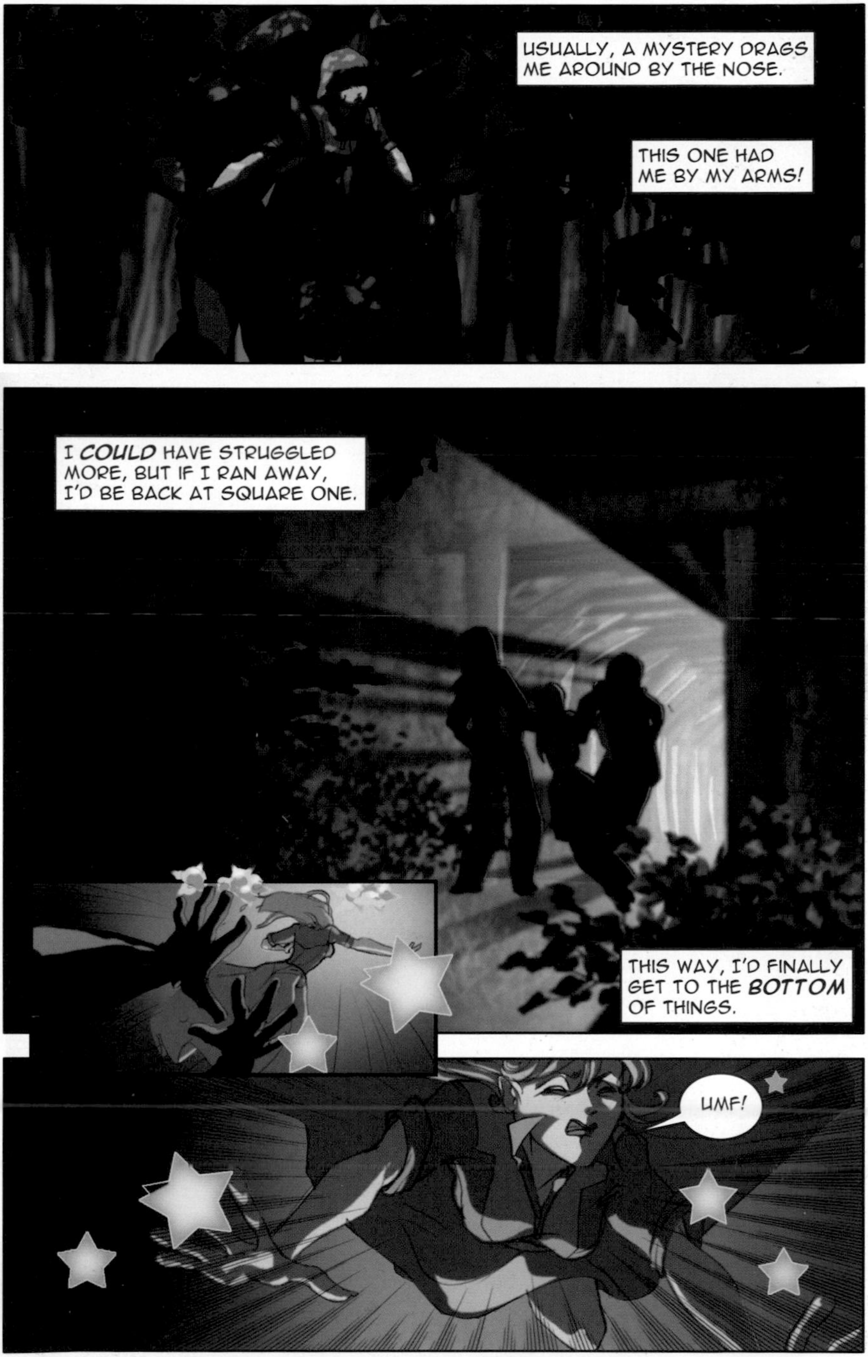
USUALLY, A MYSTERY DRAGS ME AROUND BY THE NOSE.
THIS ONE HAD ME BY MY ARMS!
I *COULD* HAVE STRUGGLED MORE, BUT IF I RAN AWAY, I'D BE BACK AT SQUARE ONE.
THIS WAY, I'D FINALLY GET TO THE *BOTTOM* OF THINGS.
UMF!

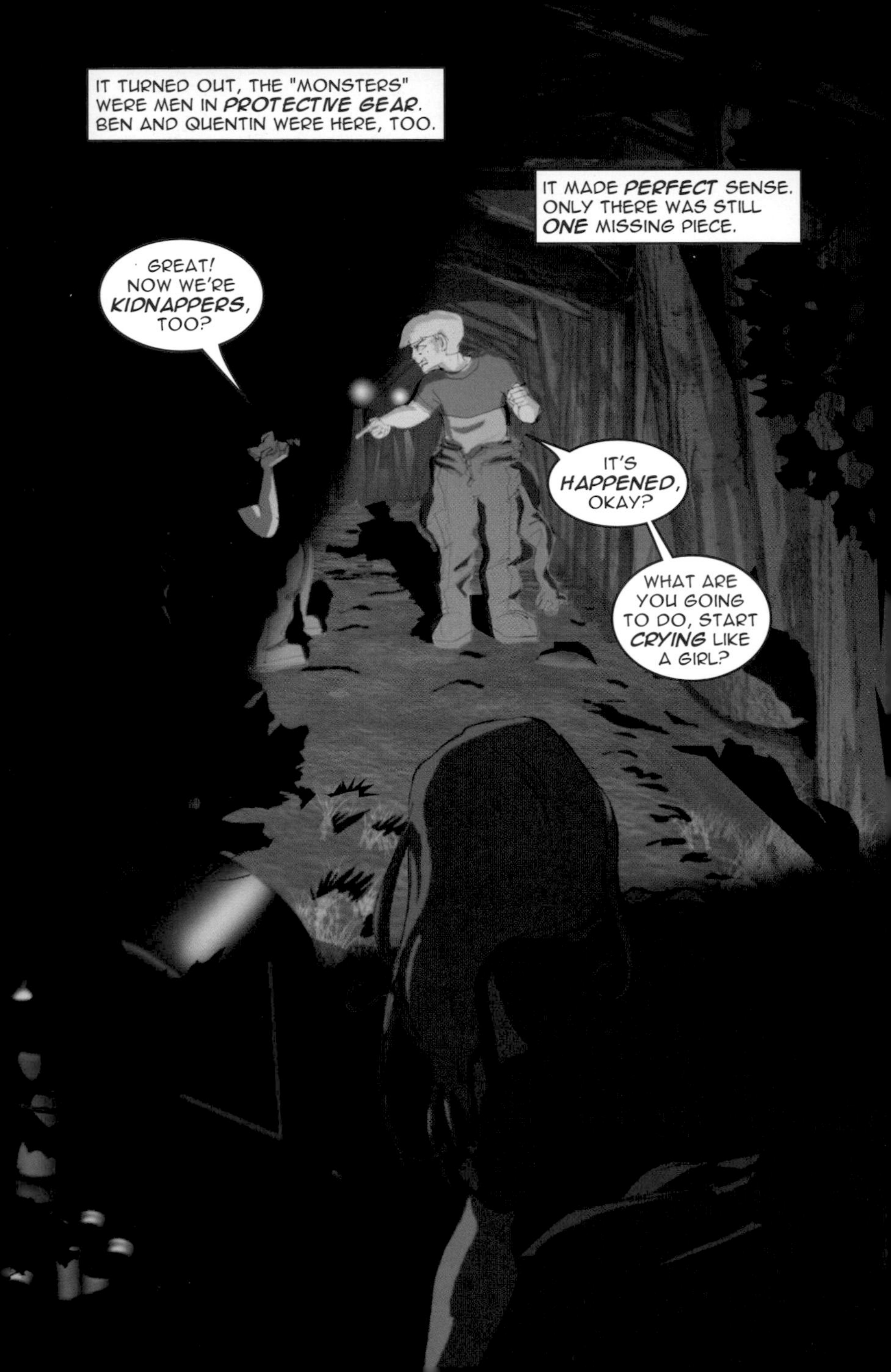
IT TURNED OUT, THE "MONSTERS" WERE MEN IN PROTECTIVE GEAR. BEN AND QUENTIN WERE HERE, TOO.
IT MADE PERFECT SENSE. ONLY THERE WAS STILL ONE MISSING PIECE.
GREAT! NOW WE'RE KIDNAPPERS, TOO?
IT'S HAPPENED, OKAY?
WHAT ARE YOU GOING TO DO, START CRYING LIKE A GIRL?

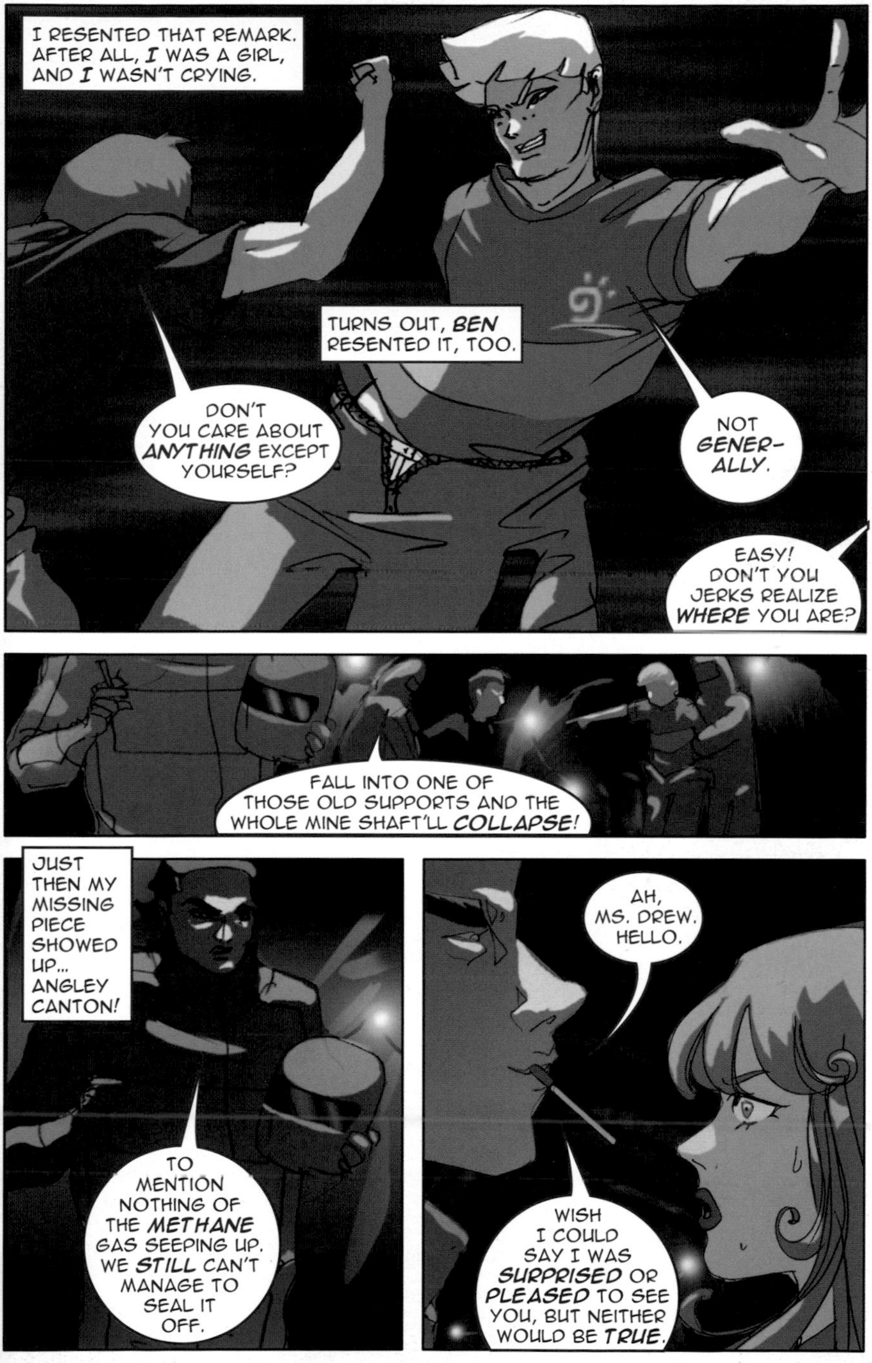
I RESENTED THAT REMARK. AFTER ALL, I WAS A GIRL, AND I WASN'T CRYING.
TURNS OUT, BEN RESENTED IT, TOO.
DON'T YOU CARE ABOUT ANYTHING EXCEPT YOURSELF?
NOT GENER-ALLY.
EASY! DON'T YOU JERKS REALIZE WHERE YOU ARE?
FALL INTO ONE OF THOSE OLD SUPPORTS AND THE WHOLE MINE SHAFT'LL COLLAPSE!
JUST THEN MY MISSING PIECE SHOWED UP... ANGLEY CANTON!
TO MENTION NOTHING OF THE METHANE GAS SEEPING UP. WE STILL CAN'T MANAGE TO SEAL IT OFF.
AH, MS. DREW. HELLO.
WISH I COULD SAY I WAS SURPRISED OR PLEASED TO SEE YOU, BUT NEITHER WOULD BE TRUE.

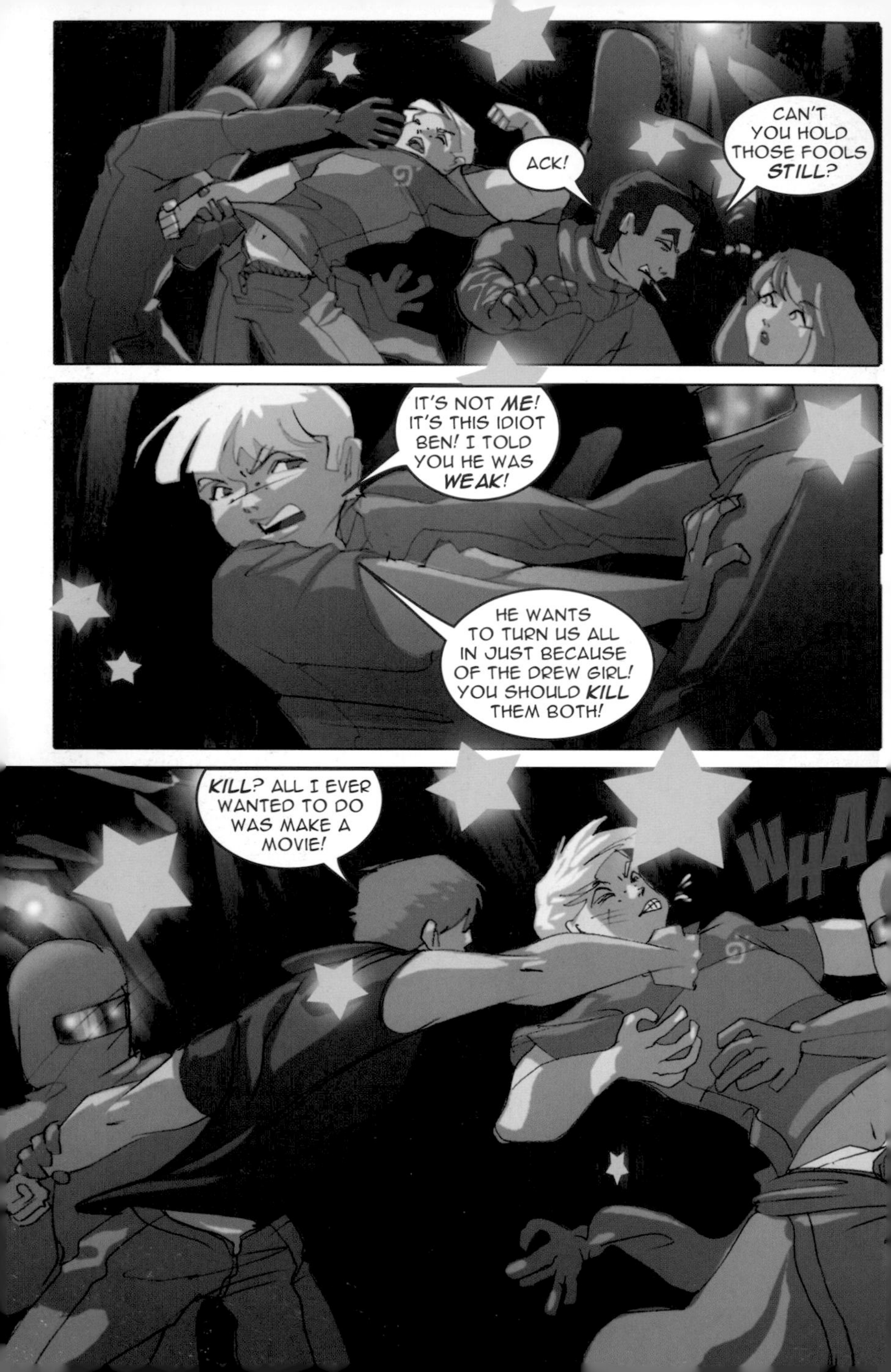
ACK!
CAN'T YOU HOLD THOSE FOOLS STILL?
IT'S NOT ME! IT'S THIS IDIOT BEN! I TOLD YOU HE WAS WEAK!
HE WANTS TO TURN US ALL IN JUST BECAUSE OF THE DREW GIRL! YOU SHOULD KILL THEM BOTH!
KILL? ALL I EVER WANTED TO DO WAS MAKE A MOVIE!
WHA

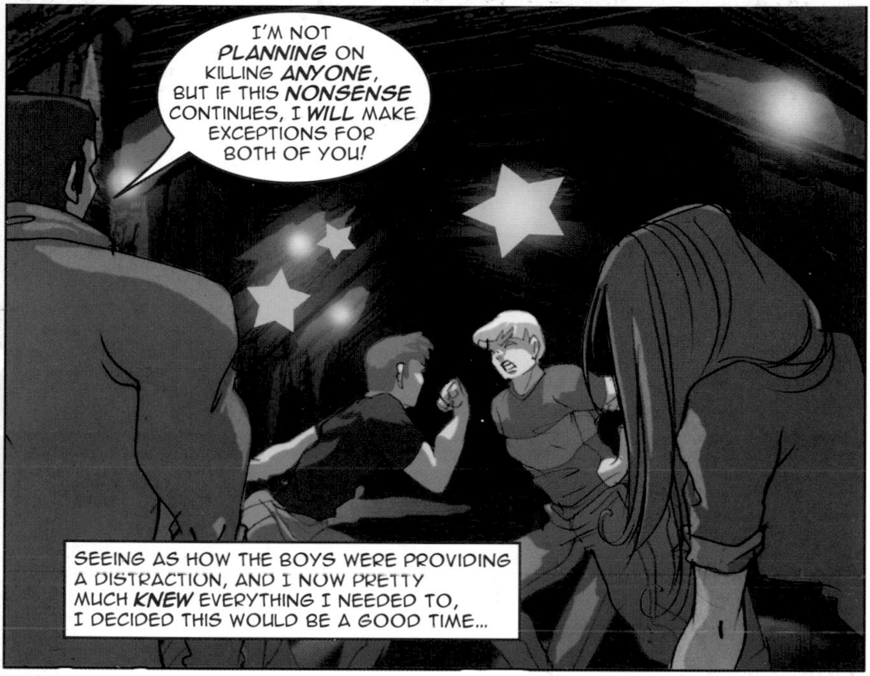
I'M NOT PLANNING ON KILLING ANYONE, BUT IF THIS NONSENSE CONTINUES, I WILL MAKE EXCEPTIONS FOR BOTH OF YOU!
SEEING AS HOW THE BOYS WERE PROVIDING A DISTRACTION, AND I NOW PRETTY MUCH KNEW EVERYTHING I NEEDED TO, I DECIDED THIS WOULD BE A GOOD TIME...

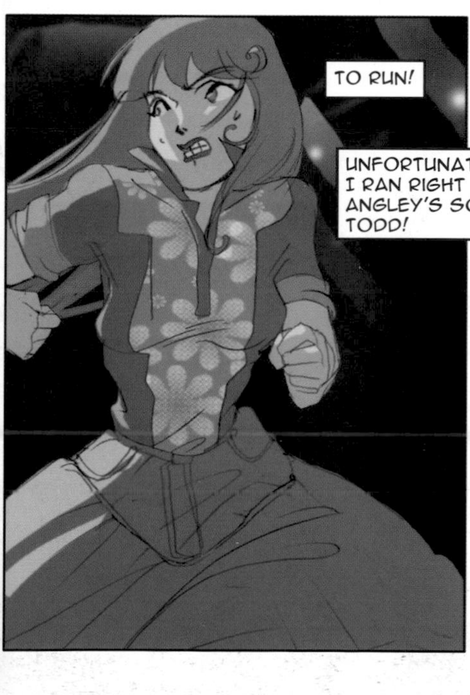
TO RUN!
UNFORTUNATELY, I RAN RIGHT INTO ANGLEY'S SON, TODD!

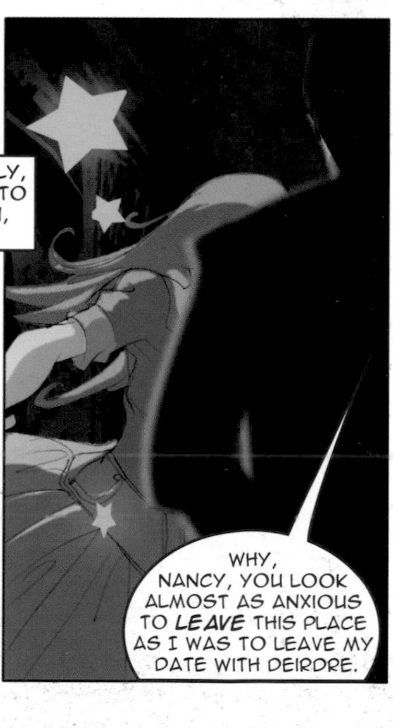
WHY, NANCY, YOU LOOK ALMOST AS ANXIOUS TO LEAVE THIS PLACE AS I WAS TO LEAVE MY DATE WITH DEIRDRE.

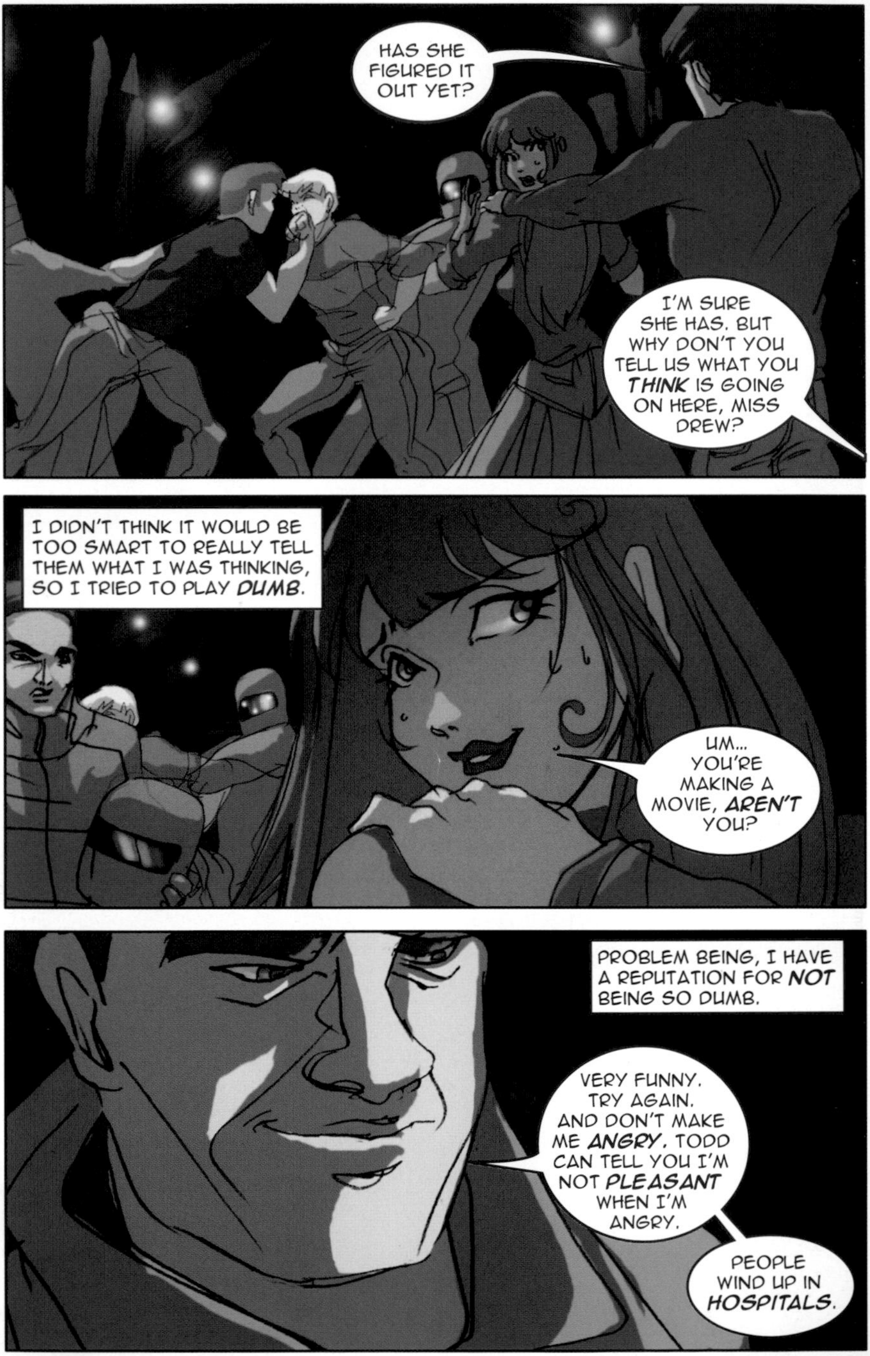
HAS SHE FIGURED IT OUT YET?
I'M SURE SHE HAS. BUT WHY DON'T YOU TELL US WHAT YOU *THINK* IS GOING ON HERE, MISS DREW?
I DIDN'T THINK IT WOULD BE TOO SMART TO REALLY TELL THEM WHAT I WAS THINKING, SO I TRIED TO PLAY *DUMB*.
UM... YOU'RE MAKING A MOVIE, *AREN'T* YOU?
PROBLEM BEING, I HAVE A REPUTATION FOR *NOT* BEING SO DUMB.
VERY FUNNY. TRY AGAIN. AND DON'T MAKE ME *ANGRY*. TODD CAN TELL YOU I'M NOT *PLEASANT* WHEN I'M ANGRY.
PEOPLE WIND UP IN *HOSPITALS*.

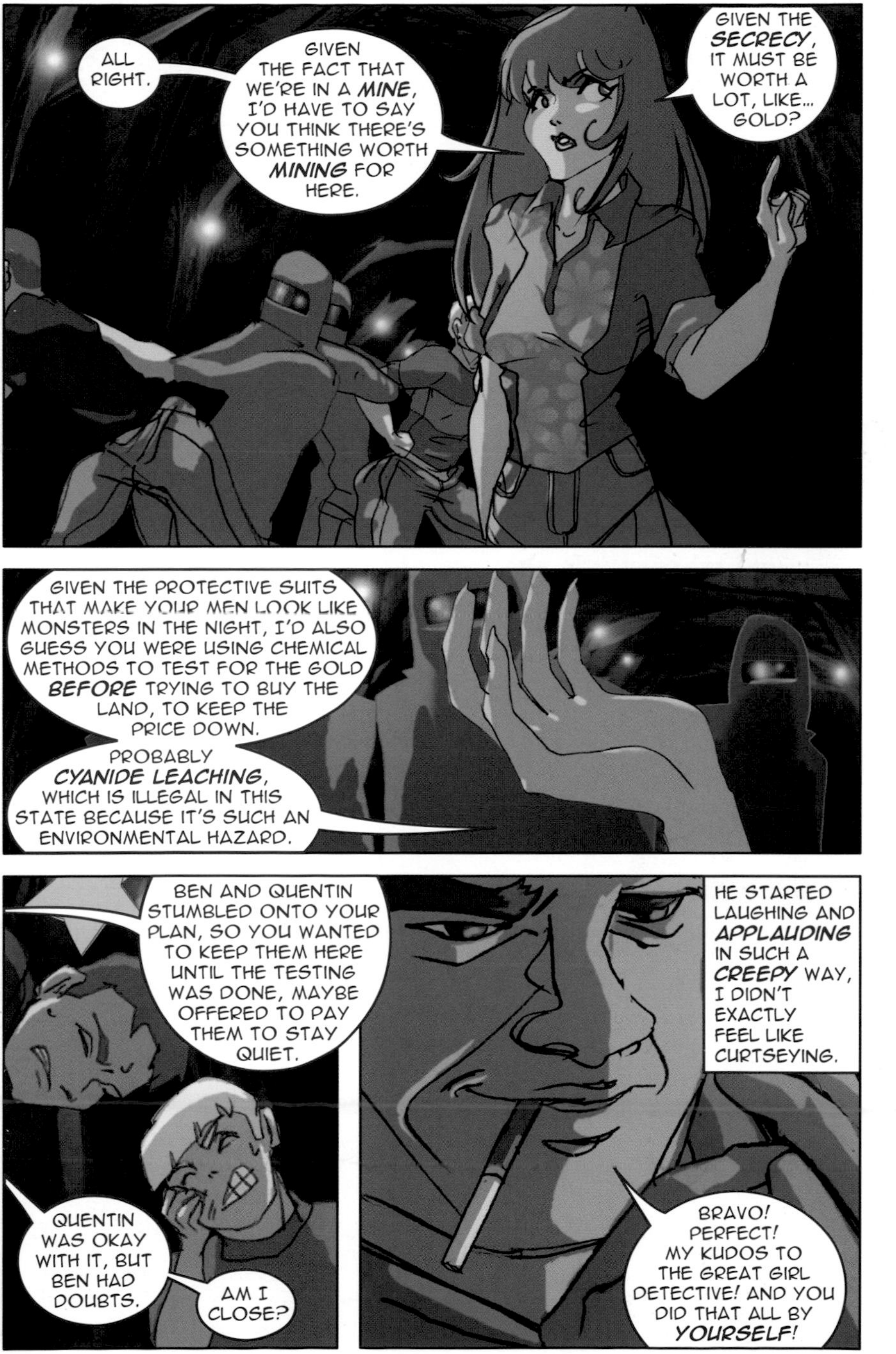
ALL RIGHT.
GIVEN THE FACT THAT WE'RE IN A *MINE*, I'D HAVE TO SAY YOU THINK THERE'S SOMETHING WORTH *MINING* FOR HERE.
GIVEN THE *SECRECY*, IT MUST BE WORTH A LOT, LIKE... GOLD?
GIVEN THE PROTECTIVE SUITS THAT MAKE YOUR MEN LOOK LIKE MONSTERS IN THE NIGHT, I'D ALSO GUESS YOU WERE USING CHEMICAL METHODS TO TEST FOR THE GOLD *BEFORE* TRYING TO BUY THE LAND, TO KEEP THE PRICE DOWN.
PROBABLY *CYANIDE LEACHING*, WHICH IS ILLEGAL IN THIS STATE BECAUSE IT'S SUCH AN ENVIRONMENTAL HAZARD.
BEN AND QUENTIN STUMBLED ONTO YOUR PLAN, SO YOU WANTED TO KEEP THEM HERE UNTIL THE TESTING WAS DONE, MAYBE OFFERED TO PAY THEM TO STAY QUIET.
QUENTIN WAS OKAY WITH IT, BUT BEN HAD DOUBTS.
AM I CLOSE?
HE STARTED LAUGHING AND *APPLAUDING* IN SUCH A *CREEPY* WAY, I DIDN'T EXACTLY FEEL LIKE CURTSEYING.
BRAVO! PERFECT! MY KUDOS TO THE GREAT GIRL DETECTIVE! AND YOU DID THAT ALL BY *YOURSELF*!

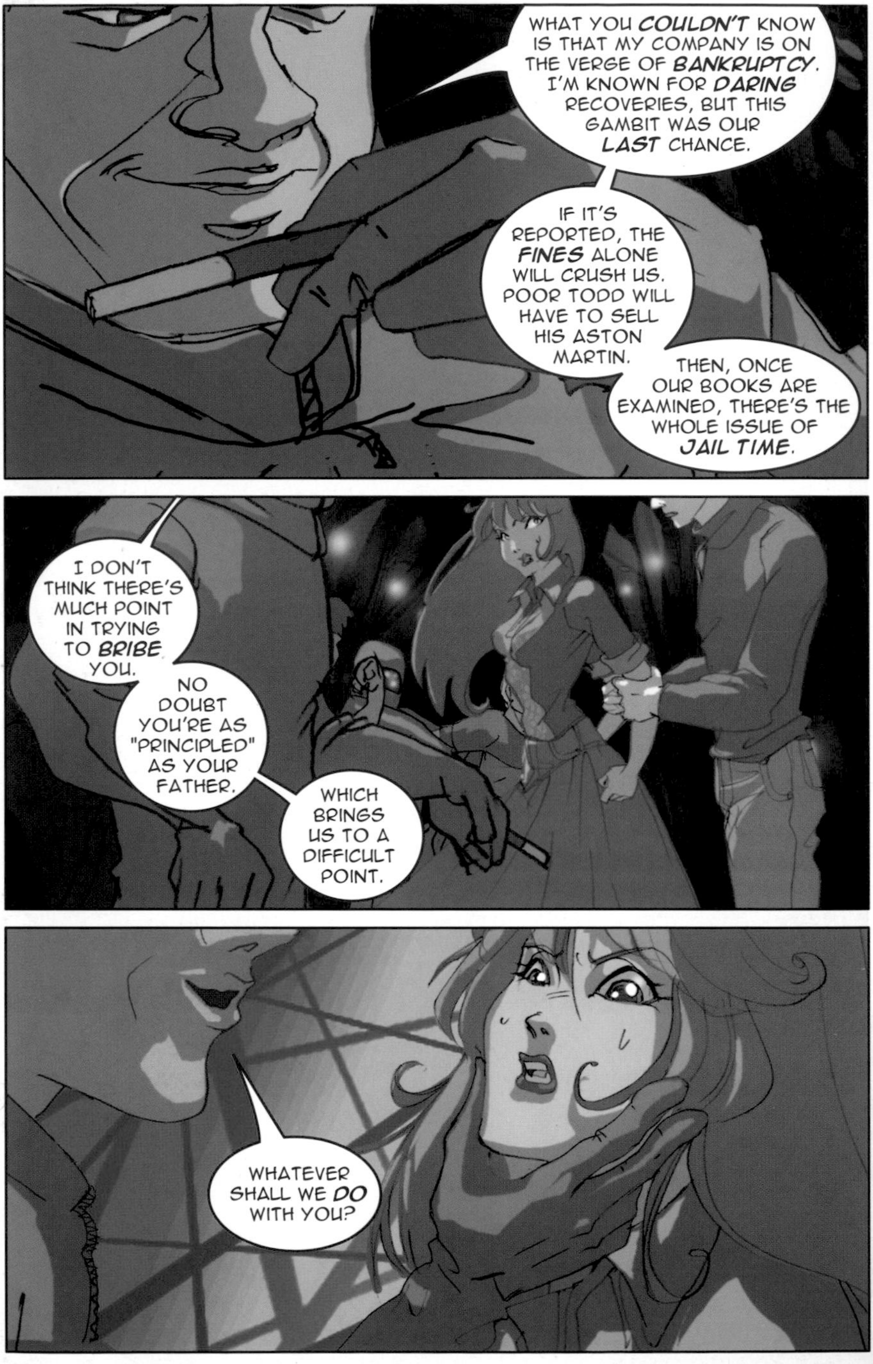
WHAT YOU COULDN'T KNOW IS THAT MY COMPANY IS ON THE VERGE OF BANKRUPTCY. I'M KNOWN FOR DARING RECOVERIES, BUT THIS GAMBIT WAS OUR LAST CHANCE.
IF IT'S REPORTED, THE FINES ALONE WILL CRUSH US. POOR TODD WILL HAVE TO SELL HIS ASTON MARTIN.
THEN, ONCE OUR BOOKS ARE EXAMINED, THERE'S THE WHOLE ISSUE OF JAIL TIME.
I DON'T THINK THERE'S MUCH POINT IN TRYING TO BRIBE YOU.
NO DOUBT YOU'RE AS "PRINCIPLED" AS YOUR FATHER.
WHICH BRINGS US TO A DIFFICULT POINT.
WHATEVER SHALL WE DO WITH YOU?

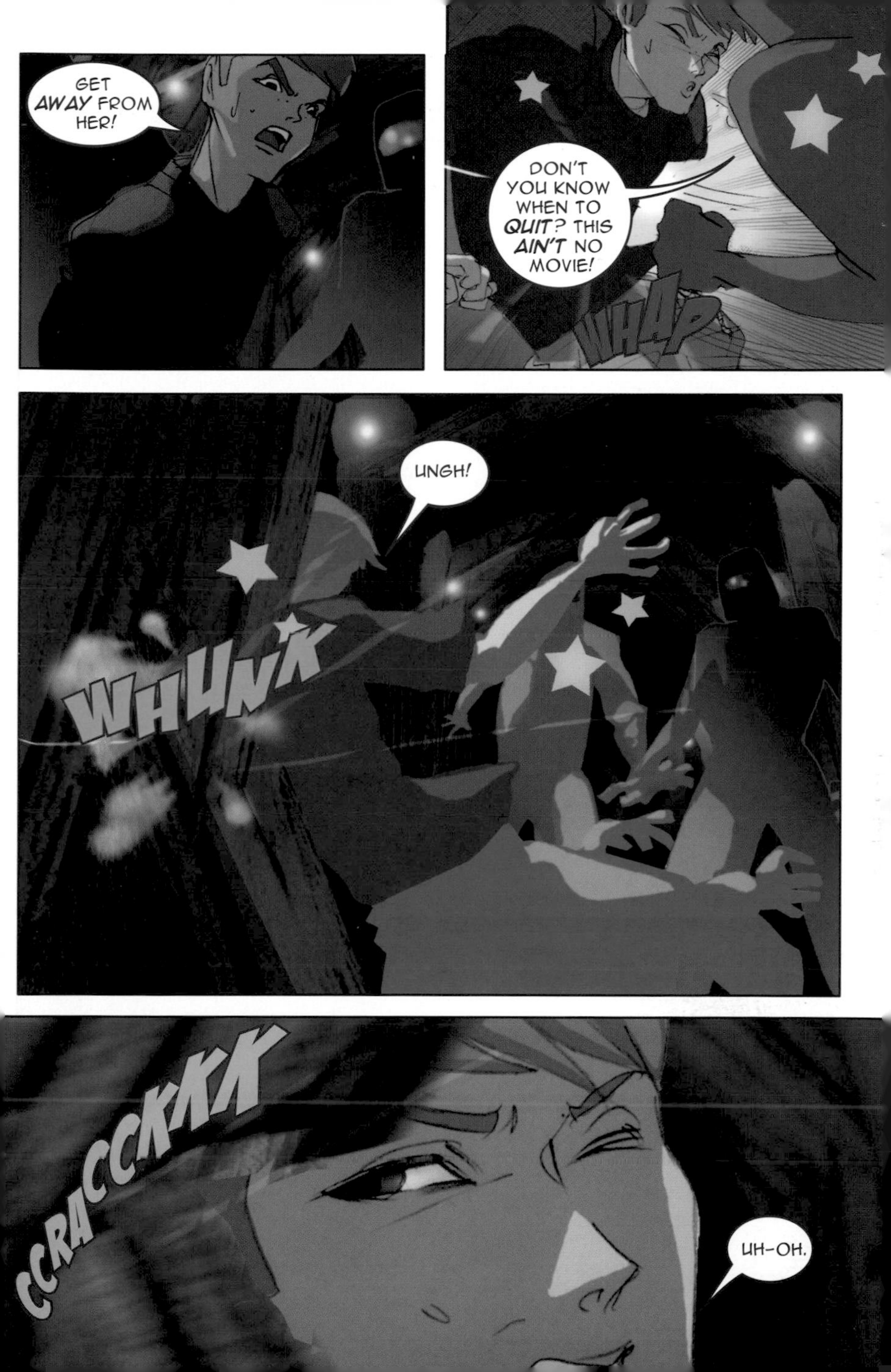
GET AWAY FROM HER!
DON'T YOU KNOW WHEN TO QUIT? THIS AIN'T NO MOVIE!
WHAP
UNGH!
WHUNK
CCRACCKKK
UH-OH.

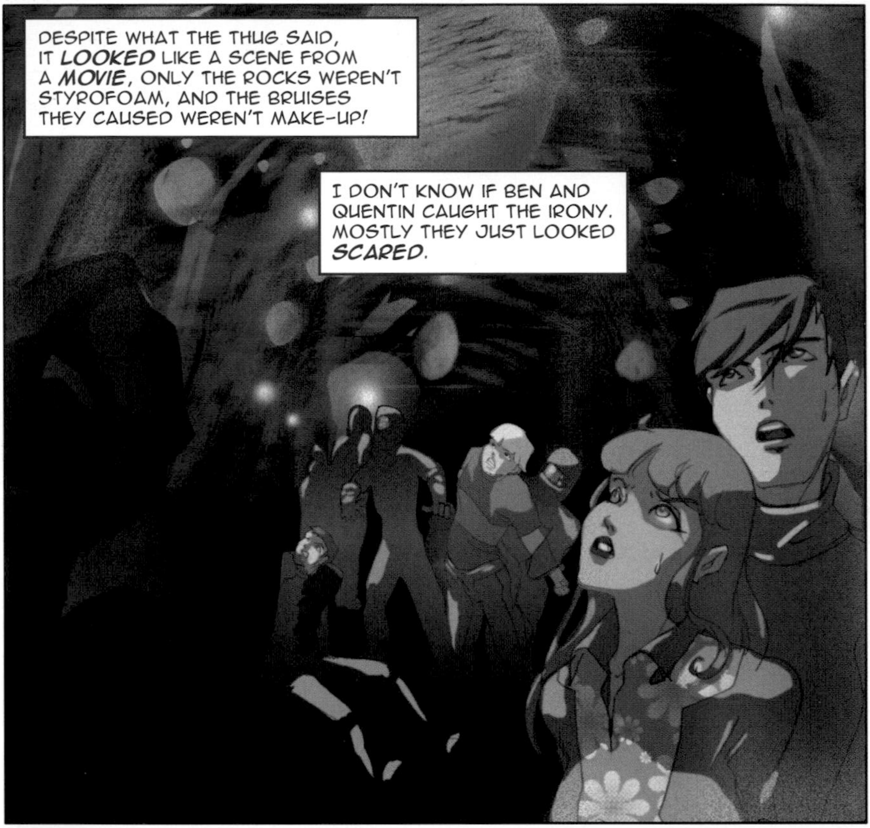
DESPITE WHAT THE THUG SAID, IT LOOKED LIKE A SCENE FROM A MOVIE, ONLY THE ROCKS WEREN'T STYROFOAM, AND THE BRUISES THEY CAUSED WEREN'T MAKE-UP!
I DON'T KNOW IF BEN AND QUENTIN CAUGHT THE IRONY. MOSTLY THEY JUST LOOKED SCARED.

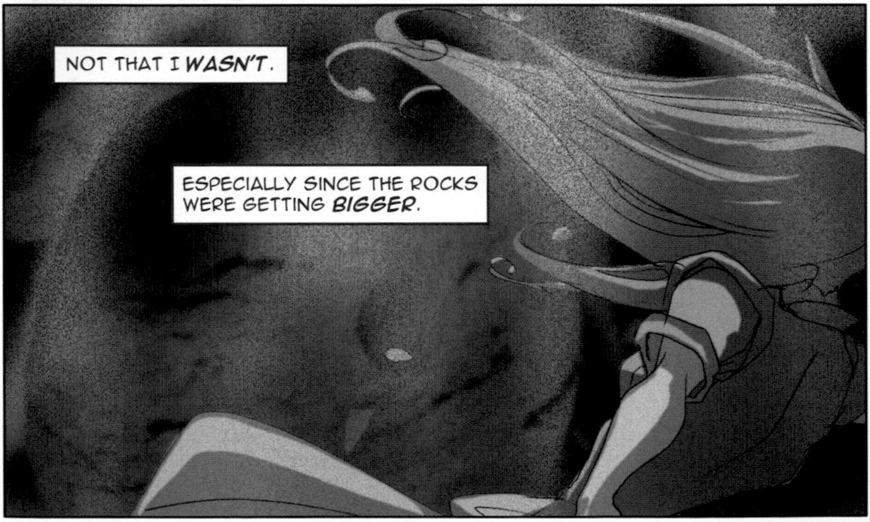
NOT THAT I WASN'T.
ESPECIALLY SINCE THE ROCKS WERE GETTING BIGGER.

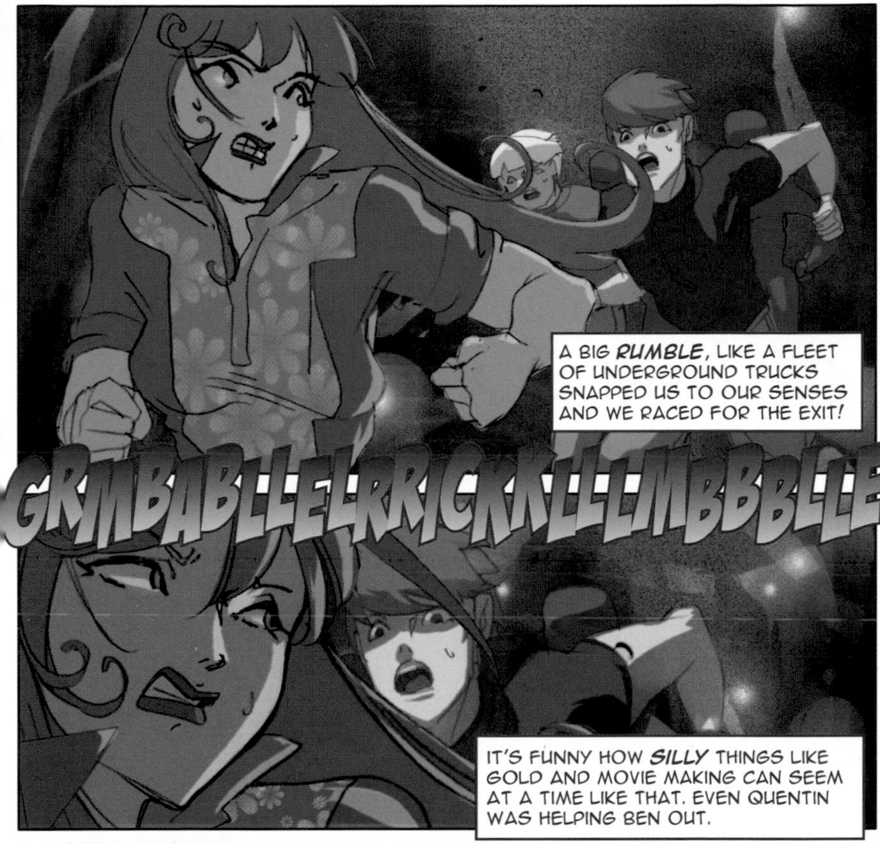
A BIG RUMBLE, LIKE A FLEET OF UNDERGROUND TRUCKS SNAPPED US TO OUR SENSES AND WE RACED FOR THE EXIT!
GRMBABLLELRRICKKLLLMBBBLLE
IT'S FUNNY HOW SILLY THINGS LIKE GOLD AND MOVIE MAKING CAN SEEM AT A TIME LIKE THAT. EVEN QUENTIN WAS HELPING BEN OUT.

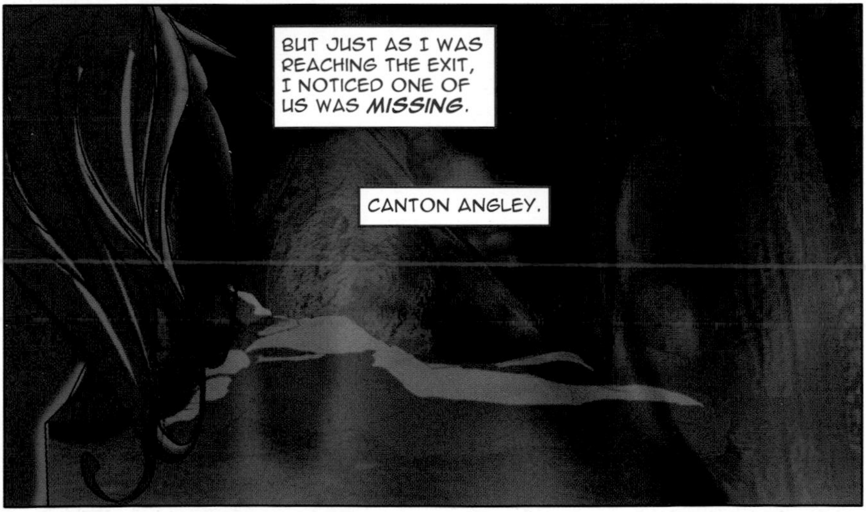
BUT JUST AS I WAS REACHING THE EXIT, I NOTICED ONE OF US WAS MISSING.
CANTON ANGLEY.

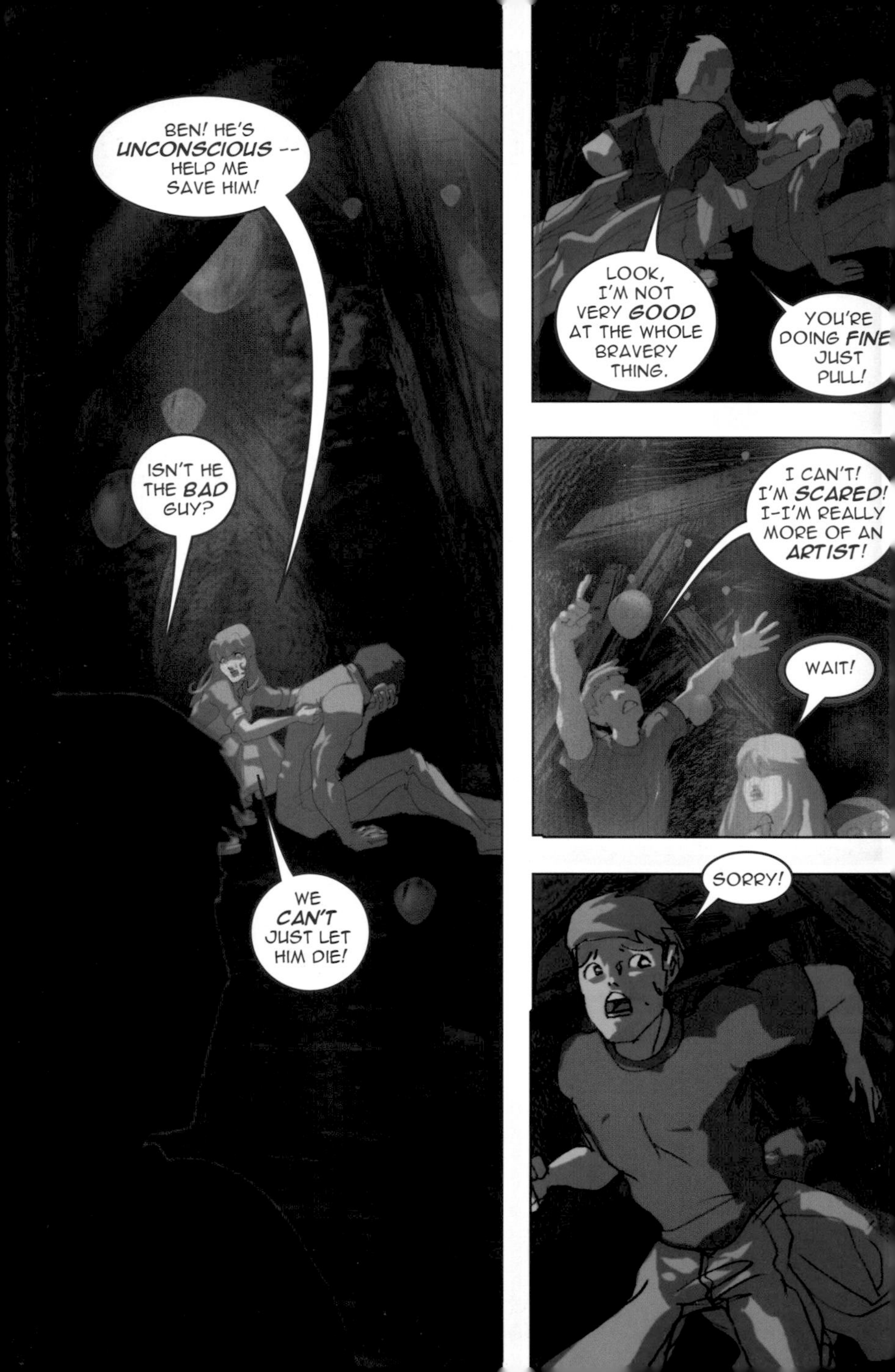
BEN! HE'S UNCONSCIOUS -- HELP ME SAVE HIM!
ISN'T HE THE BAD GUY?
WE CAN'T JUST LET HIM DIE!
LOOK, I'M NOT VERY GOOD AT THE WHOLE BRAVERY THING.
YOU'RE DOING FINE JUST PULL!
I CAN'T! I'M SCARED! I-I'M REALLY MORE OF AN ARTIST!
WAIT!
SORRY!

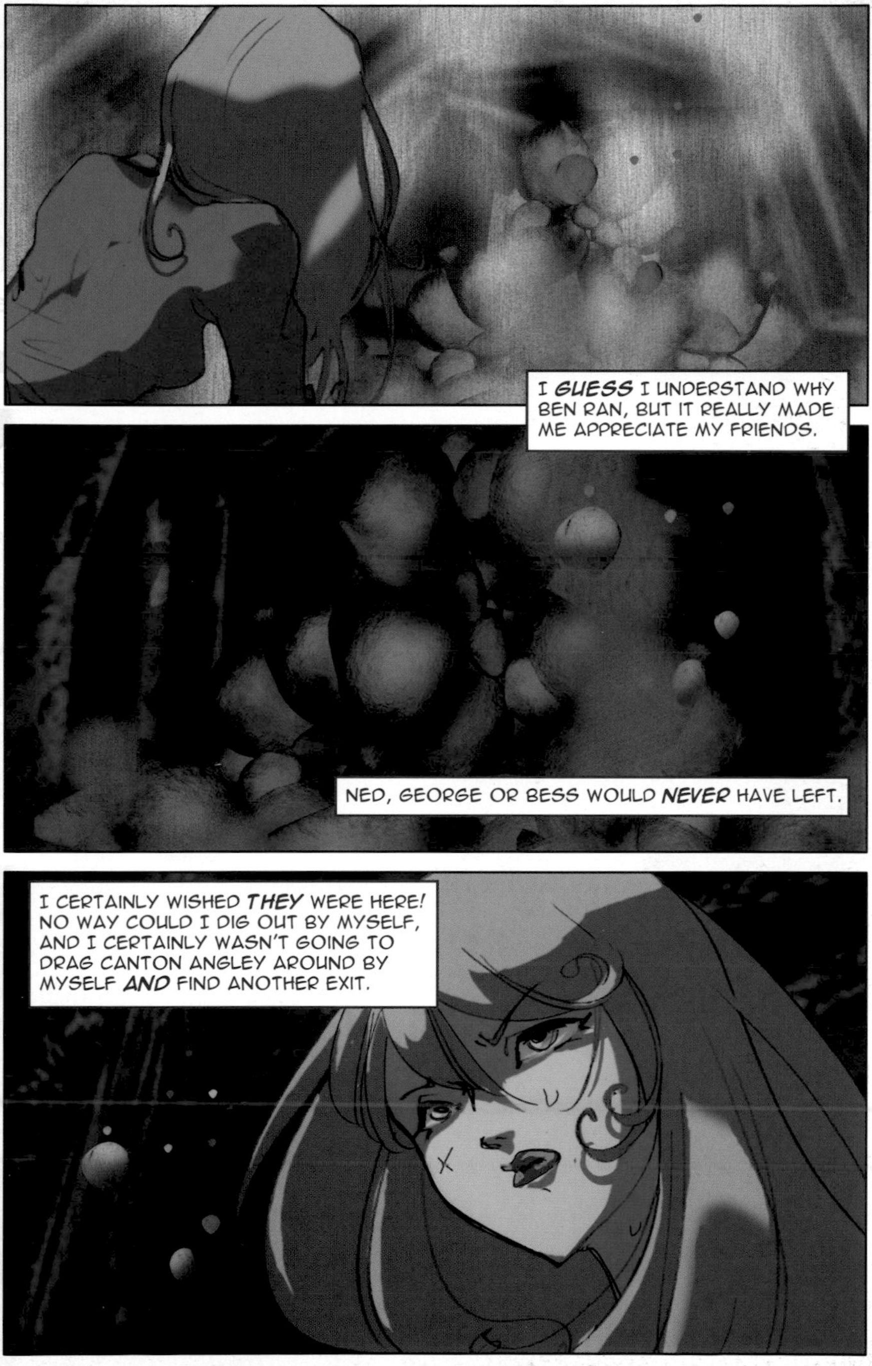
I GUESS I UNDERSTAND WHY BEN RAN, BUT IT REALLY MADE ME APPRECIATE MY FRIENDS.
NED, GEORGE OR BESS WOULD NEVER HAVE LEFT.
I CERTAINLY WISHED THEY WERE HERE! NO WAY COULD I DIG OUT BY MYSELF, AND I CERTAINLY WASN'T GOING TO DRAG CANTON ANGLEY AROUND BY MYSELF AND FIND ANOTHER EXIT.

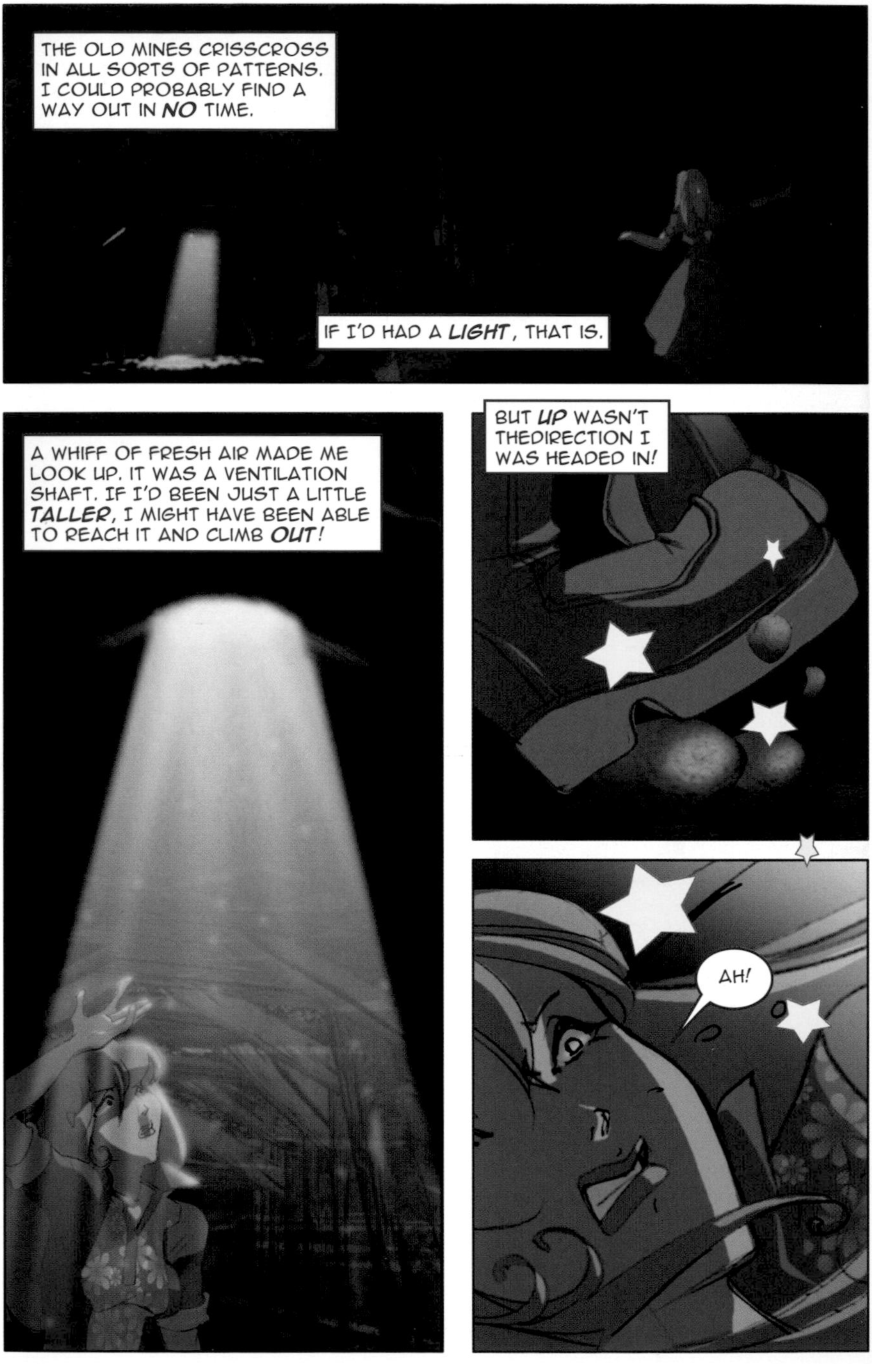
THE OLD MINES CRISSCROSS IN ALL SORTS OF PATTERNS. I COULD PROBABLY FIND A WAY OUT IN NO TIME.
IF I'D HAD A LIGHT, THAT IS.
A WHIFF OF FRESH AIR MADE ME LOOK UP. IT WAS A VENTILATION SHAFT. IF I'D BEEN JUST A LITTLE TALLER, I MIGHT HAVE BEEN ABLE TO REACH IT AND CLIMB OUT!
BUT UP WASN'T THEDIRECTION I WAS HEADED IN!
AH!

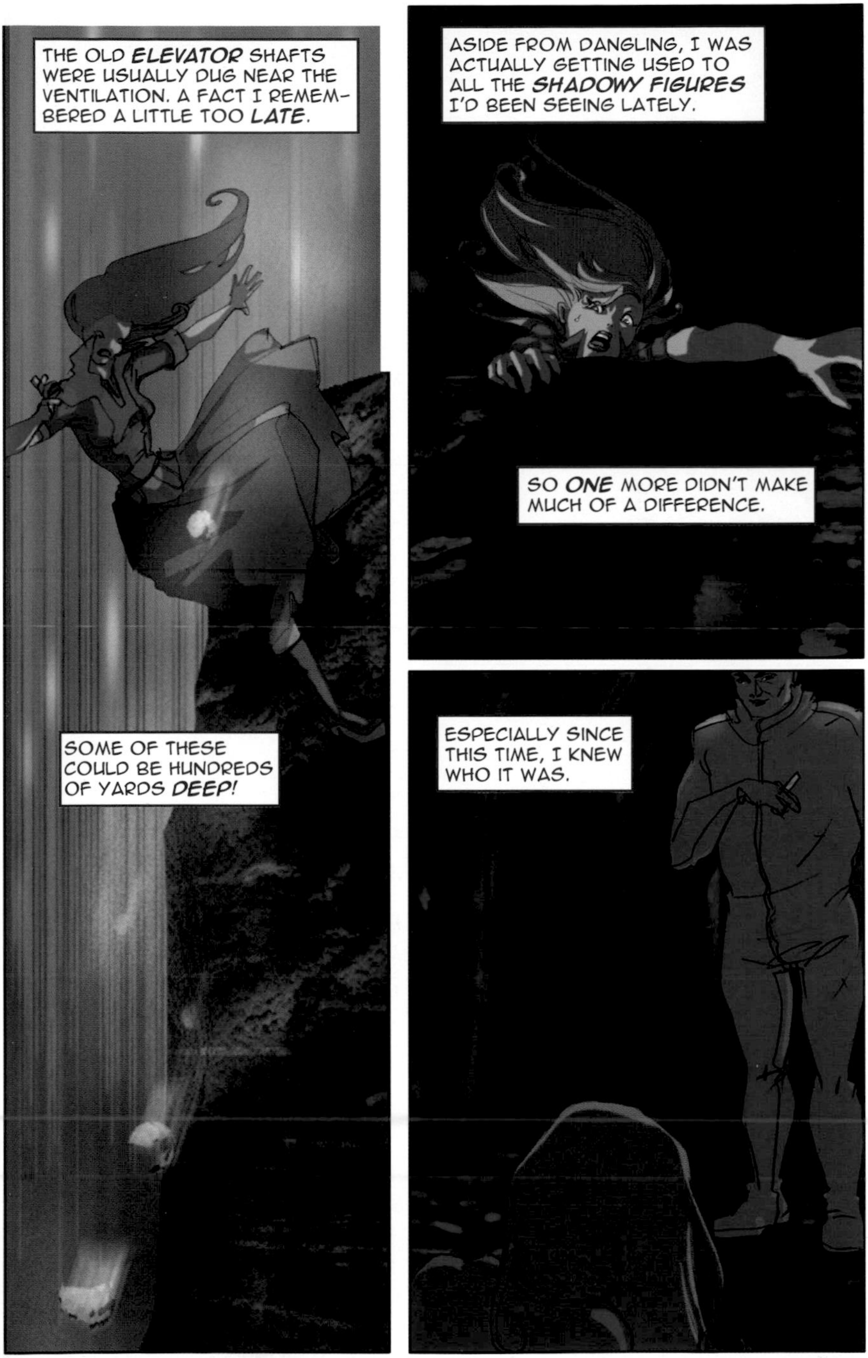
THE OLD ELEVATOR SHAFTS WERE USUALLY DUG NEAR THE VENTILATION. A FACT I REMEMBERED A LITTLE TOO LATE.
SOME OF THESE COULD BE HUNDREDS OF YARDS DEEP!
ASIDE FROM DANGLING, I WAS ACTUALLY GETTING USED TO ALL THE SHADOWY FIGURES I'D BEEN SEEING LATELY.
SO ONE MORE DIDN'T MAKE MUCH OF A DIFFERENCE.
ESPECIALLY SINCE THIS TIME, I KNEW WHO IT WAS.

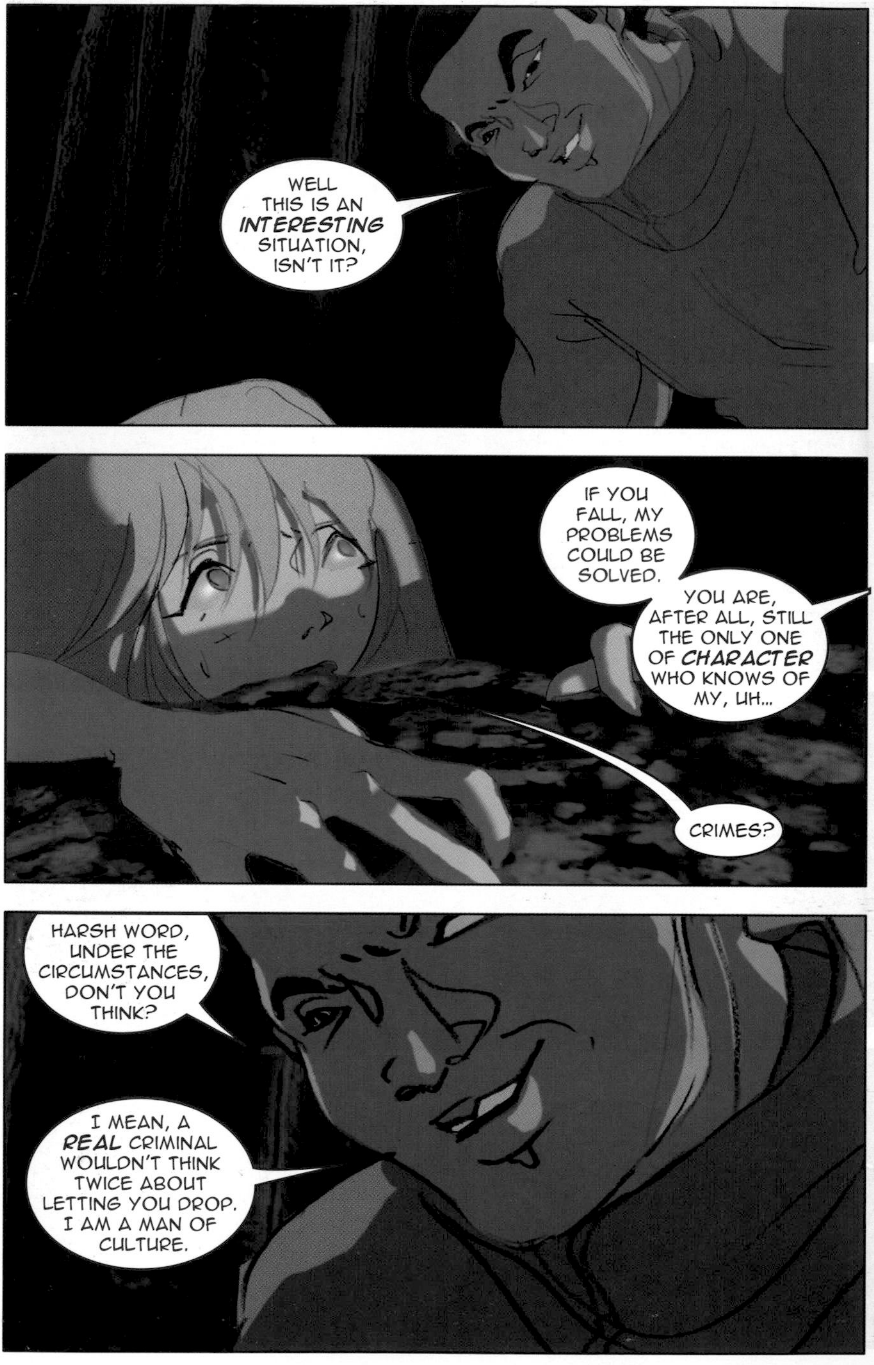
WELL THIS IS AN INTERESTING SITUATION, ISN'T IT?
IF YOU FALL, MY PROBLEMS COULD BE SOLVED.
YOU ARE, AFTER ALL, STILL THE ONLY ONE OF CHARACTER WHO KNOWS OF MY, UH...
CRIMES?
HARSH WORD, UNDER THE CIRCUMSTANCES, DON'T YOU THINK?
I MEAN, A REAL CRIMINAL WOULDN'T THINK TWICE ABOUT LETTING YOU DROP. I AM A MAN OF CULTURE.

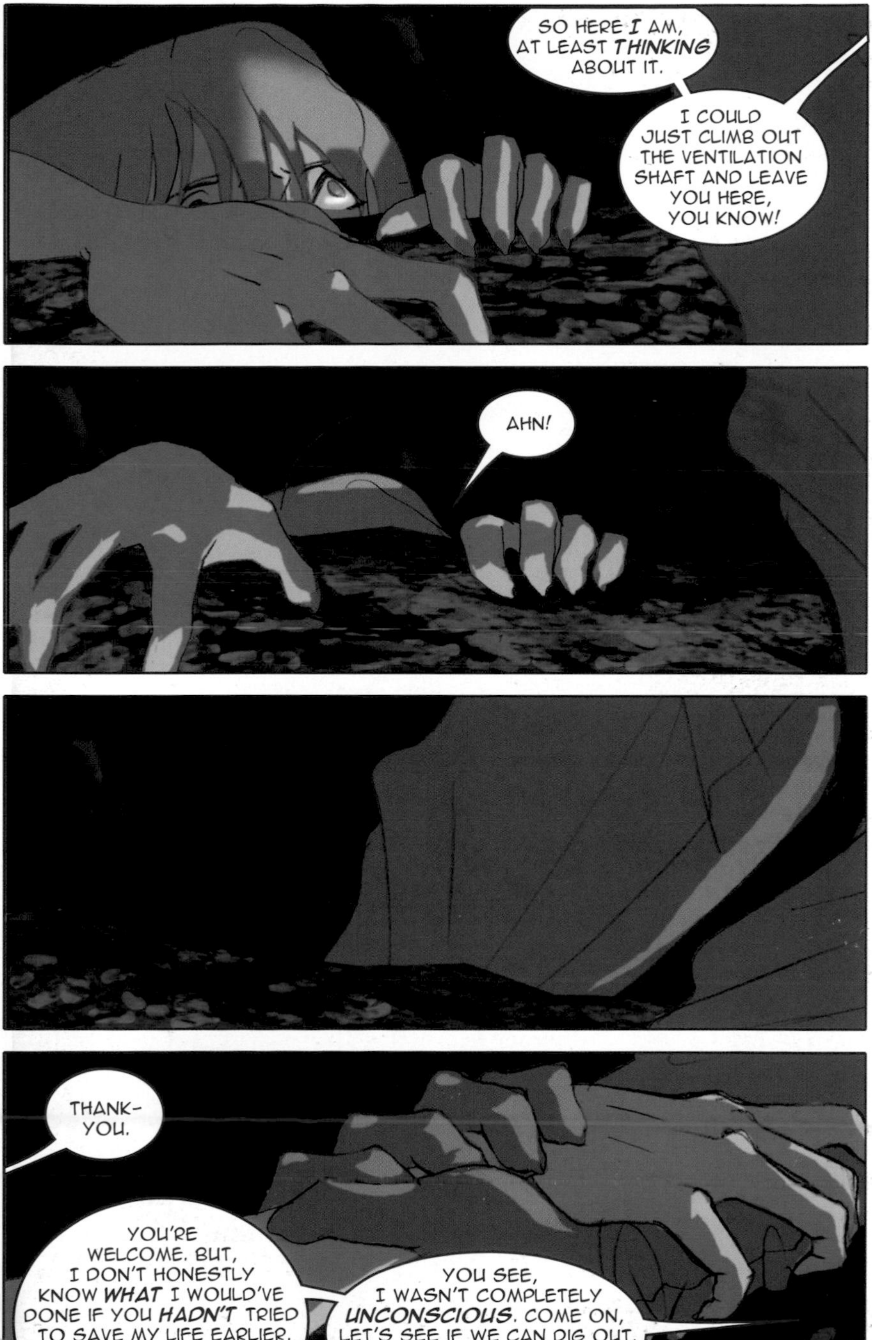
SO HERE I AM, AT LEAST THINKING ABOUT IT.
I COULD JUST CLIMB OUT THE VENTILATION SHAFT AND LEAVE YOU HERE, YOU KNOW!
AHN!
THANK-YOU.
YOU'RE WELCOME. BUT, I DON'T HONESTLY KNOW WHAT I WOULD'VE DONE IF YOU HADN'T TRIED TO SAVE MY LIFE EARLIER.
YOU SEE, I WASN'T COMPLETELY UNCONSCIOUS. COME ON, LET'S SEE IF WE CAN DIG OUT.

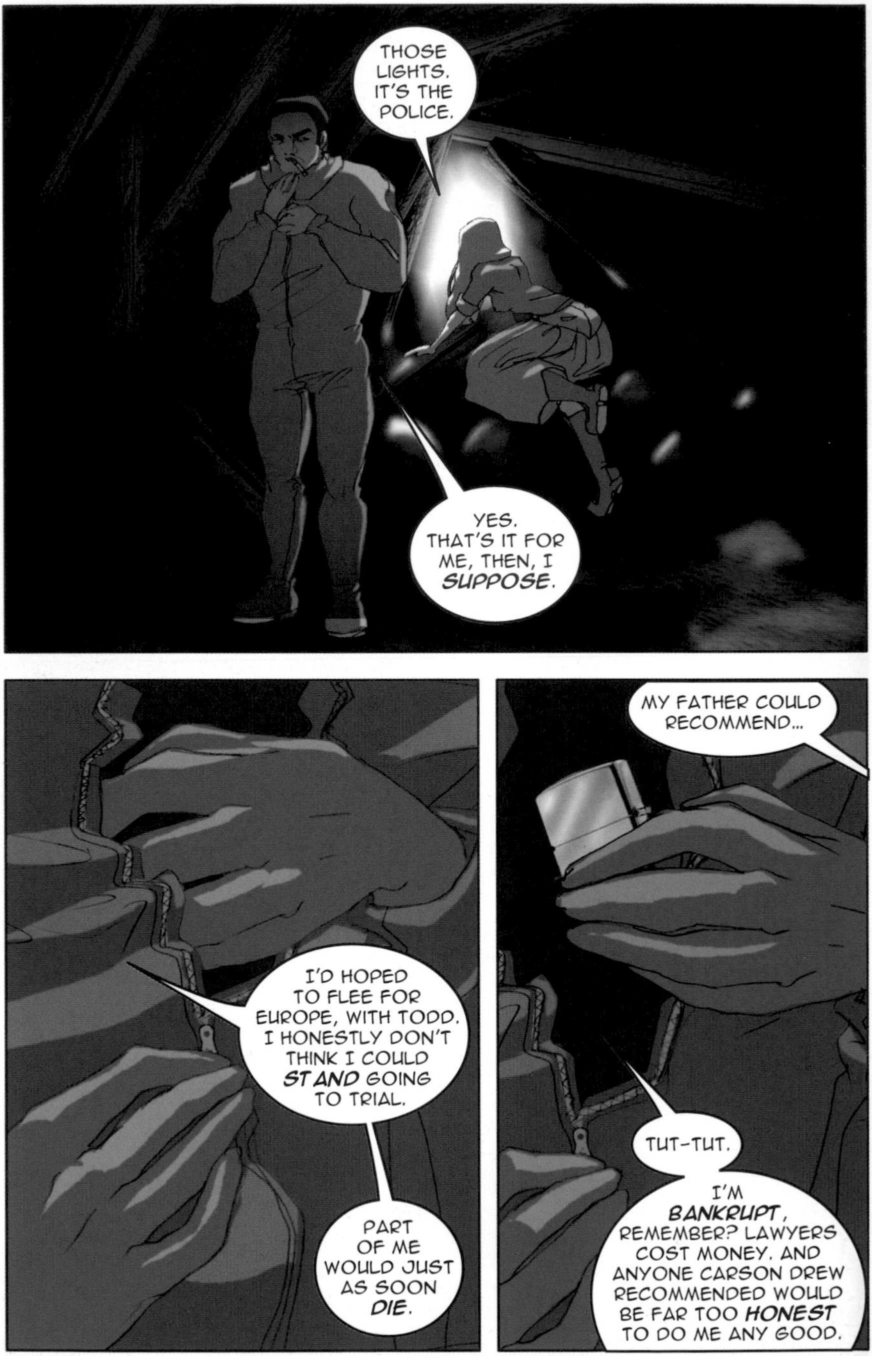
THOSE LIGHTS. IT'S THE POLICE.
YES. THAT'S IT FOR ME, THEN, I SUPPOSE.
I'D HOPED TO FLEE FOR EUROPE, WITH TODD. I HONESTLY DON'T THINK I COULD STAND GOING TO TRIAL.
PART OF ME WOULD JUST AS SOON DIE.
MY FATHER COULD RECOMMEND...
TUT-TUT.
I'M BANKRUPT, REMEMBER? LAWYERS COST MONEY. AND ANYONE CARSON DREW RECOMMENDED WOULD BE FAR TOO HONEST TO DO ME ANY GOOD.

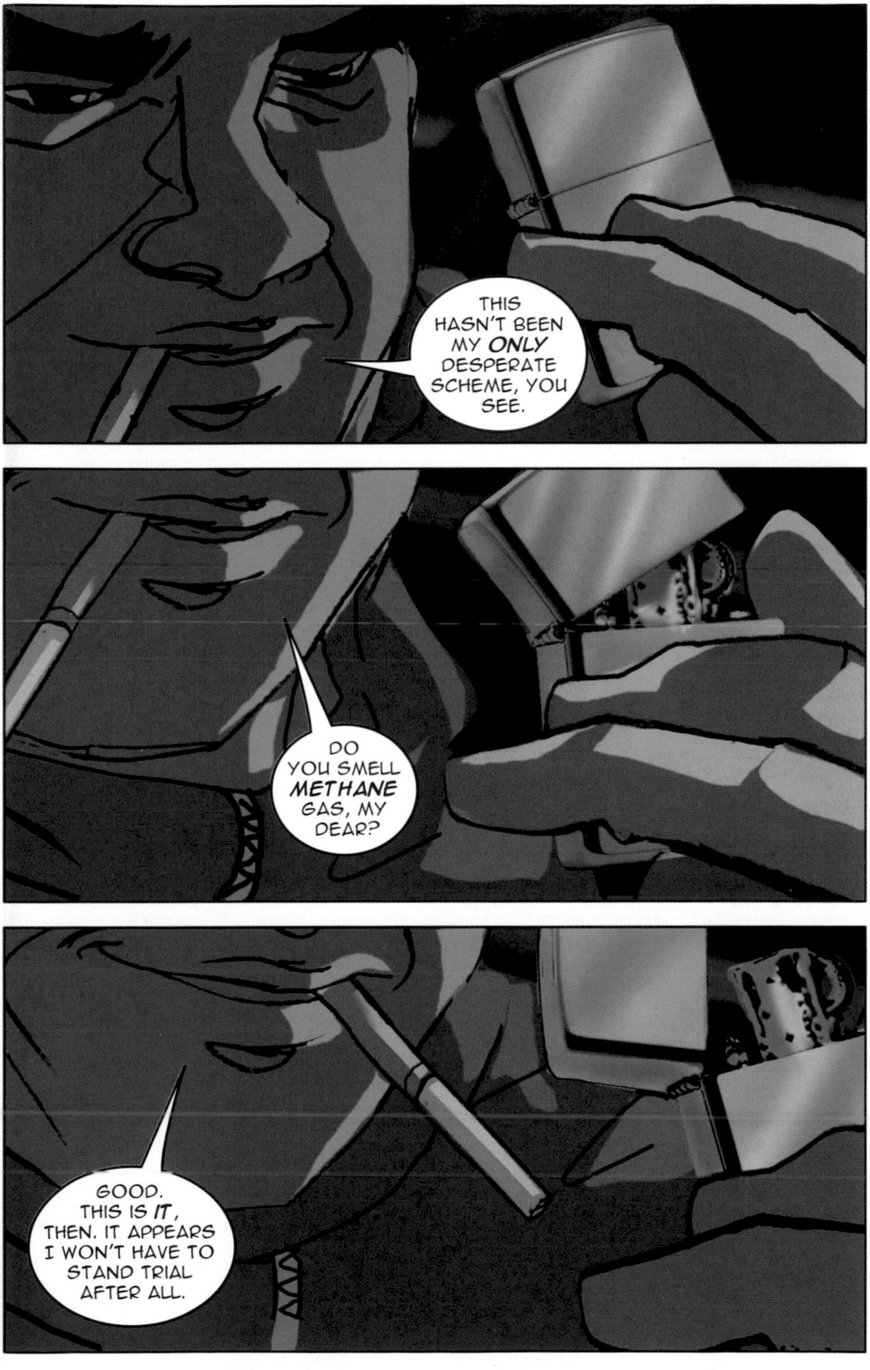
THIS HASN'T BEEN MY ONLY DESPERATE SCHEME, YOU SEE.
DO YOU SMELL METHANE GAS, MY DEAR?
GOOD. THIS IS IT, THEN. IT APPEARS I WON'T HAVE TO STAND TRIAL AFTER ALL.

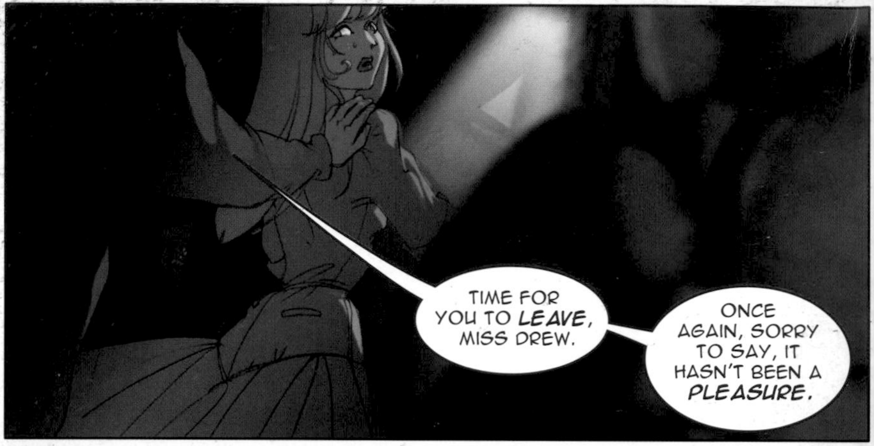
TIME FOR YOU TO LEAVE, MISS DREW.
ONCE AGAIN, SORRY TO SAY, IT HASN'T BEEN A PLEASURE.

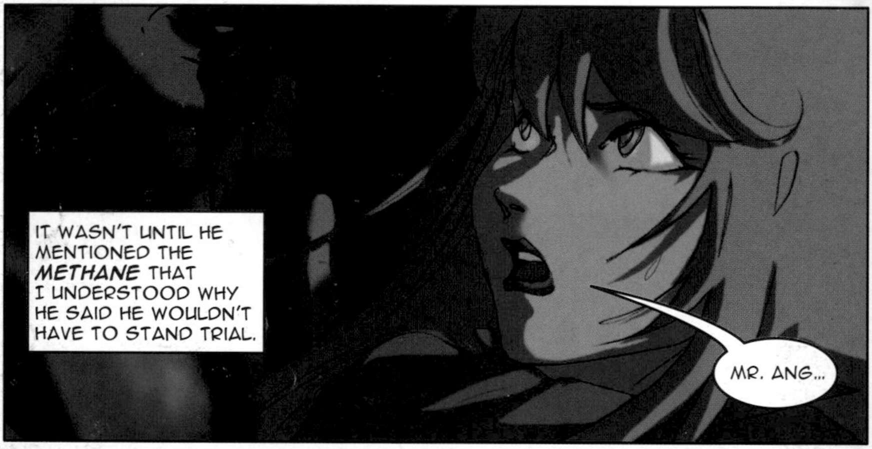
IT WASN'T UNTIL HE MENTIONED THE METHANE THAT I UNDERSTOOD WHY HE SAID HE WOULDN'T HAVE TO STAND TRIAL.
MR. ANG...

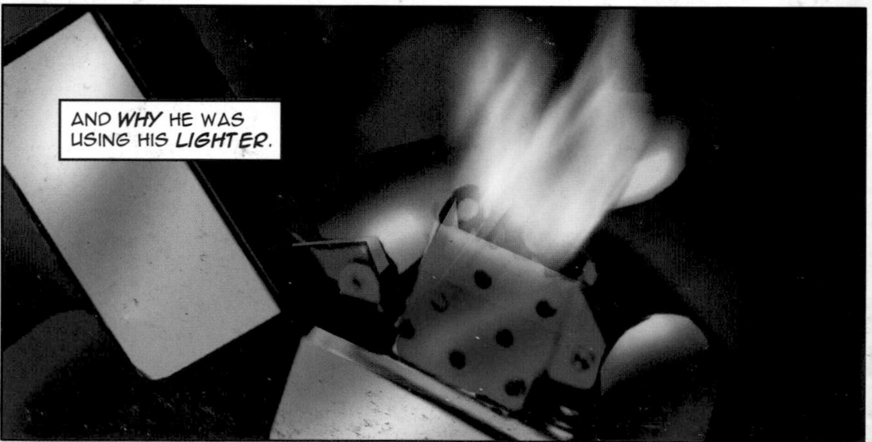
AND WHY HE WAS USING HIS LIGHTER.

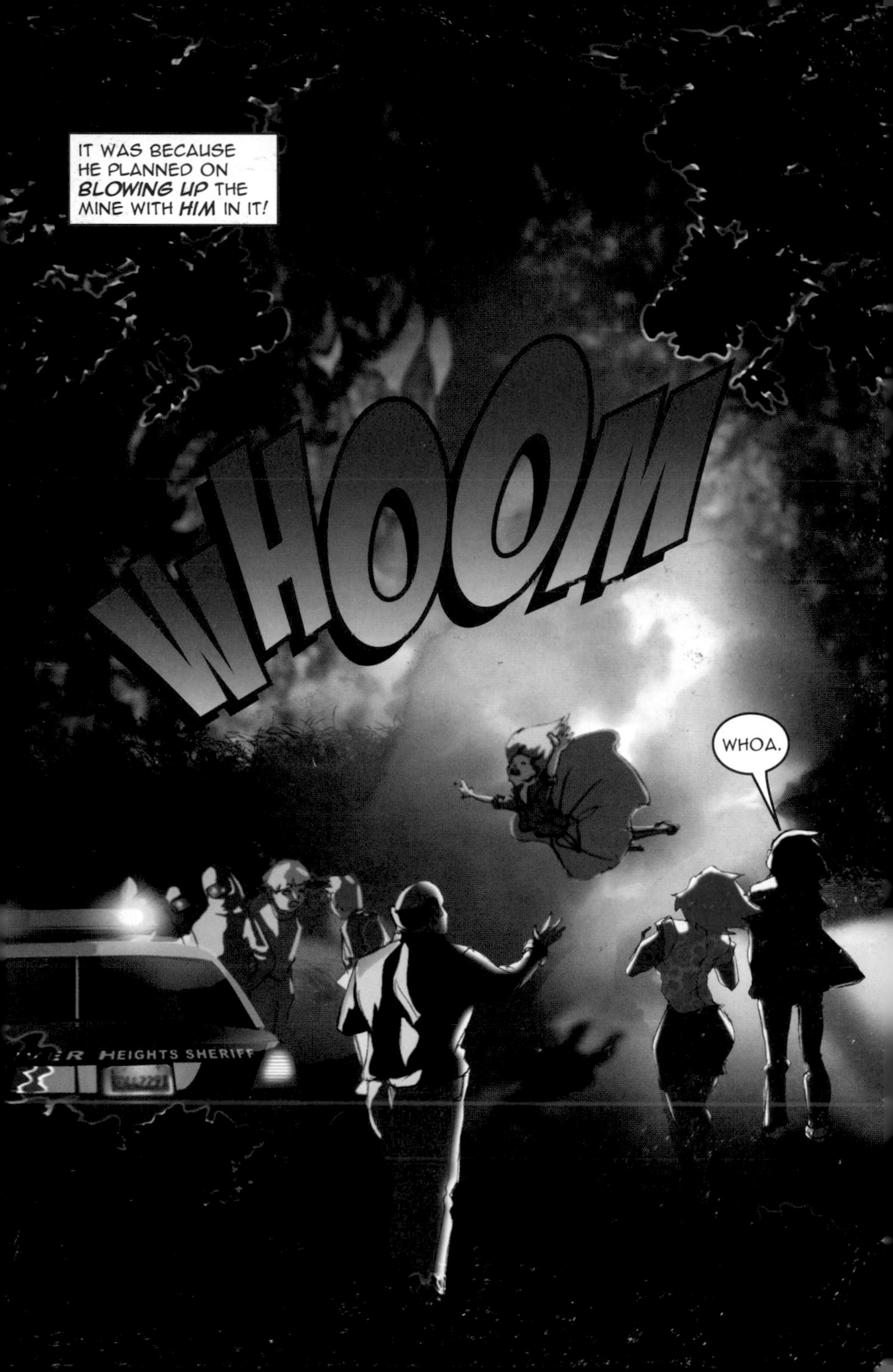
IT WAS BECAUSE HE PLANNED ON BLOWING UP THE MINE WITH HIM IN IT!
WHOOM
WHOA.
HEIGHTS SHERIFF

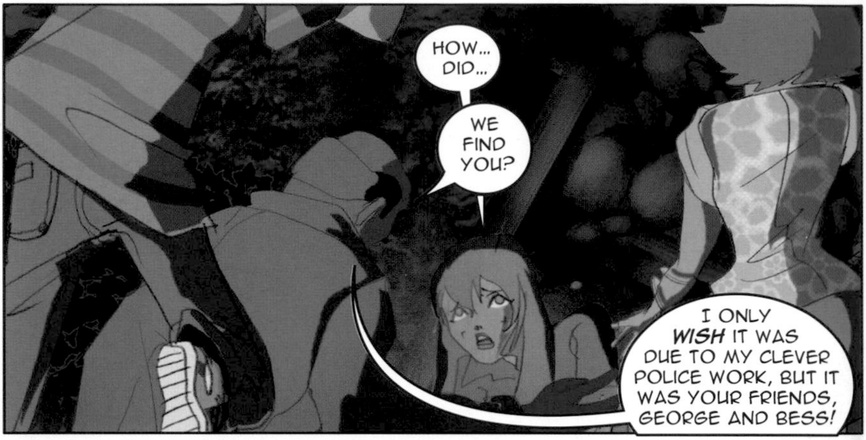
HOW... DID...
WE FIND YOU?
I ONLY **WISH** IT WAS DUE TO MY CLEVER POLICE WORK, BUT IT WAS YOUR FRIENDS, GEORGE AND BESS!
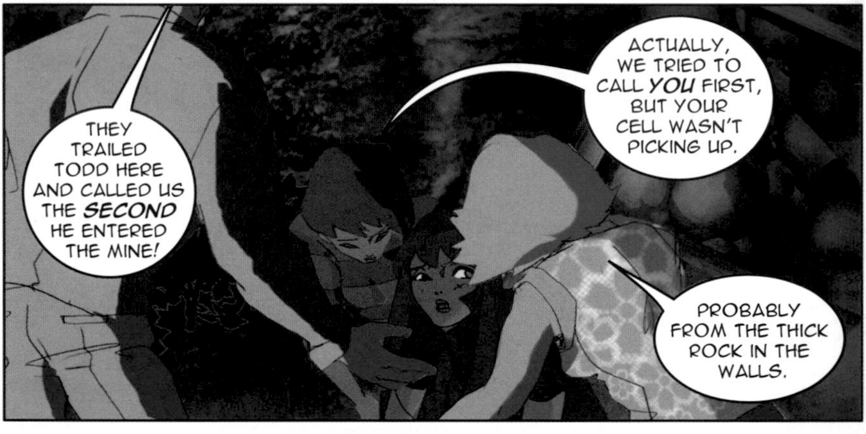
THEY TRAILED TODD HERE AND CALLED US THE ***SECOND*** HE ENTERED THE MINE!
ACTUALLY, WE TRIED TO CALL ***YOU*** FIRST, BUT YOUR CELL WASN'T PICKING UP.
PROBABLY FROM THE THICK ROCK IN THE WALLS.
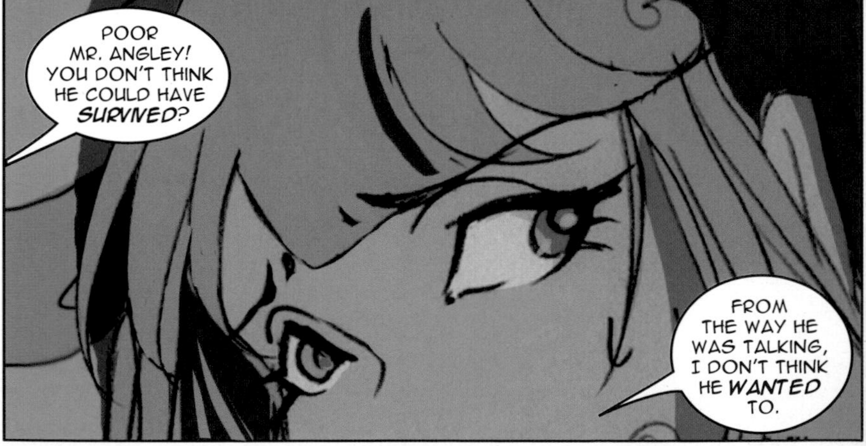
POOR MR. ANGLEY! YOU DON'T THINK HE COULD HAVE ***SURVIVED***?
FROM THE WAY HE WAS TALKING, I DON'T THINK HE ***WANTED*** TO.

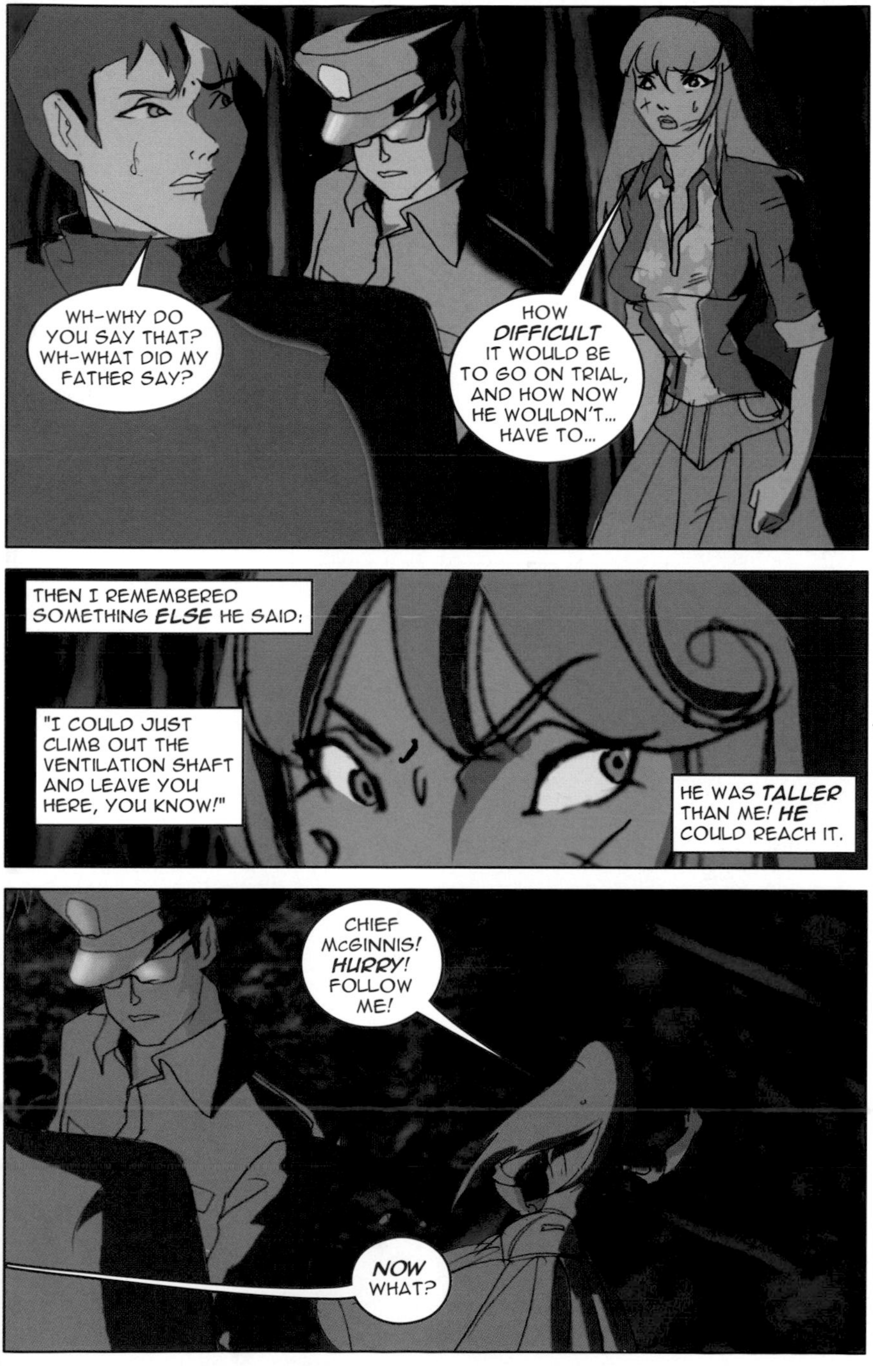
WH-WHY DO YOU SAY THAT? WH-WHAT DID MY FATHER SAY?
HOW *DIFFICULT* IT WOULD BE TO GO ON TRIAL, AND HOW NOW HE WOULDN'T... HAVE TO...
THEN I REMEMBERED SOMETHING *ELSE* HE SAID:
"I COULD JUST CLIMB OUT THE VENTILATION SHAFT AND LEAVE YOU HERE, YOU KNOW!"
HE WAS *TALLER* THAN ME! *HE* COULD REACH IT.
CHIEF McGINNIS! *HURRY!* FOLLOW ME!
NOW WHAT?

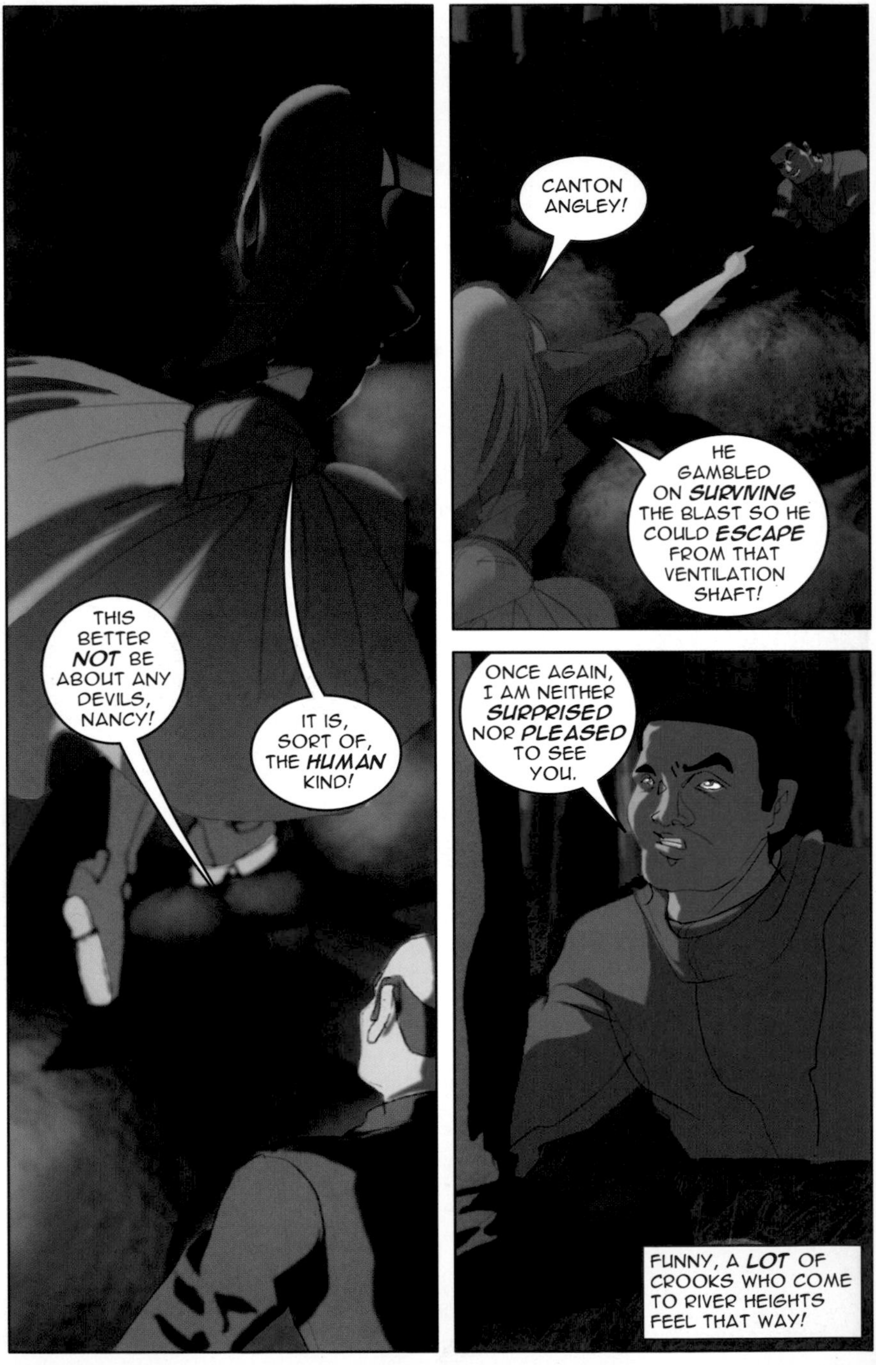
THIS BETTER NOT BE ABOUT ANY DEVILS, NANCY!
IT IS, SORT OF, THE HUMAN KIND!
CANTON ANGLEY!
HE GAMBLED ON SURVIVING THE BLAST SO HE COULD ESCAPE FROM THAT VENTILATION SHAFT!
ONCE AGAIN, I AM NEITHER SURPRISED NOR PLEASED TO SEE YOU.
FUNNY, A LOT OF CROOKS WHO COME TO RIVER HEIGHTS FEEL THAT WAY!

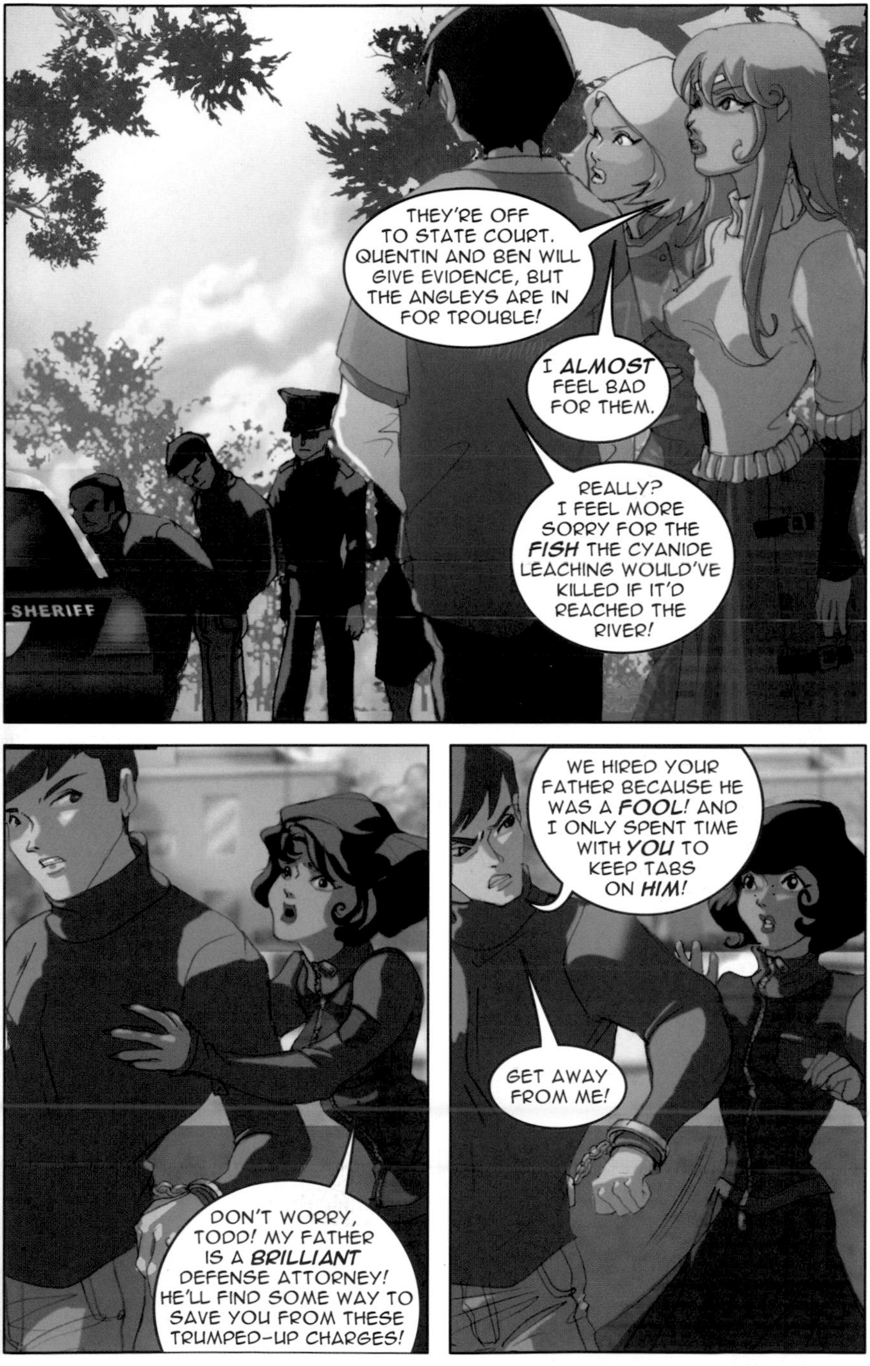
SHERIFF
THEY'RE OFF TO STATE COURT. QUENTIN AND BEN WILL GIVE EVIDENCE, BUT THE ANGLEYS ARE IN FOR TROUBLE!
I *ALMOST* FEEL BAD FOR THEM.
REALLY? I FEEL MORE SORRY FOR THE *FISH* THE CYANIDE LEACHING WOULD'VE KILLED IF IT'D REACHED THE RIVER!
DON'T WORRY, TODD! MY FATHER IS A *BRILLIANT* DEFENSE ATTORNEY! HE'LL FIND SOME WAY TO SAVE YOU FROM THESE TRUMPED-UP CHARGES!
WE HIRED YOUR FATHER BECAUSE HE WAS A *FOOL*! AND I ONLY SPENT TIME WITH *YOU* TO KEEP TABS ON *HIM*!
GET AWAY FROM ME!

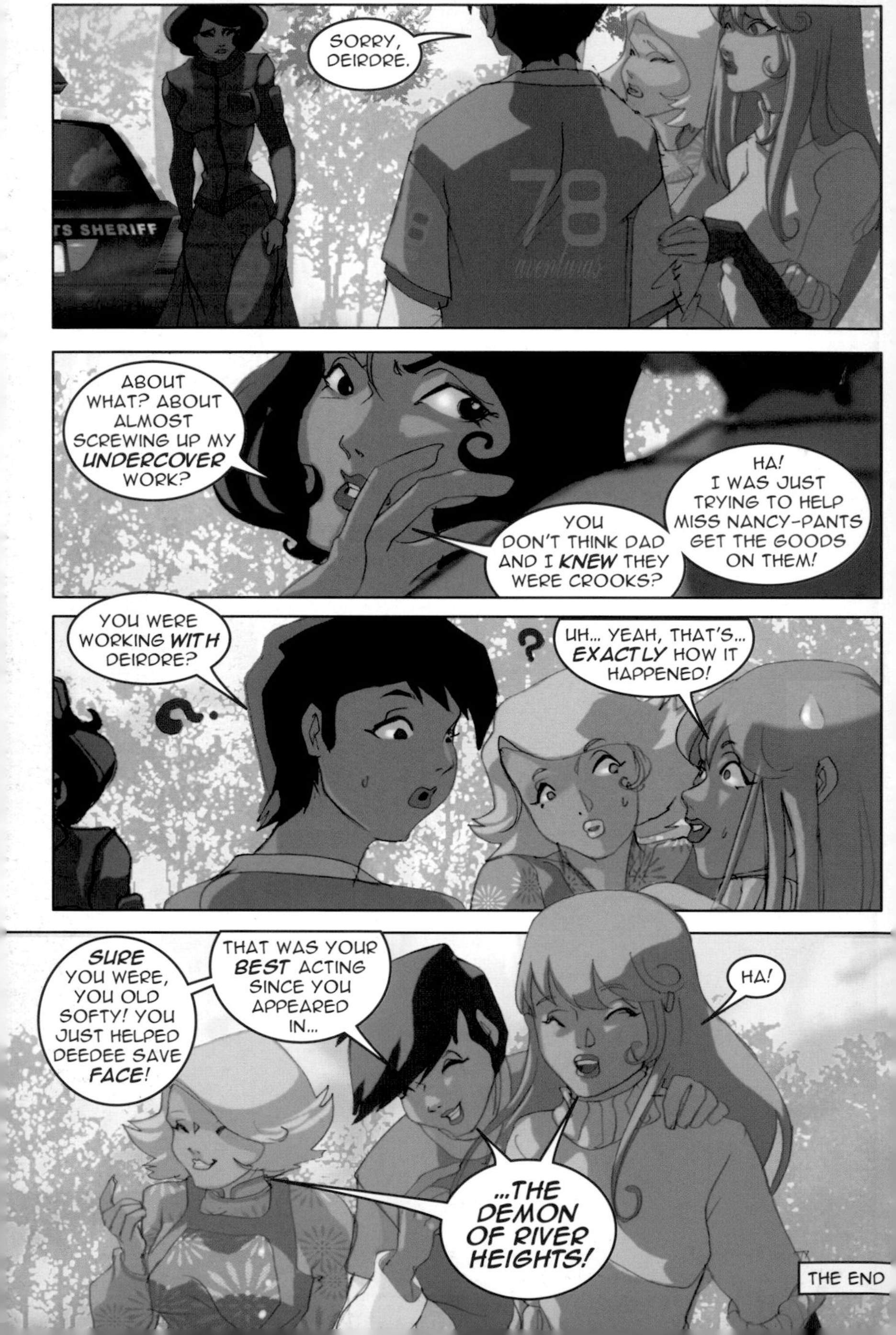
SORRY, DEIRDRE.
TS SHERIFF
78
ABOUT WHAT? ABOUT ALMOST SCREWING UP MY UNDERCOVER WORK?
HA! I WAS JUST TRYING TO HELP MISS NANCY-PANTS GET THE GOODS ON THEM!
YOU DON'T THINK DAD AND I KNEW THEY WERE CROOKS?
YOU WERE WORKING WITH DEIRDRE?
UH... YEAH, THAT'S... EXACTLY HOW IT HAPPENED!
SURE YOU WERE, YOU OLD SOFTY! YOU JUST HELPED DEEDEE SAVE FACE!
THAT WAS YOUR BEST ACTING SINCE YOU APPEARED IN...
HA!
...THE DEMON OF RIVER HEIGHTS!
THE END

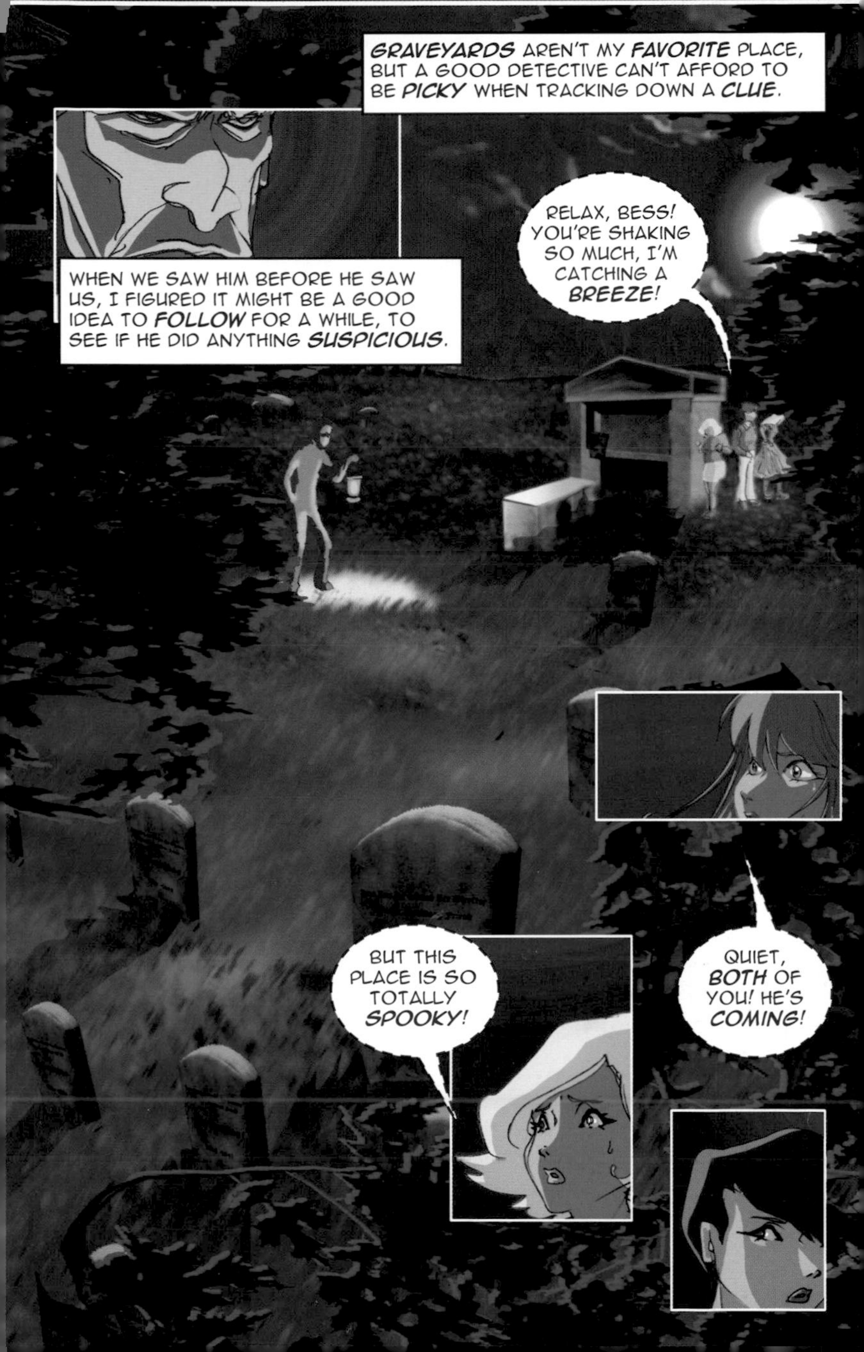
GRAVEYARDS AREN'T MY FAVORITE PLACE, BUT A GOOD DETECTIVE CAN'T AFFORD TO BE PICKY WHEN TRACKING DOWN A CLUE.
WHEN WE SAW HIM BEFORE HE SAW US, I FIGURED IT MIGHT BE A GOOD IDEA TO FOLLOW FOR A WHILE, TO SEE IF HE DID ANYTHING SUSPICIOUS.
RELAX, BESS! YOU'RE SHAKING SO MUCH, I'M CATCHING A BREEZE!
BUT THIS PLACE IS SO TOTALLY SPOOKY!
QUIET, BOTH OF YOU! HE'S COMING!

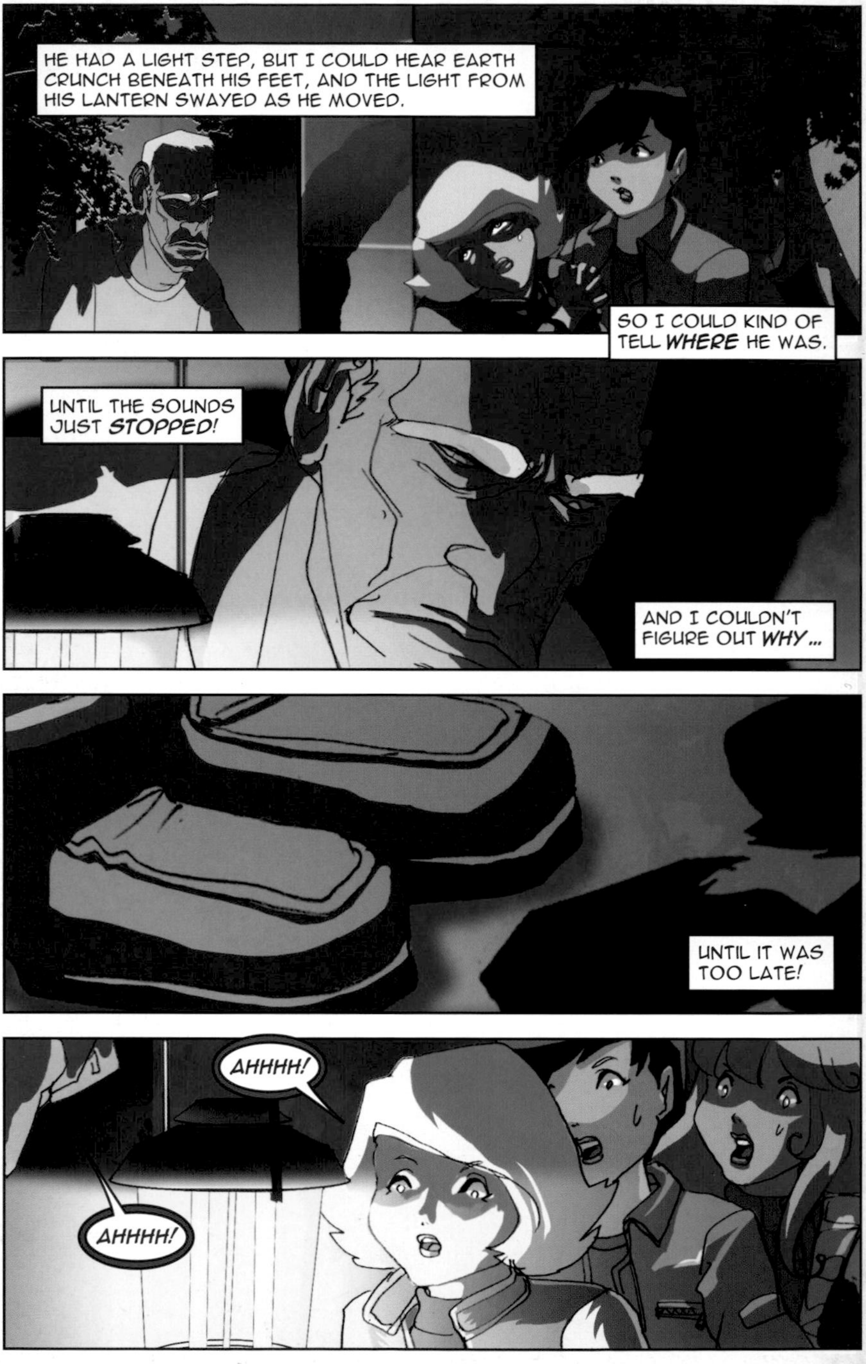
HE HAD A LIGHT STEP, BUT I COULD HEAR EARTH CRUNCH BENEATH HIS FEET, AND THE LIGHT FROM HIS LANTERN SWAYED AS HE MOVED.
SO I COULD KIND OF TELL *WHERE* HE WAS.
UNTIL THE SOUNDS JUST *STOPPED*!
AND I COULDN'T FIGURE OUT *WHY*...
UNTIL IT WAS TOO LATE!
AHHHH!
AHHHH!

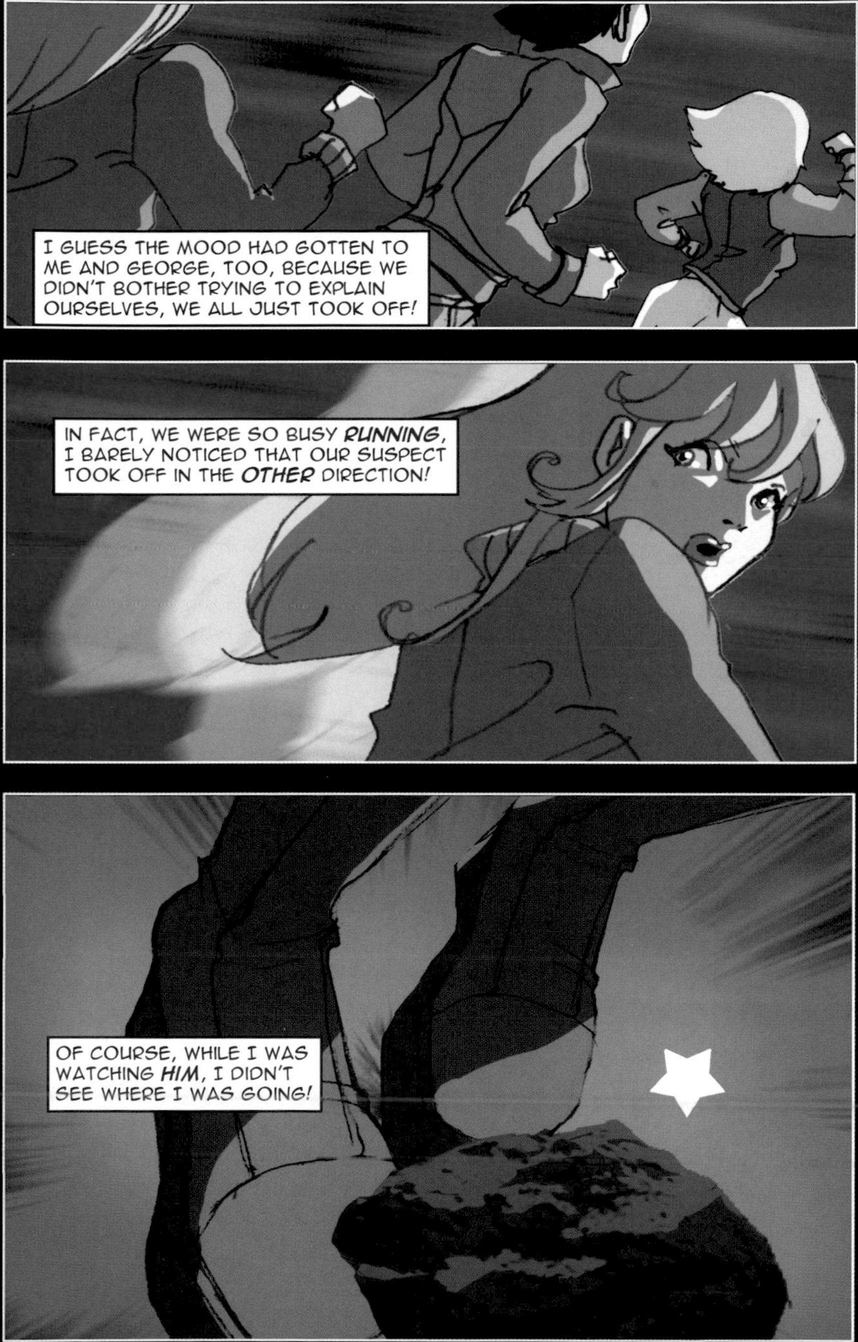
I GUESS THE MOOD HAD GOTTEN TO ME AND GEORGE, TOO, BECAUSE WE DIDN'T BOTHER TRYING TO EXPLAIN OURSELVES, WE ALL JUST TOOK OFF!
IN FACT, WE WERE SO BUSY *RUNNING*, I BARELY NOTICED THAT OUR SUSPECT TOOK OFF IN THE *OTHER* DIRECTION!
OF COURSE, WHILE I WAS WATCHING *HIM*, I DIDN'T SEE WHERE I WAS GOING!

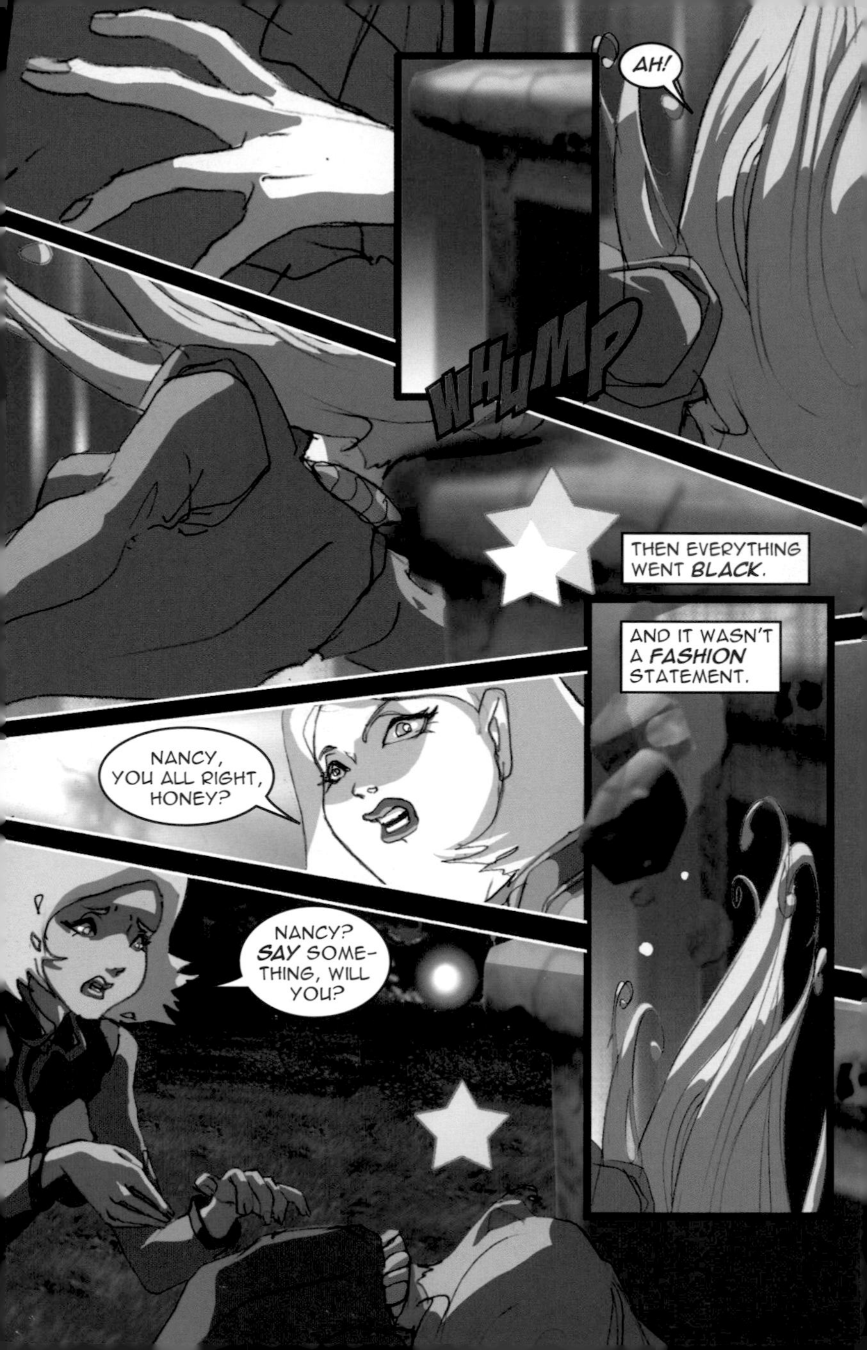
AH!
WHUMP
THEN EVERYTHING WENT **BLACK**.
AND IT WASN'T A **FASHION** STATEMENT.
NANCY, YOU ALL RIGHT, HONEY?
NANCY? **SAY** SOME-THING, WILL YOU?

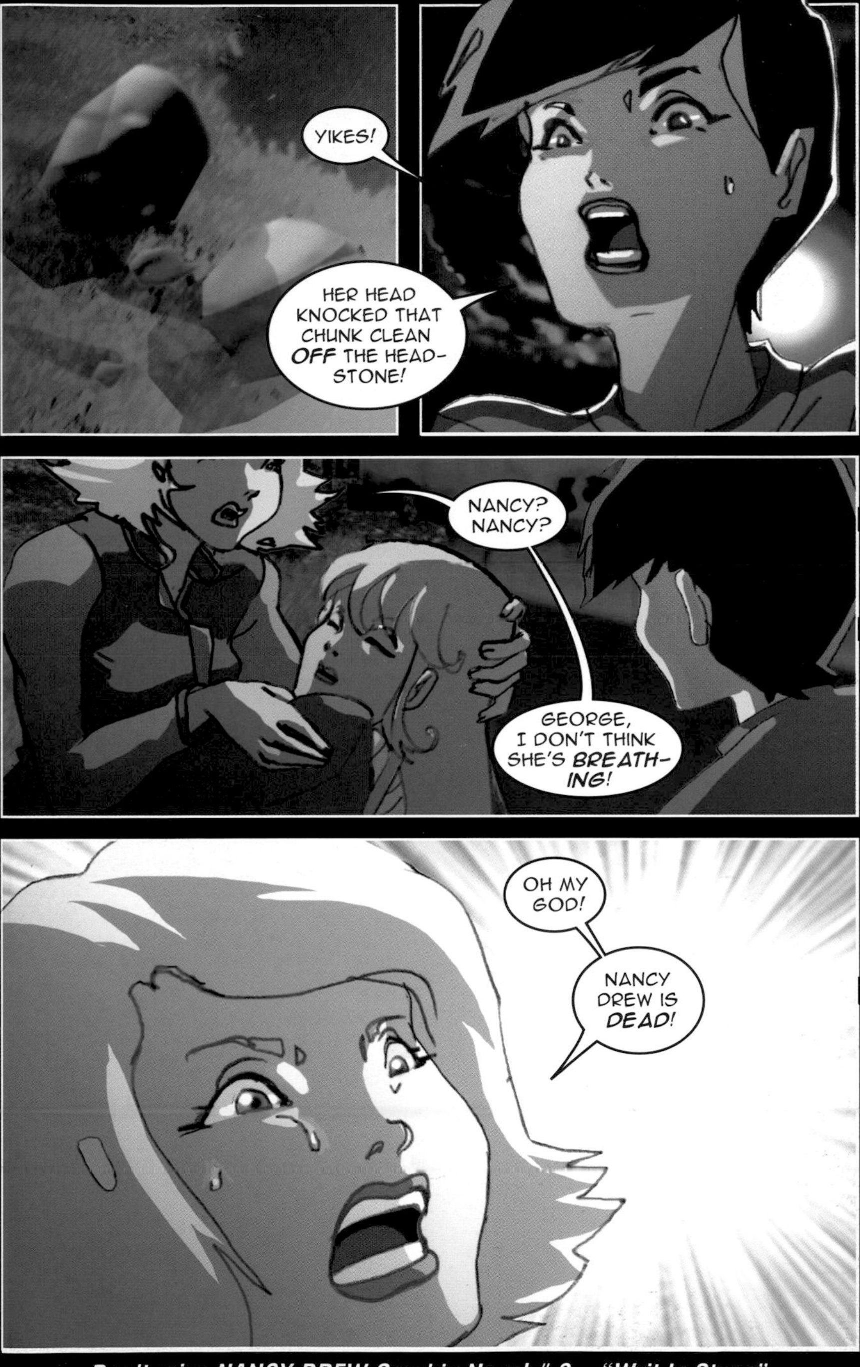
YIKES!
HER HEAD KNOCKED THAT CHUNK CLEAN OFF THE HEAD-STONE!
NANCY? NANCY?
GEORGE, I DON'T THINK SHE'S BREATH-ING!
OH MY GOD!
NANCY DREW IS DEAD!

Don't miss NANCY DREW Graphic Novel # 2 – "Writ In Stone"

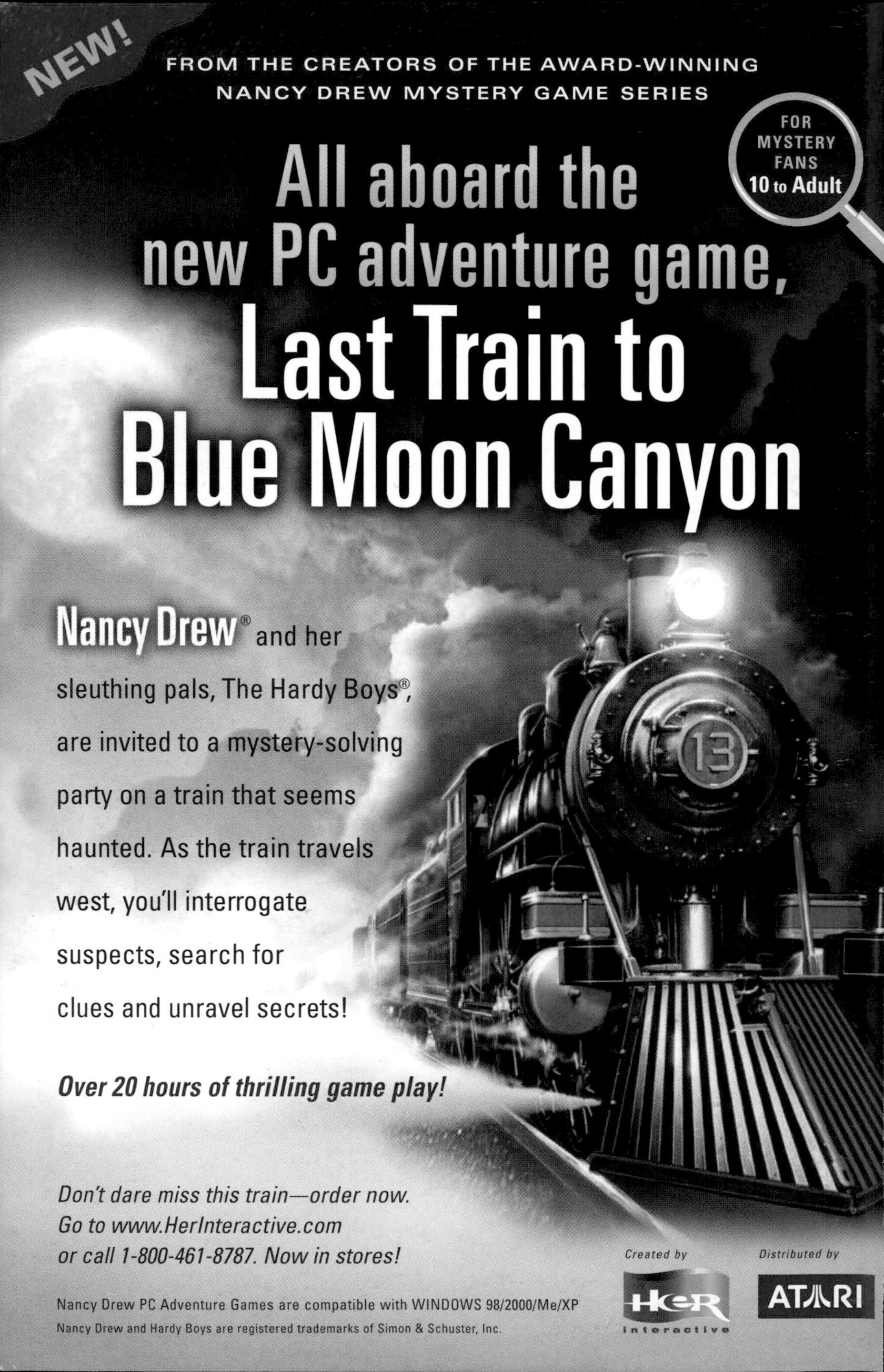
NEW!
FROM THE CREATORS OF THE AWARD-WINNING
NANCY DREW MYSTERY GAME SERIES
FOR MYSTERY FANS 10 to Adult
All aboard the new PC adventure game,
Last Train to Blue Moon Canyon
Nancy Drew® and her sleuthing pals, The Hardy Boys®, are invited to a mystery-solving party on a train that seems haunted. As the train travels west, you'll interrogate suspects, search for clues and unravel secrets!
Over 20 hours of thrilling game play!
Don't dare miss this train—order now.
Go to www.HerInteractive.com
or call 1-800-461-8787. Now in stores!
Created by
HER interactive
Distributed by
ATARI
Nancy Drew PC Adventure Games are compatible with WINDOWS 98/2000/Me/XP
Nancy Drew and Hardy Boys are registered trademarks of Simon & Schuster, Inc.

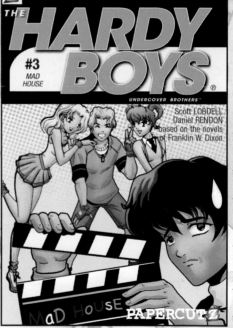

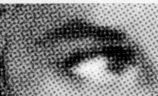

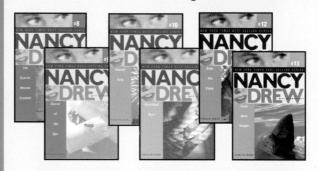